his to keep

USA TODAY BESTSELLING AUTHOR
autumn archer

His to Keep
Copyright © Autumn Archer (2018)
Published by Autumn Archer Books

The right of Autumn Archer to be identified as author of this work has been asserted by her in accordance with section 77 and 78 of the Copyright, Designs and Patents Act 1988.

All rights reserved. No part of this publication may be reproduced, stored in a retrieval system, or transmitted in any form or by any means, electronic, mechanical, photocopying, recording, or otherwise, without the prior permission of the publishers.

Any person who commits any unauthorised act in relation to this publication may be liable to criminal prosecution and civil claims for damages.

ISBN: 9781075530012

www.autumnarcher.com

To my family.
With love, anything is possible.

1

It hadn't taken long to strip off the sexy skimpy panties. They were lacey and barely there. Just the type of lingerie he imagined the sultry Lana would wear.

Even he had to admit, it was a little eerie having her so lifeless on the carpet before him. He wanted to look into her big blue eyes and see his own reflection.

His reflection, no one else's.

She was his from the second they met, even if she didn't want to accept it.

The duct tape around her wrists made her skin tinge with a cold shade of blue. He knew it was a too tight, but it was necessary. Having Lana, was necessary.

Squatting beside her pretty face, he teased the blonde locks away from her pale cheeks. Her lashes fluttered, fighting against the pull of the sedative. Her limbs were limp and her mind on shut down.

A few hours had passed, and he was becoming impatient. Being stuck in the same room was taking the edge of his thrill. Any time now, Lana would wake from her dream and he could finally tell her how it was going to be.

They were together now.
She belonged to him.
This was what she wanted from the start.

2

Lana's heavy eyelids slowly blinked open. A blurry haze clouded the room. When she swallowed, her throat felt like sandpaper.

A tingling spread to tightly bound wrists pulled behind her lower back. Her left cheek rested on pale carpet that smelt like Rory's aftershave and her chest pressed into the floor.

Goosebumps shot down the exposed skin on her restricted arms and legs. In a muddled state, she realized the jeans she had worn had been removed. She licked cracked lips, blinked rapidly and strained to focus on the surroundings.

Craning upward, she scanned the clothes and shoes that littered the floor. The tan court shoes she bought for a dinner party last month poked out from under a pair of jeans.

Her narrowed eyes flicked back and forth, noticing Rory's old alarm clock had been knocked off the nightstand. The red digits were visible, telling her it was 4 p.m. She had been unconscious for a few hours.

What the hell had happened in those few hours?

Her tingly fingers waggled as she tried to regain feeling in her hands. Tugging for freedom was pointless as her wrists wouldn't budge and when she tried to move each leg, both ankles flipped up, wrapped tightly with silver sticky tape.

Lana was wearing the lacey black dress that had been meticulously laid out on the bed before she arrived, the same dress that had caught Marcus's attention in Verto Veneri. While the drug had blanketed reality, her captor removed her clothes, including her panties and had somehow dressed her limp body in the lacey garment.

To finish, he'd wrapped duct tape around her wrists and ankles, and her hair had been freed from her ponytail.

A throaty cough came from the left followed by a plume of cigarette smoke.

"Oh, thank fuck, you've woken up. I must have gotten the dosage wrong for the sedative." The voice was smooth yet hinted concern.

The stiffness in her neck gripped her shoulders like a vice when she tilted her chin. A pair of shiny black brogues came into focus.

Hazy memories of his face flooded back. The same guy she propositioned at the club, Verto Veneri—the guy she asked to fuck her.

"Why…Carl?" she stuttered, her lung capacity restricted.

A low growl was followed by a shift in the brogues at her eye level. "Did you like the flowers, Lana?"

Her eyes squeezed shut and she groaned.

It had been him all along. He sent the stupid yellow flowers to her office and left them in Rory's bedroom for her to find.

He tugged his trousers at the knees and sank down. His fingers combed through her disheveled blonde strands.

"Your hair looks so good when it's brushed. Makes it

His to Keep 5

more shiny and neat," he mumbled, balancing a cigarette between his lips.

"Please, Carl. Untie me," she begged.

Ash tumbled from the end of his cigarette and twirled in the air, settling in her hair. "Oh, sweetheart, don't be upset. You and I will have loads of fun. I'm a great guy, I promise." He pinched the grey cinders from her silky tresses and rubbed them between his thumb and forefinger.

"Why this?" She tugged her wrists pointlessly.

He chuckled with a throaty rasp. "I know, I know. It seems a little drastic, sweetheart, but this is what we both want…what you wanted, Lana. You wanted me...remember?"

She rocked from side to side, but her body was weak and her head heavy. "Untie me!"

Carl inhaled smoke deep into his lungs and breathed it back out steadily, filling the room with an intoxicating fog. "I've been a member of Verto Veneri for years, and I've never been jilted. How do you think that made me feel?" His words came sputtering out as anger bubbled to the surface.

He raised to a stand, stubbed the butt out on the dresser and paced a track amongst the strewn clothes. "Donna Marie tried to palm me off with an ugly red head, as a replacement for you! Like, what the fuck, Lana! Why would you do that to me…why?" His voice strained like he was muting hurt. "You and I need to have a chat - to set the record straight."

He slotted his hand into his trouser pocket and teased out a lacy bundle—her pretty pink panties. Bringing them to his nose, he sniffed, long and deep into his lungs.

Her gut churned, feeling a swell of vomit rise. "What..have you.. done?" Her words stammered as tremors shook her from the inside.

"Nothing, sweetheart. Not yet anyway."

Lana watched him twist around to face his reflection in the long mirror by the window. Her heavy-lidded gaze followed his hand as it brushed down his baby pink fitted shirt that closely followed the curves of his back and gripped his lean biceps.

He neatly tucked in the fabric around the waistband of his pale blue jeans that sagged at the knees like he'd been sitting around all day. His dark chocolate eyes trailed up and down his physique while his fingertips teased the strands of hair at his forehead.

Silvery flecks scattered the shorter lengths above his ears and twinkled in the afternoon sunlight. His knees dipped as he checked out the flick of his hair from the side.

"I'm a good-looking guy, right?" He looked back over his shoulder, eyeing her struggle. "Lana, sweetheart, I'm talking to you? Stop wasting your time and answer me."

Her skin burned from the inside, heating her cheeks to an angry crimson. "I won't fucking surrender. I won't!" she panted, using up what little energy she had as the remainder of the sedative still trickled through her blood stream.

Carl swivelled and marched to her head. He crouched down and weaved the lengths of her hair around his fingers, then he yanked her head back. "I asked you a question!"

She gulped loudly, feeling the strain on her neck.

"I'm good-looking? Handsome? The type of guy you would go for, obviously, or you wouldn't have propositioned me?" His eyes searched her face seeking redemption.

Lana's heart stuttered. She wanted to bite his nose off, but she couldn't reach forward to inflict any pain, even though his face was too close.

Carl Reed had been left waiting for her in the penthouse suite, the one and only night she had gone to Verto Veneri. He had approached her at the bar after the heated encounter with Marcus.

She hadn't felt any sexual chemistry, but he had kind eyes, and admittedly, he was good-looking, if not a little too old for her. It wasn't her intention to lead him on and then leave him hanging without an explanation.

"TELL ME THE TRUTH." The force of his words hit her face in little spats of saliva.

"Yes, I thought you were attractive," she gritted out.

He released his grip and her face dropped to the floor. "I knew you fancied me. That's what makes me your hero, sweetheart."

"Hero?" she rasped.

"Yes! Against all the odds, I brought us back together. I heard your fiancé has hit hard times. Good timing, huh? He won't get in the way now!"

The fact she'd split up with Rory was none of his business and she planned to keep it that way. It was her choice to try and help Rory, her decision to leave Fermanagh without telling Marcus why, and it was her fault she ended up in the path of Carl Reed.

Her nostrils flared. "What do you mean? What did you do?" The words cracked in her dry mouth.

Carl rounded his shoulders. "I didn't do anything. He's the one who tightened his fingers around her throat and squeezed until her lips went blue. You have such a bad opinion of me."

"I ssshould be thankful…," she slurred. "You've drugged me and tied me up?"

"You're still alive, aren't you?" His tongue darted from his mouth with a snake like slither. "I feel a little sorry for that runt of a boy you were with. Jacqueline was always a kinky bitch. It was only a matter of time before she was throttled to death." His husky voice morphed into a strangled laugh.

He stepped over her bound body. With her face hovering inches from the carpet, she tried to follow his steps but her neck wouldn't permit it.

His fingertips brushed along her inner thigh. "I love this dress on you. It added to your allure that night, well, that and your hair. I have a thing for blondes."

Fear twisted in her gut, whispering to her sensitised skin to be aware. Prickles scurried across her scalp, hurtling down her back.

His hand followed the curve of her hip. She bit back a whimper as her stomach heaved. Her body jerked away from his touch.

"I want you to be sensible about this. Don't make a scene when we get outside. If you do, well, I'll have to resort to punishment and neither of us want that. Do we?" His tone was gentle. "You're so innocent to Verto and its ways. I was over the moon when you asked me to be your first." He lunged forward and planted a dry kiss on her temple. "There has to be a perfectly good reason why you didn't show up. It was your fiancé, wasn't it?"

Her lungs inflated, and she gulped back the sobs that bubbled in her throat. With every ounce of willpower, she managed to hold back the salty tears preparing to drop to the carpet.

She would never give him the pleasure of seeing how his actions affected her. She wouldn't gift this psycho with the knowledge of her fear.

She swallowed hard. "It was nothing to do with him."

"Sure it was. I would be jealous if my girl was going after a guy like me. I bet he made you go home early?"

She shook her head. "I left. Verto wasn't for me. I changed my mind."

Carl sighed removing a flick knife from his inside pocket. "You don't get to change your mind, sweetheart. Not about me."

"What do you want from me?" Her teeth chattered.

He stabbed the duct tape at her ankles, tearing the sticky adhesive from her flesh in one rip.

"I think that's pretty obvious, Lana. We need to get to know each other better, and then you'll realise the big mistake you made when you ran off like Cinderella." The sole of his shoe nudged her hip. "You didn't leave a shoe, but you certainly left an impression on me. You're unforgettable."

"Fairy tales, Carl?" Her head swam. "Don't you know the bad guy always loses in the end?"

He nodded in agreement. "Most of them do. Just as well, I'm not the bad guy around here. You'll see that soon enough." He swept a clump of hair away from her face and smoothed it down her back. "I'm the good guy, sweetheart." He paused. "Please don't make a scene outside, or I'll inject you instantly with a lethal dose. Do you understand?" His voice was calm.

Lana struggled to a stand, mumbling to herself incoherently. "Right...*Good guys threaten death*?" The words were meant to play out in her foggy brain but they fell out of her mouth with a hint of sound.

He slid her a chilling look. "I'm protecting you, from yourself Lana. Now, do you understand what will happen if you fight me?"

Steadying her with a helpful hand, he nudged her chin upwards. He squeezed her pale cheeks between his fingers and thumb, puckering her lips. "I said, 'do you understand'?" His smoky breath made her stomach tighten.

"Yes," she muttered.

Leaning into her face, he pressed his lips to her cheekbone. "Good. Things will be so much better if you comply."

3

Carl led her by the arm, out of Rory's house, a place she once called home.

He dragged her, shoeless and barely dressed, into the open. With each step, she padded the gritty concrete, and tiny stones dug into her soles. The road-fronted property was one of many townhouses; however, aside from the flow of traffic and a line of parked cars, there were no neighbours lurking.

The street was empty.

"For fucks sake," hissed Carl. "My car is blocked in."

Not knowing the layout of the busy road, Carl had parked awkwardly on the street corner and now his Range Rover was sandwiched between the neighbour's ancient rusty Ford and a black bollard.

"Change of plan. We'll take yours." His thin lips rose in an undefeated grin. He pulled a key fob from his jeans and pushed the unlock button, causing orange hazard lights to blink a few yards ahead. "A Lexus. Well, I am surprised. Living in squalor yet driving a fancy car."

Clearly, he wasn't aware that she had been with Marcus,

the owner of Verto Veneri. No one was aware of their blissful time together, other than her best friend Amanda and Marcus's chef, Freddy.

She bit her tongue, choosing not to engage with the creep who gripped her elbow before shoving her into the passenger seat and slamming the door shut. He jogged around the car bonnet with a pleased look on his smarmy face.

With her hands still bound, she was unable to put on her seat belt. Carl leant over her from the driver's side, his stale smoky breath filled her nostrils the closer he got.

He pulled the belt across her breasts, skimming them slowly with his knuckles. The corners of his mouth twitched, and he sucked in through gritted teeth.

"We would've had a good night together in that hotel suite. I know a few tricks that would make you scream."

Acid rose to the back of her throat, and the tiniest hairs on her skin stood to attention. He inched forward, stuffing his nose into her hair and inhaling loudly.

She held her breath, straining her neck away from him. Her blood began to boil as anger grew in the pit of her belly like a furious beast. The effect of the sedative had mostly worn off and jittery adrenaline jumped inside her muscles.

"Fuck you, asshole!" she spat, venom dripping off each word.

Carl leant back into his seat. His brown eyes narrowed. Running a hand over his sable hair he turned to face her. "Why are you being such a bitch, Lana?"

Baring clenched teeth, she pulled in her brows and hissed, "I'll never let you touch me, Carl. Especially like this…"

His gaze dropped, his lips quivered, and without warning Carl lunged forward and punched her in the face. Her head jolted to the side, and pain rocketed through her skull, splintering into fragments of red hot agony.

"Stop being such a bitch, or I'll dump you in the River Lagan," he barked, opening and contracting his fingers after the hard punch. "Don't make me hurt you. I'm a nice guy."

Lana's head spun, and darkness shadowed the daylight. Pain blazed across her cheek and she knew the warmth that rolled down her chin was blood oozing from her nose. The only way to survive was to stay quiet. She would bide her time until he released her hands and then wait for an opportunity to fight for her life.

She held no qualms about bludgeoning him on the head with a heavy object. As scared as she was, Lana knew she would do whatever it took to survive.

Leaning her head sideways, she watched the outside world as he pulled into the oncoming traffic and drove away from Jordanstown, towards Belfast city.

Her thoughts drifted to Marcus, his sexy lips and strong arms that had held her tightly the night before. They had sex a few times, both consumed with need, and then something had changed.

His eyes had flashed with a different emotion, and his lust had become tender. She had hoped to find out if the connection was real, but Carl was robbing her of the chance.

Her heart sank, considering her imminent fate. Lana regretted withholding her plan to help Rory and hated the fact a girl was dead by his hands. Her stomach twisted.

She cursed herself for sneaking away from Marcus. If only she had stayed at Marcus's and waited for him to return. Now her future hung in the balance and she needed to find a way to escape.

After a short, silent drive across the city, Carl pulled onto a wide, tree-lined avenue. The red bricked mansions were picture perfect, nestled amidst mature trees and shrubs.

It was a delightfully tranquil street, far removed from the

hustle and bustle of the city center. No one would ever imagine that an occupant was hiding monstrous deeds.

He pulled up outside an electric steel gate. Once he waved a card from his wallet in front of a silver box on the stone wall, the gate began to open slowly.

Trailing ivy covered the front of the impressive property, draping the sash windows and clinging to the porch roof. The freshly painted red door brightened the dreariness of the overcast late afternoon.

It felt cooler in the city, a subtle drop in climate that made her shiver. Or, perhaps she felt a chill because she was tired, sore and scared. Carl's smug face suddenly appeared at the passenger window.

Lost in her thoughts, she hadn't noticed him park up or even exit the car. He flung open the door, leant over and unclipped her seat belt, all the while humming an unrecognisable tune. He latched onto her arm and heaved her out.

"I've rented this place." He beamed. "What do you think?"

"Nice," she muttered, keeping her eyes low.

A brick wall screened them from the neighbours' view. No one could see her entering the property, but at least she had a fair idea of her whereabouts, should the opportunity to escape present itself.

"I'm really sorry, Lana. You can't stay in the house." Pushing her forward, he opened the front door. "You're staying in the garage. The owners installed a loo, so you'll be okay." He added with a half shrug.

His palm rested on her shoulder. "Straight to the end of the hall. Let's go."

She padded over the chequered floor, her gaze drawn to every detail. She navigated the long hallway with his finger prodding her in the back repeatedly, pushing her forward like cattle.

The space smelt stale and musty, like it hadn't been aired in days. She hesitated at a single framed picture of Carl and a younger woman with golden, shoulder-length hair.

"Where is she?" Lana dared to ask as they reached the kitchen.

His body tensed. "She said I had an addiction to sex with strangers and left me…the bitch," he said sharply. "Can you believe she moved in with a guy from Belfast. She chose a dick like him, over me!" He blew a puff of air from his nostrils and his hands balled. "Let's not talk about Lorraine. I have you now, Lana."

She chose to stay silent as he escorted her through the large kitchen with walnut units and sombre putty coloured walls. A circular glass table sat beneath a low hung crystal chandelier and the surrounding chocolate velvet chairs looked like they had never been sat on.

Several vases filled with dead flowers were dotted around the eerie space.

Leading her out the back door, they crossed a paved yard to the standalone garage. True to his word, it was moderately equipped with a screened toilet and sink.

Along the back wall sat a long, well-used sofa that could double as a bed. Under the steel-framed window were several drawers, neatly labelled for garden implements.

Carl shoved Lana down onto a shaggy brown rug, and she fell to her knees. With her arms still tied behind her back, her landing was awkward, but she managed not to topple over. As she knelt on the floor, she scoured the room for a way to escape.

Crouching down on his hunkers in front of her, he balanced in silence. A slight smile crept over his cheeks, but he said nothing. Moments passed and still his eyes burned into her trembling body.

"What are you staring for?" Her tone was high pitched, slashing into the uncomfortable silence.

Carl hummed in the back of his throat. "I'm so glad you're finally here with me, Lana. Everything has fallen into place, just as it should." The smile turned to a sly grin as his palms rubbed together. His unyielding scrutiny held her in place for a few more minutes, then he stood.

"I have some pressing things to take care of in the house. When I come back we can talk about why you left me high and dry and discuss how you can make it up to me. Until then, I can't risk someone taking you away from me again."

He rummaged through one of the drawers and pulled out a dirty rag, covered in oily black stains. Shaking it out, he proceeded to roll it up like a cigar.

"Open your mouth," he ordered.

Lana looked up at him, clenching her jaw so tightly that it ached. The second of a pause caused him to forcefully slap her left cheek, jolting her head to the side.

The sound cracked through the stillness and the sting brought a glitter of tears.

His breathing quickened and he grabbed her shoulder. "DON'T make me hurt you, Lana," he yelled. "I don't want to argue anymore. Please, behave yourself. I know you want me, so don't fight this." He pressed his fist to his lips and took a step back. "You do want me, don't you?"

She tore her gaze away from his face. "Okay, maybe not after I hurt you, I understand. I'll treat you better from now on, sweetheart."

Lana kept her mouth shut.

"I don't really want to slap you again, but I will, if you don't play nice," he said flatly. "Is that how you want to play?

Do you like it rough?" The corners of his mouth widened to meet his ears. "Now, open your mouth, please."

She gave in to a muted sob and her chin wobbled uncontrollably as tears stung the blazing slap mark. Her lips parted and she surrendered to his request, a small defeat for the sake of protecting herself from further immediate harm.

"Good girl. I have a treat for you, sweetheart. You and I are going on a road trip in one of my big trucks. It's waiting for us at the harbour. We'll get away from here and away from the memories of her…and finally enjoy each other's company." A broad grin stretched across his cheeks as if this was all he wanted in the world.

4

"She did what?" Marcus yelled into the receiver. "Tell me you're not serious, Freddy?"

"I'm sorry, Marcus, I've called her phone loads, but she hasn't picked up."

Marcus slammed the phone down and buried his face in his palms. "Fuck!" he growled.

She had broken her promise to stay in Fermanagh, and now she was driving head first into danger. Keeping the secret about Rory was a mistake.

A murder in his hotel was a major headache, and the fact that Lana's ex-fiancé was the only suspect, made it even worse. He hadn't expected Rory, the guy who snuffed out his bit on the side, to ask Lana for help, or that she'd run back to him.

The door to his office flung open. "Marcus, I've got some information." Marcus's PI, Arthur, burst into the room. His forehead was creased and his top lip was scarred, yet the skin on his bald head was smooth and blemish free. "Carl Reed was caught on CCTV in the hotel the night the Simpson girl was strangled, and then he went AWOL from the footage.

Something doesn't add up." He flicked a piece of gum into his mouth.

Marcus stood and rounded the desk. "He can't just disappear. We have cameras everywhere."

Arthur shrugged. "I know. Don't worry, I'm on it." He turned to leave. "You and the girl need to watch out, Marcus. I heard about the stunt you pulled in the club with the key card. The security team told me it was Carl in the room waiting for her - he might be out for payback."

"I ordered her to stay in Fermanagh, but that dickhead Rory made contact with her and she ran to him." Marcus shook his head.

Arthur cocked a brow. "You took her to Fermanagh?"

His shoulders pulled back and he crossed his arms. "Yeah. And...?"

"I'm not even allowed out there!" Arthur jeered. "You upping the game?" His smirk was light hearted, but his brows were raised in shock.

"It felt right at the time – like she's different from the rest. Who knows. No doubt I'll regret it." Marcus lifted his shoulders slightly.

"Be careful." Arthur nodded. "So far, all the evidence points to Rory. I'm just not convinced a guy like him could actually kill someone." Arthur left Marcus in his office, alone with his simmering anger.

He knew where she and Rory had lived together, hell, he'd been there himself the night he barged in on her watching porn. Grabbing his car keys, he bolted out of the hotel and into the underground car park.

The engine revved and he slammed the accelerator, urging the traffic to move faster. Hitting the motorway helped him to gather speed on a mission to warn her about Rory. He had to find her and make sure she was safe.

Sweet and sexy Lana Craig had waltzed into his life and injected him with an insatiable hunger created out of something, more than just sexual need. He didn't want to admit it, but something had changed inside him.

He sped to Rory's house by the shore. A heavy worry tightened the ventricles of his heart when he stormed into the open house and found it empty. The small living space showed no sign of her, only toppled tables and a busted television.

There was a creepy silence amidst the devastation which raised a scurry of dread across his scalp. He charged up the stairs, noted the open door to the bedroom and barged straight in.

The clothes he had bought her had been dumped in a pile on the stripped bed. Kneeling down, his pulse jumped when he picked up the snipped duct tape and caught the twinkle of a sharp blade nestled in the carpet.

Panic ripped through his muscles, stealing the ability to think logically. His imagination raced towards the cruellest of outcomes, falling foul to a seething fury.

A lethal combination for anyone who would get in his path. The only thing he could do was speed dial his brother, Jamie, his rock in all times unstable.

"Jamie, I need your help. This is so fucked up."

"What do you need, Marcus?"

"That girl I told you about, Lana—she's missing. I think her ex has kidnapped her. He's already murdered a girl from the club." His face paled as the words rambled out and the truth of the situation became real.

"Where are you now?"

"Her house in Jordanstown. She's not here. The place has been ransacked and there's duct tape and a fuckin knife on the floor."

"When did you see her last?" asked Jamie.

Marcus palmed his face. "I brought her back to Fermanagh. She was with me last night."

"Seriously? You took her home – to the Coach House?"

"Now isn't the fucking time, Jamie," he snapped. "I'm going to kill the son of a bitch if he hurts her."

"Okay, okay. Calm down. How did she get from your place in Fermanagh to Belfast?" Jamie quizzed.

"My Lexus."

"Right, then. Track it. I'll be right there in 20 minutes. Send me her address. Don't do anything until I get there, Marcus." Jamie paused. "I mean it. Chill the fuck out and wait for me."

"Fine," Marcus grunted

The thing was, Marcus had known she was in love with Rory. Christ, she had agreed to marry the asshole, but Marcus was still driven to have her all to himself.

In a fucked-up turn of events, it was Lana who had played him at his own game of fuck and run – and she ran straight back to Rory.

He typed in his location to the maps app on his phone and sent the details to Jamie. The swoosh of the sent message seemed so loud in the empty home.

He repeatedly tapped the small screen on his phone, urging the tracking software to load but a frustrating icon just flashed instead.

He searched through the clothes and slammed shut empty drawers. A picture of Rory and Lana, from a few years back, lay at his feet.

Scooping up the frame, he gazed at her happy face and shoulder length hair. Those big blue eyes were filled with hope for a happy future. Their fingers were locked and Rory was kissing her cheek like he loved her more than life itself.

Asshole.

Marcus's stomach churned. He chucked the photo back to the ground and watched it crash to the floor like a brick. He closed his eyes briefly, trying to process the crazy jealousy that plagued his mind.

"You in here?" his brother called from downstairs.

"Up here!" he shouted back. "Coming down!"

Marcus flew down the stairs, jumping off the last three and landing beside his brother. He slapped Jamie on the back.

"Thanks, mate. We need to find her ASAP. That asshole, Rory, has her."

Jamie was calm and cool, the ying to his out of control yang. "Check the location app for the Lexus."

"I can't get it to load!" Marcus growled as he repeatedly tapped the small screen on his mobile phone.

"I'll try. My internet connection is better than yours."

The app buffered for a few minutes and then reloaded. "Thank fuck!" he exclaimed.

A blue dot flashed on the map, showing the car near the Lisburn Road on the outskirts of Belfast. "Got it!"

"Is that a house?" Marcus scowled. "Rory lives here."

Marcus scrolled through his contacts and rang Arthur who answered after two rings, as he always did.

"I'm going to send you through an address. Find out who owns the house. Jamie and I are on our way there. Lana is missing. I think Rory has her."

5

As soon as Carl left the garage, Lana heard the slide of a bolt and the click of a lock turning.

She scrambled to her feet, staggering sideways and trying to balance without the use of her arms. Running to the window, she scanned the back garden.

Mature trees at the rear sheltered the property and offered privacy, the perfect place to hide a hostage. Her pulse pounded in her throat as she ran around the edges of the walls, trying to find something that would puncture the duct tape.

The plaster was smooth with no jaggy ridges or jutting nails. She dropped to her knees, trapped in a concrete prison with no way to escape.

After a few long minutes of isolation, the mechanical click of the lock shattered the silence. Carl had returned. The door slammed behind him as he strode inside.

He had changed into casual clothes and wore a pale green tee, stretched tightly around his lean torso and tucked into grey track pants. In any other setting he would appear handsome and approachable, but right now, he was a predator on a mission.

The sickly-sweet stench of cologne, combined with tobacco, made her stomach heave. She backed away, shivering with the prickles that darted across her back.

His gaze bounced around the room and he tugged at the neck of his tee, then he paced the floor like his thoughts were spiralling out of control. He dragged his fingers through his hair, back and forth.

The lines on his brow creased so deeply that his brows nearly met in the middle. Stomping towards her, he slotted both hands under his armpits and stood with his feet wide.

"I've ended things with Lorraine…it's finally over." He chewed the inside of his left cheek, skewing his mouth to the side. "Get up!" His eyes were like a raging storm, ready to whip up a powerful gale and tear down houses.

She wanted to ask what he was talking about, but her noises were muffled by the filth stuffed between her lips.

Lurching forward, he grabbed her bicep and yanked her upwards, so she was standing before him.

"I know you fancy me." His Adams apple bobbed up and down as he swallowed. He reached for her tousled hair and flattened it down the sides of her face. "Tell me what Rory said to you. What did he say to make you walk away from me?" His voice was ice cold, calm and sedate. "I want to know what he said that made you change your mind."

Her head shook and her eyes widened as he released the rag from her mouth. "He didn't say anything… I couldn't get into the room." Her words rushed out in one breath.

His head cocked. "You tried to get in?"

She nodded repeatedly. "I tried three times. Then I left. I swear I didn't mean to upset you, Carl."

The corners of his mouth reached his eyes. "I knew it! You do want me. I'm always right!"

"Will you let me go now?" She barely heard her own voice over the thrumming pulse in her skull.

His nostrils flared and a hint of fury flashed behind his eyes. "I didn't go to all this trouble just to let you go, Lana. You still left me to wait for over an hour, alone. When I went back down you were gone. You left me, like she did!" Carl began to pace, fisting his hands by his sides. "If it wasn't Rory, then it must have been that bastard, McGrath."

Lana sucked in a gust of air. "Why would he do that?"

Carl's head snapped back over his shoulder, and he stared directly into her eyes. "Those McGrath fuckers think they're God's gift. Only he could block your key card. I bet he wanted you for himself."

"No!" Her head shook, pretending it wasn't true.

In one stride he was in front of her again. "This doesn't change a thing, Lana. I want you and no one is here to interfere this time. It's just me and you, sweetheart." He shoved the rag back into her open mouth as she inhaled, ready to scream.

"Your hair is a mess. I like smooth silky hair, sweetheart." He shook his head disapprovingly and pulled out a small tortoise shell comb from his pocket.

Lana squirmed feeling the tug on her scalp when the tiny teeth dragged through the ends of her hair.

"I'll tell you a secret because relationships should be based on honesty." His movements were slow and his lips inches from her ear. "You're gorgeous, Lana. Even more beautiful than my ex-wife," he whispered. "You and I look pretty good together...the perfect power couple." His palm followed the comb from root to tip. "She's in the house, Lana." The words were spoken softly and controlled.

Her eyes bugged and uncontrollable whimpers rushed past the dirty gag.

"She wanted to talk," he scoffed. "Bit fucking late for that, don't you think?" His eyes became slits like a cautious reptile. "You're my future now. She's just a bitch who left me for a substandard guy."

Lana flinched when his hot breath met her cheek. "I knew it wasn't your fault that night in Verto Veneri. Now I know it was Marcus McGrath's greediness that took you away from me. I've decided that you and I should leave Belfast together. We'll tell everyone I was having an affair with you and that Lorraine was so broken hearted she ran off somewhere…we can iron out the details on our way."

A ripple of fear spread over her skin with every feathery light kiss he pressed onto her cheeks.

6

"So, what's the deal with this girl Lana?" Jamie asked as he checked over his shoulder and drove out into the traffic. "You seem invested?"

Marcus focused on the still water stretching towards the impressive yellow cranes at the Belfast dock.

"I can only describe it as an overwhelming obsession. I've never met a woman who could sink her teeth into my insides and make it hurt with unbearable pleasure."

"Jeez, bro. You're sunk."

"What do you mean?"

"We're on our way to rescue the girl from the love of her life. If he wasn't a murderer, this would be awkward."

A pained breath left his tight lungs. "She left him, they aren't together anymore," Marcus grumbled. "There's something about her." He rubbed his chin. "Can I commit to her, that's the question? I'm so used to having things my own way, doing what I want, when I want. Women just complicate things."

"And you want to be a lonely bachelor for the rest of your days?" asked Jamie.

"I was far from lonely." He almost laughed. "I love fucking about on my own terms. That's what I'm used to, but this girl plays on my mind even though I've already messed about with her. It's like I want to get to know her inside and out. You know, like what her favourite cereal is, that sort of random crap."

"Oh, fuck. You're so dramatic, bro. I'm gonna be sick." Jamie chuckled.

Marcus threw his brother a sideward glance. "Fine. Let's just save her from this asshole and see what happens after that."

The car raced towards the city centre, hitting red light after red light.

"For fucks sake." Marcus slammed his fist on the dash. "Another red light. It's like the universe is trying to piss me off."

Jamie strummed the steering wheel. "Look, she's probably at the house. With any luck we'll get there before the prick does anything bad."

An incoming call connected through the bluetooth speaker in the car. "Arthur, what do you know?" Marcus asked.

"The house is a rental which was recently signed for a six-month lease by Carl Reed." His husky voice echoed on loud speaker.

Marcus blinked rapidly. "Carl Reed has her?"

"One more thing." Arthur added. "His wife, Lorraine, is missing. Her new fella reported her AWOL. Apparently, Carl asked her to sign some documents. She hasn't been seen since. The PSNI are involved."

"What the fuck." Marcus hissed. "Put your foot down, Jamie, you're driving like a pussy."

Jamie had already broken the speed limit and was

dodging his Mustang through the traffic like a pro race car driver. They pulled up outside the rented property and jumped out onto the roadside.

"Wait." Jamie pressed his hand on his brother's arm. "Be sensible about this. If we startle him, he could do something stupid."

Marcus fixed his stare on the gate. "If he's hurt a hair on her head, I'll do something worse than stupid. It'll be fucking permanent," he snarled. "No one touches her."

They marched up to the gate, studying the entrance. Suddenly, two black unmarked vehicles sped down the tree lined street and halted beside the bright blue Mustang.

Several police officers exited the cars, crowding the brothers like bears around honey.

"ID please." A tall lanky officer moved closer.

Jamie and Marcus both offered their drivers licences. "Marcus. Thought I recognised you." He flipped off his hat. "Johnny Fisher." Johnny held out his hand. "Why are you standing outside this house?"

"Johnny, am I glad to see you again." Marcus tugged the officer's hand close and patted his arm. "Look, long story short, but the girl I'm involved with took off in my car, but now she's missing. I've tracked my Lexus to this place. I need to get in that house. Some guy called Carl Reed is renting it, and I know his wife is missing too."

"Who is your girl?"

"Lana Craig. She's in there."

"We're here on official business. I'll need you to step aside so we can search the property. If she's inside, I'll let you know immediately. Okay?"

Marcus scrubbed a hand over his face. "Seriously, Johnny, I need in there."

Johnny looked over his shoulder. "Can't, mate. If something goes down, it would be on my head. You'll have to wait out here. I'll get one of the guys to call in your missing girl. Give him the registration plates of the Lexus." He nodded to another police officer.

"Fine. I understand." Marcus stalked away and rested his hip on the car as he scrawled his personal reg on a pink page and handed it back to the officer.

He watched as the police men short circuited the entrance device, shoved the gate open and disappeared. Marcus marched over to the narrow gap and peered through, scanning the windows for any hope of Lana.

Every second that ticked by ate into his thrumming heart. Time felt like it had ground to a monumental standstill, like the mother of all pauses.

"It'll be okay, Marcus. She'll be okay." Jamie joined his side.

Johnny emerged from the property with a pale face. "When did she go missing?" he asked with a tremor in his voice.

"This morning."

"Right. We need to act quickly. She's not in there."

Marcus stepped closer. "What's going on, Johnny?"

Johnny shook his head like he couldn't speak, then he pressed the button on his radio. "Coroner required. Deceased female, late thirties. Cause of death, strangulation. Estimated time of death a few hours ago, maybe longer. Identified as Lorraine Reed."

"Holy fuck." Jamie grabbed Marcus by the arm. "Where's Lana?"

Marcus crouched in the driveway, holding his head in his hands. "It's not her. She has to be alive. She has to be fucking alive." He repeated with panted breaths. He suddenly jumped up to a stand, his back straight and his hands curled to tight fists. "Where the fuck is she then. Have you searched the whole house?"

"Yes. You said you tracked your car to this address. There's no Lexus here, Marcus." Johnny crossed his arms.

"They're not here." He turned to Jamie. "Quick. The app. Track the car again."

Jamie swiped his phone and loaded the app. A blue dot flashed at the harbour, twenty-three miles away.

7

The stench of fish grew stronger when Carl opened the door of the Lexus at the harbour.

"Stay in the car until I say so, okay, sweetheart." He nodded towards a forty-foot cargo trailer lined up, ready to board the ferry. "This is our new home for the next few days. I feel like I should carry you over the threshold." He laughed from his belly.

Back in the garage he had removed the rag from her mouth, freed her wrists, but then wrapped them up again in front of her pelvis so she could sit comfortably for the long journey ahead of them.

He wasn't a monster. The girl needed comfort. How else would she fall in love with him?

He flicked open a pair of sunglasses, planning to cover her watery blue eyes. Her satiny pale cheek was coloured with a wash of purple, blue and a trace of red, like a pretty watercolour.

He had tidied up most of the blood on her face, but he wasn't a fucking nurse. He did the best he could. The last thing he wanted was to mark her skin, but she deserved it at the time.

That's what happens when people don't listen—they pay the fucking price.

"This will hide that horrid bruise and stop you from making eye contact with anyone." He carefully positioned the frames on the bridge of her nose and tapped them into place.

The lenses didn't entirely cover the mark, but they suited her nonetheless. His shoulders bounced to his ears and he smashed his lips to her mouth.

Fucking hell, her mouth felt good. It won't be long until it's wrapped around my dick like a glove.

Lana didn't say a word, she'd been warned to keep her pretty mouth shut, and the good girl was obedient now. One or two slaps knocked her into line.

Her body was stiff like a cardboard cut-out. That wouldn't last long. Not when she was warm and relaxed.

Carl clambered out of the car and strolled towards the truck, whistling loudly. Raising his hand to the air, he clicked the auto lock button on the keys and heard the delightful sound of the car securing Lana inside.

He swiped a cigarette from behind his ear, thumbed the metal lighter and sparked up. With his feet wide and his arms crossed, he waited for the driver to exit the glossy white truck.

"Sure, you know how to drive this thing?" A gruff man with a white goatee beard shook hands with Carl.

"Sure do, Rick." Carl glanced over his shoulder and waved at her like they were a happy couple.

She was strapped into the car, safe and sound. Right where he needed her to be. The lovely Lana wanted this as much as he did. And if she didn't…well, he wouldn't dwell on the disappointing ending.

"All you pretty boys are the same." The lanky man laughed. "A pretty girl in every city. I'd love a good go at that one."

Carl tilted his head. "Don't look at her, Rick," he said with a blank expression. "Or I'll put my cigarette out in your eyeball."

"Steady on, boss. She's a good-looking girl, that's all." The man teased the hair of his wiry beard.

"I know she is, Rick. Now fuck off. We're done here."

The man rounded his shoulders and puffed out his chest. "Fine. Next time, it'll be seven grand for the lend of my truck." His lips tightened and he scampered off.

Carl's cold gaze instantly brightened when he turned to face Lana and waggled the keyrings attached to the truck key.

"Come on!" He bobbed his head sideward. "Your carriage awaits," he shouted.

An automatic clunk released the locking system inside the car. Fumbling with the inside handle, she shunted the car door open, swung her legs out and rolled herself out.

There were a few drivers in the distance but too far to notice her bound wrists. She paused, waiting for an escape plan to drop from the heavens.

"Lana?" Carl called over to her with a wily look on his face.

The thought of joining him was like willingly slipping into her own coffin. With a sudden surge of adrenaline, she jerked forward and bolted a few steps across the concrete yard.

The idea was to run anywhere other than by his side. One second she was running and the next she was flat on her face with his body on top. Her head cracked against the ground and she lay under his crushing weight, motionless.

She floated in a dreamy haze as he carried her to the truck and propped her up at the wheel.

He rubbed the back of his neck, his eyes searching hers. "Don't run from this, Lana." His smile dropped. "This is meant to be an adventure, sweetheart. Don't be a bitch, I won't take any more of this nonsense from you, okay?" His palm slammed the door behind her head. "Get in the fucking cab." His tone hardened.

"I don't want to go with you!" she snarled. "HELP..." Her strangled yell muffled behind his fingers when he slapped his hand over her mouth.

"Fuck sake, Lana." His fingers dug into her cheeks. "Shout one more fucking time and so help me...I'll..." A blaze of anger flickered in his cold eyes.

He momentarily held his breath and released it gradually. As if a switch had clicked in his brain, Carl gently tapped the tip of her nose with his finger.

"Come on, sweetheart. Everything will be okay. We'll be good together." His handsome smile didn't melt her heart—it gripped it in a choke hold instead.

Her stomach churned queasily and her brain shook. With short sweeps, he brushed the swollen bump on the side of her head.

She stiffened, repulsed by his show of affection.

His arms fell away and his tongue clucked. "Get in." He yanked open the hefty door. "I'm going to give you something that will keep you quiet for our boat journey. I'll go ahead and give you it now, so I can park your car away from the lorry." After forcing her inside the truck and hauling himself in behind, he pulled out a sheathed syringe from the glove box which had been left as per his request.

Flicking off the cover, he squeezed the plunger to release a squirt of liquid. Lana jerked to the side, adrenaline taking over. Carl missed her by inches.

"Sit still, Lana! I warned you not to fight me!" he growled.

Lana twisted around and pulled her knees up so the soles of her feet were a barrier.

"I swear, Lana, you're testing my patience. Put your fucking legs down before I break every one of your toes." He reached out and pinched her baby toe, inching it backwards. "Lower them, now," he hissed through gritted teeth.

The pain shot up her foot with his continued pressure, yet she kept them in place, blocking his advance. The calmness that once lived in his eyes vanished into darkness.

"You stupid bitch," he spat. Shoving her knees sideward, he clambered over her. She butted her hips and writhed under his weight. "Shhhh, little Lana." His harsh tone faded. Carl puckered his lips and planted a kiss on her nose. "You just need to give us time. There's loads of girls who would love to be in your position."

"Carl, this isn't right. Please, if you feel anything for me, let me go. We can work on this together, without all this?" She tried to move her wrists under his weight. "Please…"

"No, Lana. This is the only way for me to get what I want."

Her chin wobbled. She couldn't move, she was trapped under his oppressive weight. Her gaze flicked to the mini boxing gloves that hung from the visor, swaying gently after her struggle.

The needle punctured her flesh like a wasp sting and it didn't take long for the drug to poison her blood, again. Tiny tingles prickled her skin, dulling her reactions.

As the seconds ticked on, moving was no longer an

option, her body was unresponsive. The ability to fight slithered away, with hope riding its back.

Game over.

HE TWISTED THE PLASTIC DIAL AT THE SIDE OF HER SEAT, gradually inching her to a recline. It would look more believable like she was taking a nap.

Lana was his, and he would damn well make sure she stayed faithful. He decided Verto Veneri was the reason Lorraine left him. This time around, Lana wouldn't be allowed to fuck anyone other than him.

In fact, if he was truly honest with himself, he wouldn't let her out of his sight. It was probably for the best if he kept her holed up in the house. Ready and waiting for him to come home. Like a good girl.

The plan to leave Belfast behind was in full swing.

Clambering to the driver's seat, he stared at his reflection in the rectangular mirror, sighing with pride. Then, he leant over her limp curvy body like a hunter eyeing his prize kill.

He peeled the hem of his tee upwards, freeing his torso from the tight fabric as he tugged it over his head. His ribs jutted out and his belly was paved with muscles.

"I'm sorry about all the drugs, sweetheart!" He rested his cheek over her heart and absorbed each shallow breath. "I was the one who signed us up for the club a few years ago," he muttered. "It was such a buzz having sex with all those women, they lapped it up. I was hooked on the rush of random sex while I was married. Like having affairs with no complications. But then she left me for a puny fucker. He's half the man I am. I gave her everything and she still fucked me over." His hand drifted to the edge of her black dress. A shiver rocketed down his spine, anticipating the feel of her fleshy folds. A groan left his throat. "I noticed you the minute you strutted into Verto Veneri, Lana. I knew we would end up together, one way or another."

The drug had turned her muscles to jelly. No matter how hard her mind begged her to fight, her body just laid in a heap. It oozed through her arteries, dulling her senses.

The drug was different this time. She could see him and watch him, but she was powerless to move away from him.

Floating away from her paralysed form, she watched from above. In her mind, she screamed at her prone body to push him away.

He fluttered kisses over her jaw like a caring lover. The stink of tobacco was masked by peppermint gum, but the staleness permeated his skin.

Slowly, he teased down the front of her dress and freed her breasts. His tongue slithered across the plump flesh, and he released a rasping groan of gratification.

"Don't worry. Our first time won't be at the dock in a stinking truck...and your hair...it will smell like vanilla not diesel."

Lana fell into the depths of her mind, locating a dark hideaway that protected her from his torment.

Marcus thumped on the glass window of the truck door when he caught sight of the pathetic little cockroach Carl. He almost ripped the hefty door off its hinges as he swung it open.

"What the fuck?" Carl snarled, scuttling back from Marcus in a hasty retreat.

Jamie bounced in through the driver's side and pounced on Carl's half-dressed form, dragging him backwards like a rag doll.

Marcus heard the cries of pain when Carl's bones hit the tarmac but his sharp intake of air was held captive when he assessed the gut wrenching scene before him. He hauled off his hooded top and carefully shielded Lana's chest.

His heart crashed against his ribs as his shaky fingers brushed her blank face, swiping strands of hair away from her chilled skin.

"Holy fuck, Lana. Talk to me. Please, Lana, tell me you're okay?"

She just hummed and her glassy eyes rolled in her head. A cracked groan escaped her throat, but she didn't reply.

He quickly rectified her dress, covering her bare breasts and tugging it down to her thighs.

"Kill the motherfucker," he growled like thunder to his brother Jamie, who wrestled with Carl and slammed him face first onto the car bonnet. He kept his hard gaze on Lana's soft features and lightly thumbed her jaw. "Did he...? Was I too late?" Marcus's husky tone was strained.

Marcus fixated all his senses on Lana. Scrutinising her breathing—listening, feeling and watching as her chest rose, ever so slightly. He counted each breath, in fear she missed even one.

The harbour swarmed with police officers. One read Carl his rights and another cuffed him before shoving him in the back of a police car. Marcus was oblivious to it all, including the sirens that signalled the arrival of an ambulance.

He held Lana's little hand like she was dying, pressing his forehead to hers. A female medic assured him that Lana needed to be treated in private, forcing Marcus to let go of her cold fingers.

"Come on, mate." Johnny tapped his shoulder. "You can tell the sarge what happened. You'll have to give a statement."

"Jamie." Marcus nodded to his brother. The two men had a brief unspoken agreement. Jamie stood guard at the rear of the ambulance.

Lana blinked in slow motion.

Her eyes were gritty and tingles rushed to her limbs like the blood was in a race. A brunette woman carefully strapped her onto a narrow bed in the back of an ambulance.

"Did he l…l…leave?" she mumbled.

"Yes, Lana, the man was arrested," replied the medic. "It seems like he gave you a low dose."

The woman was talking but her words just drifted in the air between them. Lana was struggling to pinpoint one thought from the hundreds whirling inside her mind like a surreal motion picture.

"Why? They arrest M…Marcus? He save me…" she babbled incoherently, each word slurred and lazy. Tight straps held her weakened body in place. "Please. Marcus."

"Marcus is okay. He's talking to the police. Rest now. The drugs will be out of your system soon."

She nodded, barely understanding. The pounding in her head, became an overwhelming ache that exploded in her skull.

"My head sss…sore," she whispered. "Sick…" Her eyelids drooped.

A deep male voice joined the conversation. "When will the drugs be out of her system?"

"I'm guessing it was Ketamine, but we won't know for sure until they take a urine sample. It will take a while to work its way out. But don't worry, we'll look after her."

"I'm sure you'll take great care of her."

"M…?" she stammered, drawing in her fuzzy lips and sucking.

The tall male moved closer, he looked familiar—almost like Marcus but his features were finer. He had the same strong jaw and honey coloured skin, with short, thick sandy hair and fair stubble.

He was attractive, like a muscular male model, but not as ruggedly handsome as Marcus. Still, he was devilishly striking with pensive, almost black, almond-shaped eyes and a solitary dimple on his right cheek.

"Marcus will be over soon, he's giving a statement to the police. I'm Jamie, his younger brother." The corners of his full lips curved upwards in a wicked, yet caring, smile. "Just rest up. You're safe now, love."

8

Marcus jumped into the back of the ambulance, fixating on her bruises with an antsy fury scurrying under his skin.

His fists balled when her head lolled to the side.

That motherfucker needs a bullet in the balls and left to bleed out.

Lana drifted in and out of consciousness as Carl's drugs pumped through her bloodstream and took full effect. Her porcelain skin was marred by violence and icy cold.

She mumbled, garbling nonsense while her eyes rolled in her head like a china doll, scattering tremors of dread through his rigid body.

She was so fragile and vulnerable, now abused and beaten.

The drive to the private hospital was only a few minutes but every second that ticked by felt like a painstaking hour. The longer he had to watch her struggle, the angrier he became.

In the past he hadn't wanted the responsibility that came with a relationship. That was the very reason he kept his heart out of the game. Now he had feelings for Lana and hated the worry and helplessness that was eating him alive.

The tests and examinations she endured only made his anger blacken into tar, sticking to every organ, suffocating each breath, and seeping around his heart.

Once they were complete, he demanded an update. The short female doctor, drowning in an oversized white lab coat, looked up at Marcus through rectangular lenses.

"Are you her husband or a relative?" She blinked rapidly like her heart was fluttering.

He shook his head. "Neither. I came in with her last night. I rode in the ambulance with her."

The doctor cleared her throat as her lingering gaze drifted to the floor. The artery in her neck pulsated like she was nervous.

"Then I'm sorry, I can't tell you anything. How did you get in here?" She sucked in her lips like she was trying to remain professional yet lost under his confident spell.

"The police gave me the all clear at the reception. You can check for yourself. My name is McGrath." Marcus pulled his wallet from his pocket. "Look, how much will you take? I need to know if she's okay." He was growing impatient.

Her brows pulled together. "I don't accept financial bribes Mr. McGrath. I shouldn't talk to you." She paused while she chewed the inside of her mouth. Looking back over her shoulder as if scouting for listeners, she sighed. "Fine."

Her framed stare cut back to him, trailing up his towering physique and resting on his strong jaw. The slight twitch of her mouth gave the distinct impression she was eager to wrap her lips around his dick.

Usually, he'd be only too willing to charm the little doctor into the store cupboard, but right now he wanted answers. He wanted Lana.

"I'll tell you this much - she wasn't sexually abused. If you're the one who found her, then she has you to thank for that. Overall, her physical injuries are minor."

Relief forced a long slow exhale, which puffed out his cheeks. His gaze focused on Lana, lying in the hospital bed, weak and defenceless. The drug had made her irrational and woozy.

She'd babbled nonsense and vomited a few times. Finally, in the early hours of the morning, her body gave in to a peaceful sleep. Marcus had waited with her the entire time, ordering the nurses about like they were his staff.

He nodded. "I'm covering the bill, so make sure she has what she needs."

The doctor snatched a pen from her front pocket. "Of course, Mr. McGrath."

His eyes flicked to hers. "Thanks," he said in a sombre tone.

The doctor's eyes were wide with curiosity, but they were dull and unappealing in comparison to Lana's.

He stared into the room from the corridor, just to catch another glimpse of Lana's fragile state. She was the most beautiful woman he had ever met, with a personality to match.

Her silky alabaster skin would make a goddess jealous, and her startling, bright blue eyes were like precious gemstones. His emotions were spiralling out of control and the doctor was just a nobody.

The doctor quirked an eyebrow and clicked her pen. "Right then, Mr. McGrath. I must finish my rounds. I'll not mention the fact you shouldn't be here, for her sake. She'll need a lot of support when she wakes up." She smiled faintly and walked off.

Marcus strode into the private room, weighed down by

his anger. He never expected that one of his wealthy, popular members would resort to kidnapping, or even murder. Now he sought justice, and he knew exactly how to get it.

Lana laid perfectly still, tucked in loosely. Her pale skin glowed under the morning sun flooding the small, sterile room. The only sound was the heart monitor beeping at a steady rhythm.

His eyes focused on her chest, watching her lungs expand and contract. It was a macabre scene for a man who loathed hospitals. Now, he despised Carl Reed even more. His head hurt with a mash of anger and worry.

Adjoining the room was a modest washroom with a shower, hand basin and toilet. He ran the cold water tap until the water was icy cold, then splashed his face and patted it dry with a paper towel.

He slumped into the high back chair at the foot of her bed and shut his eyes. A subtle vibration in his pocket forced him to a quick stand. He jogged to the hallway and accepted the call.

Skipping the pleasantries, he firmly asked, "Jamie. What's the latest?"

"Carl is such a creep, Marcus. I don't know why you kept him in Verto!"

Marcus pressed his forehead to the pale green wall and kicked the skirting. "How was I to know he was a royal fucking dickhead?"

"I've been talking to Arthur. You should know that Carl is a member of an exclusive organisation from back in his private school days. They're sworn to protect each other in any situation, solicitors, judges, policemen, businessmen—you name it. Total shady bastards. He's got connections everywhere. Last week, he was spotted at a restaurant with Paul Adair, the head of the Law Society."

"Are you serious?" Marcus snarled.

"Whatever you pull together on him has to be watertight."

"There's no way they'd let him out after he murdered his wife! He'll rot in prison no matter who he shakes hands with."

"That guy, Rory, he asked Arthur if Lana could visit him when she gets out of the hospital," said Jamie.

An atomic bomb of anger ignited in his gut. How dare that prick even think about seeing Lana after what he did? "He made a run for it until the police caught up with him. Tell Arthur that she won't be within a mile of Rory. Period." His voice began to lower into a deep growl.

"Hey, bro, don't you think that's up to her? They were supposed to get married after all."

"She broke it off. He's in her past now." He argued. Jamie had a good point. Marcus couldn't just make decisions on her behalf, but she wasn't in the position to make decisions right now and he was. "Once she can think straight, then she can decide for herself, but for now, he can fuck right off."

"Marcus?" Lana's sweet voice whispered softly from inside her room.

"Got to go, bro. Catch you soon." Marcus ended the call, straightened his back and exhaled a long deep breath before entering the room.

Lana blinked, focusing on Marcus's clenched jaw and tight lips.

When he strained to sit, a bolt of pain stabbed through her shoulder. The creases on her brow deepened as her wide eyes flicked to the door.

Was she safe, was Carl locked up? Fear gripped her throat as she scanned every corner of the small room.

"Hey." His deep voice brought her gaze back to him. "You're in the hospital."

A lock of black hair draped his creased forehead and his dark green eyes were unreadable like a hurricane was whirling in his brain.

"Marcus…you're here." She licked her dry lips, then ran her tongue along her teeth. "How long have I been out?"

He folded his arms across his broad chest and the jersey material clung to his taught biceps. "You came in last night. They'll give you pain relief for your shoulder in a few hours. The Ketamine should be out of your system soon," he replied softly.

She frowned slightly. "Ketamine?"

A scowl passed over his face. "Yeah, that's the drug he used."

A puff of air juddered from her lungs. Not because she'd been drugged. It was the way his mouth curled and his forehead creased with a sexiness that stole her breath even now.

The fist squeezing her stomach released a little when she realised her wrists were no longer tied. She was free from Carl and most importantly, Marcus was right there. He was her saviour. The real hero.

"You saved me from him, didn't you?" She rubbed her forearm feeling a surge of gratitude blend with a need to be held.

The sunlight teased the side of his face and he scratched his dark stubbled jaw. "Yeah, beautiful. Thankfully he didn't rape you." His eyes were dark and serious.

Lana's fingertips shot up to her face, delicately patting the swollen skin around her eye.

"The doctor said it looks worse than it is. It will mostly be an emotional recovery. I've lined up a female counsellor for you." He stepped closer to the bed.

Throwing back the sheet, she swung her legs off the side, ready to slide off the bed. "Can you help me stand, so I can see what he did to me?"

"No, Lana." He lunged forward putting his palms on her shoulders. "You're hooked up to the machine."

Her eyes flicked left to the frantically beeping heart monitor then she lunged into his chest. "Thank you. Thank you for being here with me." She sobbed, pressing her damp cheek into his hard muscles.

His powerful arm floated around her neck, cuddling her close. "You're coming home with me, to Fermanagh, so you can rest properly."

She sucked in a ragged sob when his arm dropped, and the sensation of his commanding strength fell away. Patting her nostrils with the back of her hand, she muttered, "Where is he now?"

His stance widened and his hands slotted into his pockets. "He's locked up. Rory was picked up by the police. He was on the run when they caught up with him at the border."

Her limbs tingled as the blood rushed to her feet. "Are they charging Rory with murder?"

Marcus nodded.

Rory's fate tore at her heart. "I'll have to call Amanda. She needs to know where I've been. What time is it?" Her gaze drifted to the window, noting it was daylight. "Could you call her for me? I don't feel like talking."

The shock was seeping into her bones. A shiver made her teeth chatter. Marcus raised her ankles back onto the bed, then covered her body with the flimsy blanket.

"I'll call Amanda later and tell her you're staying with me."

"We barely know each other, Marcus," she mumbled as tiredness swept over her body.

Her eyes fluttered shut as Marcus ordered, "You're coming home with me. No arguments."

"Okay," she mumbled into the pillow.

He leant forward and pressed his warm lips to the curve of her jaw. "That bastard will pay for what he did to you, Lana. He'll fucking rot in hell." His words rolled around in her brain amidst the flashes of Carl's menacing smile.

9

Lana's eyes pinged open.

She bolted upright and held the bed sheet to her tight lungs. A bead of sweat trickled down the clammy skin at her temple. Scanning the dimly lit corners with the same speed as her racing heartbeat, Lana recognised the large room. She was back in Fermanagh.

"Lana." Marcus's voice rumbled from the armchair beside the bed. His torso hunched forward and his elbows rested on his knees. "You're safe. I'm here."

Her breathing was ragged, each little intake of air rasped in the stillness. Pulsating adrenaline jumped in her throat and her chin wobbled. "Marcus?"

The pale moonlight peeked through the wooden window slats, shadowing half of his features like a mask and sparking the gold flecks in his eyes, making them glisten like shards of amber. Her eyes narrowed to slits, fixated on his broad powerful form.

Marcus yawned, rubbing his prickled jaw with both palms. "It's okay, beautiful." His tired voice was husky.

"It's you...thank fuck." Lana breathed in his familiar

musky scent and detected his perfect white teeth behind a warm smile.

Palming the bedside table, she fumbled for the lamp. The edge of the bed sank down and Marcus leaned over, flicking the switch. Light flooded the room, casting shadows on the walls like monsters.

"Go back to sleep." He ordered with a calmness to his rasp. "I'm right here."

She gulped, cowering under the protective sheet with only her face peeking out. "Are you sure he's not here…hiding in the house?"

"He's locked up." His face was pale, almost grey, and dark crescents hung under his sleepy eyes.

Even though his jet-black hair was messy and his unbuttoned shirt hung loose, he still looked sexy as hell. She desperately wanted to crawl onto his lap and curl around his muscular torso for safety, but she couldn't fathom why he was sleeping in a chair when she was lying in a king-sized bed, alone.

"Why were you sleeping in that chair, Marcus?" She slid him an uncertain look.

The corner of his mouth raised with a sexy smirk. His hand drifted to a lock of hair that hung in front of her face. Gently and carefully he tucked it behind her ear.

"I didn't want to crowd you, Lana. I heard your screams and wanted to stay close."

Her face pinched. "Why don't you share the bed with me?"

Marcus brushed his knuckles across her jaw, his eyes soft. "We haven't worked out what this is yet."

His gentle touch prompted a seductive shiver that stirred an unexpected heat between her legs.

"Us?" she asked, curling her fists.

The look on his face was dark and dangerous as his eyes drifted down her body. "I was giving you time before…"

"What?" she barely whispered.

His hand retreated and he sat tall. "It's been a long few days."

She nodded dizzily, feeling a surge of adrenaline heat her from the inside out. "The tablets the hospital gave me were really strong. The past few days are a blur."

A smile tugged his lips. "I'm sure they're out of your system now."

The sheet floated to her waist and she edged closer to his thigh. Resting her hand on his arm, she delicately brushed his skin with the pad of her thumb.

"Lie with me." Lana shuffled her hips down the bed. "When the nightmares take over, I'd like you to be right here. Will you lie beside me?"

For the first few nights she had relived Carl's torment, helplessly letting the terror fracture her dreams. Sometimes, she screamed like the demons were breathing fire down her throat and other times she jack-knifed with her mouth wide open and only a strangled squeak bubbling out.

Patting the empty space on the bed, she nodded for him to join her. "Please. Lie down with me."

"Sure." He clambered over her legs and pulled back the cover, removing her protective barrier.

She shifted, feeling exposed without her safety blanket. He slid his arms free from his shirt and tossed it to the ground, then he sank down on the mattress and fixed the bedding just below her ribs. His nails skimmed her braless breasts making her thighs instantly clench.

Holding his hand centimetres from her quivering skin, he paused. The green of his eyes darkened like the churning ocean amidst a frenzied storm. Pulling back, a puff of air blasted from his lips when he stretched out his legs.

A wave of protection lightened her fear the minute Marcus joined her side. She shivered as tiny sparks exploded through her muscles and she sucked up the wicked energy that vibrated between his body and hers.

"Thank you for bringing me back here," she said softly, grazing his bicep with her fingertips.

He turned on his side to face her, expelling a hoarse sigh that rumbled like distant thunder making her stomach whirl. "Don't mention it, beautiful."

A slight wink sent her heart into melt down. "Marcus?" Erratic palpitations fluttered wildly in her throat and a slow burn between legs was quickly becoming a hungry necessity.

She pressed her pelvis against his hard body, enthralled by his warmth. "What are you doing, Lana?" he rasped.

His chest was carved and firm, silky and inviting but his strong muscular arms were like shields. She longed to be swathed in his embrace, held by his masculine strength and devoured by his wickedly sinful mouth.

Just the simplest touch from Marcus was enough to rescue her from the disturbing memories.

"My body is yours if you want it. Brushes with darkness have made me realise how much I need this right now." She was almost panting. "You can wipe out his hell, Marcus. I give you permission to burn your touch onto my skin."

Marcus hummed low in his throat. His head lifted from the pillow and his tongue swiped across her open mouth.

"You're too fragile. Too broken for the things I want to do to you."

Her stomach fluttered. "What do you want to do to me?"

The corner of his mouth raised in a sexy half smile and a

shadow danced behind his eyes. Drifting his hand to her waist, Marcus jerked her closer with a firm jolt.

"I want to hear you scream my fucking name, Lana." His husky voice was thick and inviting. "I want you, on your knees, with your hands tied behind your back and your pussy on my face."

Her tongue darted free from her dry mouth, anticipating his commands. A slight flutter of fear escaped her throat. Did she want to be tied up again?

The fleeting apprehension was quickly erased when he nuzzled her neck and growled, "Fuck, Lana. I've wanted to spread you apart from the second I brought you home to this bed. Is that wrong?" Tingles scattered her spine with his delicious wicked rumble. "I've watched you sleep for hours and each time a sexy little groan left your throat, I wanted to press my dick to your lips and shove it in your damn mouth." He grabbed her hair at the scalp and yanked her mouth closer. "I want to ruin you." With a slow lick, he teased the tip of his tongue with hers. "And I want to own you."

The swell between her legs grew so intense that she began to gasp. Nudging her pelvis into his thigh, she rubbed against him. A desperate groan filled the electrified air. "Touch me, Marcus. Be my gravity. Own me."

His hand drifted to her silky shorts and his long fingers slipped underneath the elastic.

"Those fucking sounds you make, Lana. They make my dick so hard." He slid a finger around her slick heat, teasing her entrance as his teeth nipped her earlobe. "I want to smack your ass so hard it shakes." She arched against him, melting as his finger pushed deep inside. "But that's for another time."

He grabbed her hand and raised it to his mouth. With long leisurely sucks, he took each finger in turn until she whimpered. This was exactly what she needed. Marcus McGrath was her protector, and her teacher.

Even after she endured Carl's torment, all she could think about was having Marcus inside her, surrounding her, taking her. His playful tongue traced her lower lip until he drew back and pushed up to his knees.

His gaze dropped to her face as he dipped his fingers in and out with a firm pressure. "Come for me. Let me watch you. Let me hear you." His voice thickened.

With a flick of his thumb, she shuddered into his hand, gasping for breath as a powerful orgasm surged through her core. She tilted her hips a fraction, so he could satisfy her with a deeper connection.

His deep sultry growl made her chest rise off the bed bringing her mouth to his shoulder and her nails to his back. She panted hysterically, unable to scream as her teeth dug into his skin.

Before she floated back to reality, he pushed her back to the mattress and held her jaw between his fingers and thumb.

"This time, you'll do what I ordered. You'll yell for *me*, Lana." His eyes narrowed holding her captive with his authority.

Sliding his fingers across her cheek, he pushed them deep into her mouth, so her lips stretched wide and her own musky taste mixed with saliva. His hand pulled away and he lightly tapped her cheek.

"You'll do as I say," he commanded with a bark.

Her breathing became quick sharp bursts when he leant across the bed and snatched a condom from the nightstand. He peeled open the foil with the same speed as she tugged off her tee, letting the cold air pebble her nipples.

The shadows were no longer a threat as her building need became overwhelming.

"If my name doesn't pass these lips loud enough, then I'll fucking make sure it does after." The look on his face was stern and stormy like he was battling his own demons.

Her heart leapt into her throat as his fingers rubbed over her lips, then dragged across her cheeks and threaded the lengths of her hair, holding her head securely before him.

Locking eyes, Marcus held her gaze and repeated, "I want my name to spill out of your dirty little mouth. Got it?"

Lana nodded wildly, anticipating the feeling of him buried deep inside her. The tip of his cock pressed against her entrance, then bit by bit, he shunted forward until he filled her completely.

She craved his lips all over her tingling skin, but his pensive gaze waited for her reaction. Plunging in and out, Marcus growled with a savage roar. His hands moved to her wrists, pushing them into the mattress with an unforgiving grip.

A powerful intensity built to the point of a sudden explosion in her core. She yelled his name, not because he ordered her to, but because he was her everything.

Marcus was the one thing she longed for. The only man who could torture her with pleasure, wrap her in safety and guard her from the shadows.

As soon as his name arced through the electrified air between their hot bodies, Marcus pumped into her quivering insides with a dominant fierceness that she had come to expect. His forehead dropped to the hollow of her neck as he snarled with a release.

"Fuck sake, Lana. I tried to keep a distance for your own good." He bit out, and as he did so, the sexy sound of a low chuckle encased her heart and squeezed. Taking each hand in turn, he pressed a tender kiss to the insides of her wrists. "I'm sorry," he whispered.

His warm lips kissed away the hideous memories of duct tape and his loving touch banished the fact she was once held prisoner by a mad man.

"You didn't hurt me, far from it. I needed to feel something other than fear, Marcus."

A lingering apprehension of the shadows returned, making her body tense when he lifted from the bed to dispose of the condom. Pulling the sheet over her prickled skin, she nestled into the pillow and watched his confident strides return to the bed.

"Marcus."

"Uh-huh?" he hummed, settling on his back and closing his eyes.

"How did you know where I was?"

"I have a tracking device on all my vehicles. It's linked to an app on my phone."

She knew he was exhausted because his usual sultry tone was all but a gruff murmur. "Marcus…I'm sorry I left here that day, after I had promised to stay. I know it looked like I was running back to my ex, which technically I was, but I wanted to find out the truth and then help him, if I could."

His eyelids blinked open and his head swivelled to face her. The softness to his features tightened. "You broke your promise."

She swallowed, feeling a pang of guilt ripple in her chest. "I know, and I'm sorry."

The corners of his mouth straightened and he swept a hand over his face. "Don't worry about it." He squeezed his eyes shut again like he wanted to block out the world.

Lana took a deep steadying breath. "Marcus?"

"I said, don't worry about it." His tone dropped to sub-zero.

She opened her mouth to speak, but what could she say to

make him understand. "Rory was adamant that he didn't kill that girl. I believed him." She nibbled the side of her fingernail. "Maybe Carl had something to do with it?" She shuddered as a chill skittered down her spine.

His eyelids never lifted but his lips parted and an extended gust of air left his lungs in a rush. "Look, Lana, I've told you…I'm dealing with it."

Uncertainty knitted her ribs together and she twisted her hips around. "Why are you pissed off?" She silently begged him to open his eyes and look at her.

"I'm not." He threaded his fingers with hers and pulled them to his lips, but his gaze remained hidden. "He's banged up with the low lifes. You need to focus on yourself, Lana, and let me take care of the rest."

She walked her fingernails over his taught chest. "I feel better knowing Carl is in prison. I guess I've just been in shock."

"I can arrange for a counsellor to come here?" he suggested.

As tempting as that sounded, she had to get out and about sooner or later. It had been three days since the whole ordeal and the world kept spinning regardless. "I can't hide away here forever."

He hummed in agreement. "I'll drive you to Belfast for the appointment."

"Thank you." Scooting her hips closer, she angled her body snuggly to his. Her cheek rested on his pillow, inches from his head.

"You don't need to thank me. No matter what happens in the future, I'll always look out for you."

Her heartbeat paused. Her brain shook like the universe was giving her a wakeup call.

Did they have a future together?

"That's good to hear." She added quickly not wanting to think of a life without him.

The muscles in his face relaxed and his breathing deepened. His skin smelled like vetiver. That sexy musky scent she knew so well. It was both alluring and masculine.

She wanted to cling to his weary body and never let go, mostly because he was warm and inviting but the other part of her was freaked out by the deathly silence that came with the silent night.

Irrationality paid her a visit. Crazy thoughts haunted her thoughts. *What if Carl finds out where I am and pays us a visit in the dead of night? What if he poisons Marcus while we sleep and takes me again?*

As if sensing her fear, Marcus drifted his hand to her belly. The tender caring movement was just what she needed to sooth her distress and his lightening touch zapped her with a bolt of dirty desire.

"I hope he gets locked up and they throw away the key," she muttered, soaking up his protection.

His head snapped to the side and his eyes flicked open, brewing like storms. "Carl is a dead man," he gritted out like he was holding a ball of anger inside his mouth.

"What if they let him out?" Her voice trembled.

"Listen to me, Lana. He will never be near you again. EVER." He over emphasised the word.

He nuzzled the tip of her nose with his. "After what he did to you...the guy will pay with his own life."

Lana wasn't quite sure what he meant by that statement. *Surely, he wasn't going to take matters into his own hands and beat the crap out of Carl himself?*

Nevertheless, knowing he had her back gave her comfort and helped to appease her persistent worry.

"What about his wife," she asked.

"I didn't know how to tell you this, but…" He paused briefly. "He strangled her. She was found in the house, dead."

The memory of Carl's surreal calmness flooded her mind, taking her to the very minute he told her his wife had run back to him. An avalanche of words rolled like waves and crashed violently against her skull. Her mouth drained of saliva.

"She was in the house?"

"Yeah." He jerked her tight against his chest, drawing her trembling body into his shielding embrace.

Her hand slid over his washboard abs and her leg drifted over his thigh, so she could be even closer. "I feel sick. That poor girl was killed, and I could've helped her."

"You couldn't even help yourself, Lana," he snarled. "You're alive and that's the main thing. I couldn't deal with another woman I care about dying."

"Like your mother?"

He pressed his lips to hers in a quick kiss. "Get some sleep, Lana."

"What happened to her, to your mother?" She felt his sharp intake of air and noted how his body went rigid.

He slumped an arm over his closed eyes. "Now's not the time to talk about her."

"Okay," she said politely. "Maybe another time." Her voice thickened.

Marcus sighed. His eyes pulled open and he lifted his head to reposition the pillow. "Aren't you tired?"

Hell, was she tired. All she wanted to do was sleep, to slip under the covers and screen herself from the black silhouettes, but the nightmares waited for her, every damn time.

"I'm exhausted," she admitted.

He threw her a sideward glance as she shuffled beside him and her knee brushed over his cock. "It's all a bit raw,

Lana. After what happened to you. When you were in the hospital, it brought back memories of when she died. It's hard for me to talk about it, so I don't."

Details were important to her. Lana had stumbled into his life, she was part of his present, but she yearned to know the details of his past. She wanted to learn the story of the man before her and find out what paths he faced to make him her hero.

"It's okay if you can't open up." Her tone dropped with obvious disappointment.

His shoulders tensed and his lungs visibly deflated. "My mother was killed." His voice cracked in a hoarse whisper.

She absorbed his warmth, holding her breath for his gravelly voice to give her a glimpse into his soul. A shadow passed behind his eyes like shutters were preparing to fall and lock the past away. His nails dragged across his stubble.

"She was killed by a drunk driver on her way home from work." He paused to clear his throat. "I had a bad dose of chicken pox, the worst of it had eased. She had to work a late shift at the bar - I was pissed that she left me. She called during a break, and I begged her to come home. I was a stupid selfish kid. We needed the money, but she got the rest of her shift covered and left. The drunken scumbag went through a red light and hit her car side on. She didn't stand a chance." His husky voice faltered. "Worst of all, he'd been having an affair and was rushing home to his wife after being with some random woman at the bar." Marcus dropped his chin.

Now Lana understood. "And Verto Veneri is a place for couples to have consensual affairs, without lies and deceit?" She cupped his cheek. "Did you start up Verto Veneri to stop married couples sneaking around?"

He gave a crisp nod. "Pretty much. A safe place for them

to fulfil their fantasies without ruining their lives, or anyone else's."

"Was it just you and Jamie after that? What about your father?"

"Jamie was young. The little guy was crushed. He had these big fucking brown eyes that tugged at my heart strings." A laugh bubbled in his throat. "The kid followed me around everywhere. Seriously, he was lost without her. And it was my fault. I was like his only anchor, and in a way, he was mine. Our dad fell apart. Threw himself into his job and worked around the clock to bring in extra cash. It was tough for a few years." His shoulders raised in a negligible movement that agitated the velvet headboard. "I worked my way up the food chain and became the business man I am today. When Jamie was sixteen, I taught him about business and we've worked together as the fucking million-dollar dream team ever since." His eyes gleamed with pride.

He brushed her lips with his thumb, dragging her bottom lip downwards. "Little did I know that my club would introduce me to the hottest girl in the world."

A soft groan gusted from her mouth. Her eyes closed, savouring his touch, trusting his actions completely.

His fingers dropped to the locks of hair resting on her shoulders. She lowered her head and smoothed her palm over his heart, tracing the black ink.

"You make me feel safe, Marcus."

10

It escaped him how the sexy tone of her voice had teased his limited self-control.

When she gave him the green light, he lost track of right and wrong. He needed to hear her scream his name, he wanted her to think about him, and only him.

Afterwards, he failed to mention that his mother's death had put him off relationships for life. Looking after Jamie had been a challenge.

He stressed every fucking day about the kid getting knocked down or drinking too much booze and falling into the lakes. He thought when Jamie got older, the worry would ease, but it just plateaued.

Nowadays, they are best friends, but responsibility still weighs heavily. Their father had retired and wasn't the man he used to be. Another obligation could just tip the fucking scale and knock him off balance.

Regardless, Marcus had welcomed Lana back to Fermanagh without much thought of where it would lead to. The urge to keep her safe was like a flesh-eating virus, spreading through his heart and making him crazy. Lana was under his roof and his for as long as he wanted her.

This was a first.

Having a woman in his home was a first.

Wanting to keep a woman was a first.

Fuck sake, Lana was a damn first.

Nurturing wasn't exactly a quality he expected to have, nevermind nurturing a woman, but Lana had this unknown way of revealing multiple facets to his otherwise one-dimensional personality.

The intense need to protect her, awoke a whole new depth to his character, other than working hard and playing even fucking harder.

Over the past few days it had been a challenge for him to not tear off her clothes, especially at night when she was lying in bed wearing skimpy shorts and a barely there top with no bra, or when he knew she was in the shower, lathering her perfect breasts and softly rounded hips.

It took all his will power not to barge in and scrub that bastard, Carl, off her skin because he thought his touch would scare her.

Now, with her cheek pressed to his chest, his fingertips stroked the hollow of her back. Her shallow breathes were the giveaway sign that she had fallen asleep.

It was oddly comforting to feel her warm puffs against his skin and smell the fresh soapy scent of her lavender shampoo.

Just as his eyelids became heavy, his mobile phone vibrated. He'd left it on the nightstand earlier, flicking it to silent so it didn't wake her. He carefully reached out, snatching the noisy device before it buzzed off the shiny surface to the floor.

"Everything okay?" He tried to whisper but his deep voice reverberated in his chest.

"This is it. Varia is having her pups – right this minute!" Roger yelled down the phone.

"I'll be right there. Don't leave her," he said in a rush, knowing full well his staff were diligent.

Lana stirred like a sexy siren. Maybe she felt the excitement bubbling in his chest or sensed the nervousness he harboured for his little dog. Her black lashes fanned her pale skin and a tiny moan left her lips when he slid his arm away.

"Hey." He stroked her jaw. "Varia is having the pups. Do you want to come with me to the stables?"

She propped herself up on her elbow with tousled hair tumbling over her shoulders and her smooth skin warm and inviting. She gazed at him with a dreamy, half-asleep smile.

Her fucking little tongue moistened her lips before she croaked, "I'd love too!"

His dick twanged. She was so sexy with that just fucked sleepy look. He wanted to suck her wet tongue right out of her mouth. Closing his eyes briefly, he tried to realign his dirty mind and return his focus back to Varia.

"Let's go," he urged.

They scrambled off the bed and tugged on jeans and hooded tops. She pulled her hair back into a loose ponytail and dragged the hood over her head. Under all the layers she looked lost and scared.

Marcus halted her in the doorway. "You okay?"

Her mouth twitched. "I'm okay, when I'm with you."

He pressed his lips to her forehead and sought out her small hand, wrapping it with his. Whatever was happening between them had rapidly picked up pace, almost skidding out of control.

The fear dilated in her eyes, plucking at the same heart strings that Jamie once had.

Marcus took a steadying breath when Roger updated him on the situation. Varia was happy and content. All of the pups had survived the labour.

Knowing Varia was in the stable, only a metre away, should've spurred him inside, but he couldn't trail his eyes away from Lana.

A light wind danced with her hair while the moonlight gilded her blonde tresses making the strands appear almost white. She peered over the stable door, the corners of her red lips reaching her wide sparkling eyes.

She laid a hand over her heart, watching Varia meticulously clean her new born puppies.

Marcus had ensured his little faithful friend was safe and content. He'd waited for this very moment for weeks, but now, all he could do was spy on Lana's joy. His throat thickened as her happy gasps whispered in the still night air, replacing her recent sombre sobs.

"They're amazing." She kept her voice low, stepping back as the wooden door creaked open.

Marcus trailed his fingers through his hair. "I guess there's just as much good in the world as there is bad." *And that bastard Carl won't find much good in life after I see to him.*

Her smile lit up the shadows. "I'd love to get my own dog, but it's not fair to keep one cooped up in an apartment all day."

Varia was sitting under a heat lamp with six little pups nudging her belly. He crouched down. "Good girl, Varia. You did well. I'll make sure they bring your favourite dinner." He wanted to pat her soft head, but he knew it was better to leave the new mother in peace. "You want some shepherd's pie,

Varia?" His voice was soft and gentle, loving in fact, even though his head was filled with vengeance.

The little dog was tired but her eyes were thankful as she stared over at him.

Lana set her hand on his shoulder and squeezed. Her light touch penetrated his muscles and made every nerve ending tingle.

A NIPPY BREEZE WHIRLED AROUND THE STABLE YARD, dancing with loose wood shavings and disturbing the squeaky weather vane on top of the clock tower.

Marcus drew Lana close to his side in a shielding hug. "Let's go back."

His warmth and strength were fast becoming a crutch for her fear. So when he marched out of the stable, leaving her all alone, her gut clenched in a death like grip. A shaky hand floated to her stomach, holding herself up as the walls closed in.

Her eyes narrowed, burning into the dark corners and locating every unopened door as she darted out of the stable behind him. *Carl could be hiding anywhere, watching, waiting...*

Scurrying to his side, she reached out for his arm and hugged his bicep. "I don't mean to be so jittery."

He tipped her chin upwards with a firm pressure, so their eyes locked. "It's understandable." A slight smile tugged his lips, turning her organs to goo.

The pads of his fingers traced the faded bruising on her cheek. "I hate seeing what that bastard did to you, beautiful." His voice was harsh and jagged.

Dizzy and nervous, she pressed her pelvis into him. His

hot gaze trailed over her wet lips. "I'll not let him near you again." He broke her dazed spell and leant back. "If we don't go inside now, I'll end up fucking you right here, right now." His breath warmed her skin, showering her spine with tingles.

With his arm wrapped around her waist, he escorted her past every eerie shadow and spooky tree, matching her small strides and staying within inches of her hip.

The house was warm, flushing her cheeks when she burst through the door, thankful to finally be indoors. The dying embers in the wood burner formed a soft orange glow that made the room feel welcoming and safe.

Marcus prowled around the edges of the room, turning on every lamp, lighting the kitchen up like a summer's day. She snuggled up on the couch, drawing her knees to her chest.

Her eyelids felt like tiny weights were tugging them to the floor and her mind was foggy with suggestions of sleep. A warm blanket covered her weary frame and caring fingers swept the lengths of hair free from her lashes when her head sank sideward.

"Want to go to bed, beautiful?" His voice was a distant murmur.

Blinking rapidly, she focused on the powerful man at her side, holding two giant mugs of steamy hot chocolate, topped with mini marshmallows and a squirt of cream. She had fallen asleep.

"Not yet. I'd like to drink one of those." Her mouth curled and she raised her arms in a satisfying stretch.

There was a light thud as the mugs met the coffee table, then his fingers threaded hers. She was exhausted and quickly losing awareness of her surroundings, pleading with her eyes to stop rolling in their sockets like bowling balls.

The heaviness of her limbs suddenly became weightless

and her arms instinctively snaked Marcus's neck as he scooped her into his arms.

"I love you." The words tumbled from her mouth in a hazy dream and nestled into the hollow of his throat.

While the sun was teasing the clouds, Marcus coaxed Lana from the Coach house to walk in the fields. Last night, she had mumbled words that vaguely resembled, 'I Love you.'

Is that where all this was leading to? Could he really be 'that' guy?

The crazy thoughts galloping in his mind made his chest implode. Sure, Lana was a gift from the gods, but those words—those fucking three words were like atom bombs detonating in his head.

The golden sunlight sprinkled the wooded path, peeking through the tall trees that swayed gently. He wasn't sure if she had meant to reveal her feelings. She'd been half asleep, after all. Perhaps, they were a mistake and best left floating around in the past unaddressed.

He had hidden her away from reality, even keeping his chef, Freddy, at arm's length until she was ready to have visitors. Now, it was time to introduce her to the world again and lessen her growing reliance on him.

She clung to him like a broken animal. It was both welcomed and fucking claustrophobic. His head was telling him to back off, but his heart was revelling in her need for him. In a weird turn of events, he almost got off on the power of her dependency.

"I asked Freddy to make lunch for us…you okay with

that?" He watched her from the corner of his eye. She dragged her gaze from the sprawling fields from where they had just come from.

"I can't wait to see him again!" Lana said, twirling under his arm before slamming back into his chest with a girly giggle. He loved hearing that little giggle, it was sweet and cute and fucking sexy.

When he thought about it, it wasn't just the colour of her eyes that was so incredible. Sure, they glittered like the sun reflecting on an azure ocean, dilating with passion and fortitude but it was the inner strength that hid behind them.

They stopped by an electric wire that partitioned a couple of chestnut coloured horses. Lana ripped up a clod of grass and held it in her tiny palm, letting the horse's big lips fumble messily.

He rested his hand on her shoulder blade. Turning into him, her breasts pushed into his ribs. The soft mounds felt so damn good. The muscles in his back were rigid, holding back the urge to throw her on the ground and fuck her senseless.

She leant back, hesitating before him. He circled her shoulders with his arms and tugged her back into his chest. He wanted to ask if she still loved Rory, but how could he ask if she loved an alleged murderer and get a clear answer?

He had never considered commitment before and had no clue how to maintain a monogamous relationship, but with Lana, anything was possible. That thought alone gave him hope. Hope for some sort of togetherness.

She gazed up at him like a vulnerable, sexy temptress. "Why did you bring me to Fermanagh?"

Marcus cleared his throat and gave her an uneasy smile. Was he ready to have this conversation? Especially after she knocked the wind from his lungs with those fucking three words last night.

"I wanted to see where this would lead to." He sighed softly as a pang of uncertainty twisted in his stomach. "I'm not making any promises, Lana. I'll be shit at this stuff. I never wanted a relationship. Well, not until I met you." His voice became unintentionally firm.

"But you want to try?" She licked her dry lips and looked up with her fucking big eyes that instantly made his gut wrench. Hope was written all over her pretty little face.

"All in good time, beautiful. The most important thing is getting you back on your feet. Then we can work on the rest, but yeah, you have this way of reeling me in."

Lana craved the sensation of his wet lips blazing a heated trail from her mouth to her belly button. The need crackled through her core, right to the tips of her toes.

Her stomach flipped as the sensation of his body tight to hers fired up the synapses in every muscle. An intense look flashed in his eyes as her tongue darted between her lips.

His warm breath sent a flurry of chills down her spine. She closed her eyes, anticipating his touch.

A low buzz from his pocket snapped them apart. Marcus adjusted the bulge in his trousers and pulled his mobile from his back pocket. He sighed loudly and accepted the call.

After a second, he covered the mouth piece with his palm and nodded towards the house. "You go back in. Freddy's in the kitchen. I'll join you after I take this call."

Lana ambled up the path and into the house. The savoury smell of herbs and spices wafted up her nose and she found Freddy adding the finishing touches to a poached salmon.

"Nice to see you again," he called out, as she approached the large island unit.

"Hey, Freddy." She beamed, her cheeks blushed pink from her almost intimate encounter. "This looks too good to eat."

Lana was so happy to see his delightful handsome face again, with sparkling amber eyes and a roguish grin.

His eyes popped. "Don't say that, I've spent all afternoon prepping. You 'have' to eat it." He rested his hands on his hips. "Take a seat."

She perched on a bar stool and unzipped her track top. The late sun had penetrated the glass dome roof and heated the room like a greenhouse. The herby aroma intensified in the heat and shards of light reflected on every surface like splintered rainbows.

"How are you holding up?" he asked.

She shrugged loosely. "Fine, I guess. Marcus has been amazing."

Freddy tossed a final sprig of garnish on the fish and looked up. "You're such a trooper. I'd have been carted off to the asylum by now."

"I'm not quite ready for the funny farm just yet." She wondered if she was actually okay, or if she was just holding it all inside for one massive explosion.

A hand rested on her shoulder. Marcus pressed into her back and tilted his face into her hair, initiating a delightful quiver.

"Lana, I have to head out for a few hours. I need to take care of a few things at Verto Veneri. There's shit flying around because of what happened and I need to deal with it. I'll only be away for the afternoon." His lips teased the shell of her ear and sprinkled hundreds of prickles over her scalp.

"You're leaving?" She gasped.

Marcus trailed a stool closer and sat down. "Yeah. Freddy will be here the entire time I'm away. Won't you, Freddy?"

Freddy looked at her sympathetically. "Sure thing." He set two plates down before them and nodded with reassurance.

She nibbled the edges of her fingers and mulled over the idea of being alone at night. The last time he left her here, the unthinkable happened.

Guilt for leaving blended with the fear of the horrific consequences. This time she would only go as far as the stables and that was it. She'd been spoiled by his one on one company, but it was time she stood tall, and they all knew it.

Her gaze stuck to the floor and her heart beat thrummed in her throat.

"I'll drive to Belfast now, and I'll be back as soon as it's sorted." He cupped her chin. "You'll be okay. I promise. I have the best security system installed."

"I don't mind staying with you, Lana. We can watch movies and stuff our faces with crisps and chocolate?" Freddy suggested.

Lana sighed lightly as relief washed over her. She was happy to spend time with Freddy rather than be on her own. It softened the blow of being left without her safety blanket of Marcus.

"Thanks, Freddy. I'd love that." She forced a smile and Marcus lowered his head.

She shuffled to the edge of the stool, inching closer to him. "Please come back the minute you get finished." She gazed into his emerald eyes. "I feel safer when you're here."

His lazy smile heated her core and sparked a warmth that only he could resurrect. The cloud was evaporating and Marcus was shining through with a promise of a future.

He bent forward and placed a chaste kiss on her forehead. Her insides jumped to attention as the electricity from his lips surged through her muscles.

She wanted to throw herself onto his hard strong body. Hell, she wanted to taste his lips and feel his soft mocha skin rubbing all over hers. The wild sizzle between them was morphing into a thunderstorm that was beginning to crackle and rumble.

11

Lana had become all too dependent on Marcus's powerful presence and lost in his strength and protection.

Having him so far away was like having an artery sliced open. And she bled loneliness. However, the blood kept pumping and she got stronger in her own skin.

Apprehension still clung to her like a sickening stench. She hated looking over her shoulder when the shadows crept into the room.

That afternoon Freddy arranged a movie marathon, with hot dogs, bowls of crisps, handmade truffles dusted in golden powder and plenty of beer.

"What have you been up to all day?" He flopped down beside her on the couch.

She reached for a truffle and licked off the sparkly dust. "I read in my room for a while and then went for a walk to check on the puppies. They're so cute."

Scrolling through the movie list, he asked, "What movie do you want to watch first?"

"Oh, that one! I love action movies. It's an all-time classic." She popped the chocolatey ball in her mouth and clapped with glee. A soft groan left her throat as the truffle melted on her tongue.

"Me too. That guy Michael is *awesome*."

She hid her muddy lips behind her fingertips as she mumbled, "Ummm, dark haired and dangerous."

"Much like another guy we both know, right?" Freddy pouted. "You pair have really hit it off."

"We're taking it slow, especially after everything that happened. He told me he's never been in a relationship before but he's willing to try." She sipped a refreshing cold beer and swallowed the thick fudgy goo.

"That's all you can ask for, honey."

"Freddy, these choccies are to die for." She swiped another truffle and nipped a bit off.

"Awk, they're nothing. I just whipped those up for you, hon." He rearranged the snacks and moved the tray of truffles closer.

"You have a real talent in the kitchen, Freddy."

"Aww shucks." His teeth sparkled behind a wide grin. "The long term plan is to have my own restaurant. Marcus has been helping me with a business plan, but it's a long way off. I need the finances in place."

"Sounds amazing. Where would you open it?"

Freddy tilted his head. "Ideally, New York, but realistically that will never happen. The funding alone would be more than I could cope with. Marcus pays well, and he gives me a *huge* bonus every Christmas, but I would still need a massive business loan."

"Maybe you should start small and look for somewhere in the Belfast city centre area?"

He shook his head. "I want to move on from Northern Ireland, Lana. I'm young, free and ready to take on the world.

Plus, I want to find Mr. Right Now, and the pool of potential guys has been exhausted." Freddy chuckled.

Lana tucked her knees into her chest. "All the rich, hot guys have commitment issues, don't they? It's like a requirement these days."

Freddy chucked the TV remote on the armchair and reversed into the couch beside her. "Your pee must be made of liquid gold 'cause the guy is obsessed with you."

"I hardly think he's obsessed." She laughed softly. "Anyway, I drink gallons of water. My mum had the importance of water drummed into me from a young age. My pee is crystal clear."

Freddy grabbed a fist full of crisps. "Sneeze diamonds then?" he mumbled through loud crunches.

She clucked her tongue and swatted his knee. "I suppose it's got nothing to do with my first-class personality? Not that I've got much of that lately. I hate feeling like this all the time. I'm constantly looking over my shoulder and flinching when I hear a noise. It's doing my head in."

His laughter lines softened to serious creases. "What would you say to me, if I was in your shoes?"

She hummed in her throat and waggled her brows. "Oh, you're good. Reverse psychology. I get it." Lana clubbed his chest with a cushion.

"Marcus went away at a good time. It'll make you realise that you're stronger than you think," he told her, while he plumped the feathers in the cushion and tucked it behind his head.

Her knees drew into her chest. "I'm worried it's all too good to be true, and maybe he's getting bored, like I'm extra baggage. You know, the stuff you chuck out at the airport when your case is weighed and it's too heavy." She scraped her nails down her arm anxiously.

"Has he compared you to dirty knickers or old flip flops?" His smile snapped wide.

She slumped into him and pressed her forehead to his shoulder, giggling low in her belly.

"Oh, Lana." He paused theatrically pressing his palm to his heart. "You're like a well-used pair of knickers," he said, imitating Marcus's deep husky tone. "Look, out of all the women in the world, Marcus has you waiting at home for him. That's saying something."

She beamed. "I'll have to make it up to him when he gets home." Her stomach flipped when she thought about being in his arms again.

Freddy slapped his hands over his ears. "Too much info. La, la, la, not listening…"

Her phone vibrated amongst the snacks on the coffee table. "Oh, there's lover boy now." Freddy snorted out a laugh.

A silly grin ached her cheeks as she snatched up the phone. "Finally," she muttered beneath her breath.

Looking at the text message on the screen, she shook her head lightly. "It's Amanda. She wants to know what I'm up to because she just saw Marcus going into The Fitz Hotel with a woman."

Lana's heartbeat paused in limbo as all the scenarios ran through her brain at a million miles per hour. The phone dropped from her hand when she settled on betrayal as the only possibility. She jumped up and hurried out of the room with tears misting her eyes.

Hiding under the duvet in her bedroom, she sobbed into her pillow.

Why did he bother to make me feel special and wanted, only to run off with another woman the minute he left my side?

"I've been played," she muttered to herself between ragged breathes, clinging onto the pillow like it was a life raft. "I love him," the painful words whispered into the tear sodden pillow case. "He doesn't love me back. This just proves it."

Marcus was everything she ever wanted and more, but now he felt distant and out of reach.

"Lana?" Freddy called from the doorway. "Can I come in?"

She sniffed loudly and revealed her blotchy red face. "Yes."

He trotted into the room and bounced on the bed beside her. "You need to call him. That woman could be anyone. He owns Verto Veneri, Lana. There will always be women hanging around."

Rubbing her wet face, she nodded. "I guess so. It's just a shock. I'm just feeling really fragile without him here." Her voice cracked and tears streaked her cheeks.

"I brought your mobile. Call him, honey." He chucked the phone onto her lap as she heaved herself up the bed and propped herself up at the headboard.

She plucked a tissue from the box on the nightstand and blew her nose. With a heavy sigh she selected call and waited. After a few seconds the ring tone disconnected and went straight to his voice mail.

Her muscles tightened when she hit redial and reached his answer machine again. On the third and final attempt, the line went dead without even ringing.

12

She was wide awake and propped up with pillows when Marcus entered her room after midnight.

He sauntered across the room sporting a playful grin on his dark speckled jaw. "Hey, beautiful!" he drawled.

As he drew closer, his eyes looked puffy and tired.

"Were you ghosting me?" Her voice was shaky. "I called a few times."

His back stiffened and the grin subsided. "I was caught up with business."

"Right." Her gaze dropped to her fingers that wrapped her mobile phone. "You could've called me." She chucked the phone to the edge of the mattress. "You were spotted going into The Fitz with a woman."

He scowled. "And…?"

"Who was she, Marcus?"

His expression hardened. "An employee, Lana. That's all."

"Really!" she scoffed. "I might be a little vulnerable at the minute, but I'm not a fucking idiot. Who is she to you?" A warning bell clanged in her skull. "Was she the business that needed you in person?"

His eyes narrowed. "This is stupid, Lana. It was Donna Marie. The Verto Veneri general manager. I was with her most of the day, sorting out PR for the club."

A whoosh of air left her lungs. She knew who Donna Marie was, but, for some irrational reason, the idea of him being with her all day made her insanely jealous.

"Guess what, Marcus, I got on fine without you." She half lied. "If you thought I was at home pining for you, then you're wrong!"

Marcus closed his eyes briefly and exhaled slowly through his nose. "I was sorting out all the shit that went on in the club with Carl and Rory."

Lana sucked in a gasp.

"I was working, Lana. It's not as if I ran back to my ex!"

Her jaw dropped. "What the hell is that supposed to mean?"

His face hardened. "Let's face it, Lana, you were going to marry Rory, and even when he told you that he woke up beside a dead girl, you still ran to him like a love-struck puppy."

"Marcus, I've told you, I was trying to help him, that's all, and I nearly paid for that decision with my life. God, I paid for it, and I'm still fucking paying for it. Every damn night. Every time I hear a noise, or whenever I'm alone that bastard Carl is there, taunting me." Her shoulders hunched and she wrapped a protective arm around her stomach, seeking lonely comfort.

The pain of her memories added tenfold to the hurt of Marcus's possible betrayal.

His jaw slackened as ragged sobs bubbled from her throat. The creases on his forehead deepened.

"Look, Lana I own the fucking club. I'm responsible for people's wages. I'm not going to let all the bad publicity ruin what I've built up over the years."

"So it's more important?"

"More important than what, Lana?"

"Me..." She trailed off, her heart left damaged and aching.

Marcus stepped back like she'd slapped his face.

"Why didn't you call me? I was waiting around like a fool." Her mouth was dry and the words sounded strangled.

Marcus took a step closer. "I was working." He reinforced through gritted teeth.

"I just don't know if I can trust you, or anyone for that matter."

His hands bunched like he was holding back. "Right. I've got a shit load of work to follow up on."

Gulping back the swell in her throat. "That's all you're going to say?"

He stood at the foot of the bed like a statue. "You've made up your mind. There's no point arguing about it." His sigh was barely noticeable.

"You didn't text me or return my calls, then Amanda saw you with another woman. What else am I meant to think?" Her voice took a high-pitched tone almost breaking. "Did you have sex with her?"

"Fuckin' hell, Lana!" he snapped.

"How can I trust you, Marcus? For all I know, you could've been shacked up with her all day and that's why you didn't call me!"

His shoulders drew back. "Jesus Christ, this is too much. I haven't even been away that long and you're accusing me of fucking around. Are you saying you don't trust me?"

She shrugged slowly. "How can I? You've always been a

player, and it's not like we're actually in a relationship."

He cleared his throat. "I can tell this is upsetting you and that wasn't my intention. I'm gonna head out…"

"Why?"

"To give you space."

"Oh my god, Marcus. Obviously it's you who wants space."

"Right now, I do need space. I thought we had something to work with…but I just don't know now. I opened up to you, Lana. You know my past, and yet, you still think I'd sneak around behind your back and fuck someone else. You actually think I'd lie…like a fucking spineless cheater?"

"What the hell, M…"

"Yeah, I'm an asshole, I get it," he interrupted. "I didn't cheat on you, even though we aren't in a relationship. I was working alongside Donna Marie and I'll continue to do so. And to think, I was actually really fucking happy to come home, to you."

Lana saw the anger and the hurt in his eyes. Her gaze fell to her clasped fingers and her shoulders sagged.

"I'm sorry, Marcus. I just got really pissed when you didn't return my call. I'm not thinking clearly at the moment." She tucked her knees into her chest and wrapped her arms around her shins.

She hated feeling clingy and needy. In the back of her mind she had always felt an irritating niggle that he wasn't boyfriend material.

Moving in had felt like a step too soon, temporarily or otherwise, and hoping he would be faithful seemed like an even bigger error. Now, emotions were involved, and he was pulling the reins on a runaway horse.

A strand of hair hooked his forehead, teasing the furrows. "You don't trust me, and I can't change my past. I've put you first from the minute we met, Lana. I've tried my best to change my old ways, but it isn't easy. It shouldn't be this hard. It's no shocker this was going to go to shit. If we don't have trust—then we have nothing." His words spliced through the atmosphere like a fighter jet.

"You make it sound like you were doing me a favour, Marcus. I never asked you to change," she snapped, raising her chin high and rounding her shoulders, even though she was far from fine with his cold brush off. "You're right, if we don't have trust then I shouldn't be here. I'll stay with Amanda." She crawled off the bed and reached for a navy hoody that was slung on the floor.

There was a second or two of utter silence before he said, "No, you won't." Marcus stuffed his hands in his trouser pockets.

"Yes, I fucking will," she protested, even though the desire to kiss his lips burned from her heart to her core.

She fought against the natural instinct to throw herself into his arms and beg him not to push her away. Poking her head out from the neck hole of the hoody, she peered out at him. "I'm leaving…right now. Go to hell, Marcus."

Before she could slot her arms into the sleeves, Marcus marched around the bed frame and loosely tied the sleeves in a knot. "You're staying, Lana."

In the faded moonlight the tiny flecks in his green eyes swirled like gold leaf. She could stare into his eyes for eternity and never get bored.

"I'm not going to stay where I'm not wanted," she said with a surprising calmness, almost sedate. The lengths of her hair mapped her face. She puffed air from her pouted lips in a bid to blow the strands out of the way.

His fingertips gently swept her face free. "You're not leaving," he insisted. His fiery gaze curled her toes.

"Why should I stay..." she whispered raggedly, daring to believe he really did want her to stay.

He thumbed her chin. "We'll work this out, some way or another. You just need to trust me." Each word rumbled out from his chest and settled in her happy ears. "I have women on my payroll. They're employees, that's all they are, whereas you're something else."

She teetered on tip toes, so they were almost face to face. She inhaled, drawing in his familiar musky scent. "Fine." She blinked with a teasing acceptance. "Kiss me, Marcus. I need to feel something other than this fear."

His fingers ploughed through her hair and rubbed across her scalp. Cupping her head in the palm of his hands, he paused millimetres from her parted lips.

Her belly clenched while her hands slipped out from under the top and gripped his taught arms. His hot mouth blazed a path along the hollow of her throat until it found her hungry lips. With leisurely sweeps he licked and sucked, dipping inside her mouth to play.

She breathed into him, thankful he was home and happy to let him break down her rigid barriers. He lightly sucked her tongue into his mouth before breaking their kiss.

"I know Rory cheated on you outside of the club rules. I wouldn't do that. If I had hooked up with another woman, I'd tell you straight out." He told her, his eyes serious.

"I know." She gazed up under heavy lids, melting under his seductive spell. "I'm sorry. My head is all over the place. Being with you is the only thing that makes it all okay, so when you're gone, I'm hit with a double whammy of fear. I was scared, Marcus. I know it's all in my head, and I need to deal with it, but you make me feel safe." She nuzzled into the crook of his neck. "Let me make it up to you."

"What do you have in mind?"

"Pancakes!" she announced, leaning back to catch his eyes.

His forehead dropped down and pressed lightly to hers. "Pancakes?"

"Yeah, with strawberries and syrup." She laughed quietly.

His eyes suddenly darkened with lust. "Forget the pancakes. I'd rather drizzle warm syrup all over your pussy and lick it off," he said gutturally.

The black circles in his eyes expanded, sucking her into his expectant gaze. A nervous laugh bubbled in her throat. "That's a better plan," she whispered.

He yanked the hooded top back over her head and placed his index finger on her solar plexus. "I've missed that cute laugh. It's been a while since I've heard it."

Her lips curved upward and she fell back onto the bed with one nudge from his finger. Blonde locks fanned the sheets as she lay there, exposed and ready.

Lana sucked in sharply, feeling the warmth of his palms that slipped under her silk shorts. He inched them past her hips and over her knees, sweeping a heated gaze over her ivory skin.

The moisture from his wicked tongue sizzled on her skin, igniting little bombs of pleasure with each savoured lick. His fluid movements were slow and intoxicating, fuelling her anticipation.

Stopping his satisfying torture, Marcus arched over her body. "Are you ready for this?"

Her insides quivered making even her speech shaky. "Yes, Marcus."

A deep throaty growl gave away his gratification, making her stomach clench. "You want me to fuck you?" His hot lips dragged across her collar bone, venturing down to her fleshy breasts, then his gaze cut to hers.

She hummed with delight as his teeth grazed the tendons in her throat, lingering at her mouth. Each addictive kiss filled her core with a red-hot intensity. She needed more, and he was happy to oblige.

"Beg me to fuck you," he commanded.

Lana whimpered, widening her legs as he slanted his groin, positioning himself between her thighs.

"I need you, Marcus. I need you to fuck me."

Lowering his head, his mouth covered over hers. The scorching kiss was sensual and sexy, with slow tugs and licks. Her hands floated to the buttons on his jeans.

His hips tilted so she could pop open each button. Rolling to the side, Marcus ripped off his shirt. He pulled open the drawer in the nightstand and hunted around for a condom. She scooted up the bed and took the gold packet from his hand.

"Let me do it." She knelt before him, dizzy with need.

He nodded and sat back on his hands with his throbbing hardness on show. She tore open the packet with her teeth and removed the round rubber.

With tentative movements, she placed it on top of the satiny head. A contented gust of air released from his mouth and he studied her delicate fingers as they rolled it down his long shaft.

"What are you going to do now, beautiful?" he asked in a low rasp.

Her lips quirked. Nerves flurried in her belly. "I need you to take control."

Pressing a finger to her lips, his eyes flashed. "Whatever you want."

He pushed her shoulders, shoving her back to the mattress while he twisted on to his knees. Prowling across her body, she trembled beneath him.

Their eyes locked and an eager moan left her lips. The tip of his sheathed cock pressed her entrance. He muttered into her neck,

"You need me to take control, don't you, beautiful? You like it when I fuck you hard."

Her pulse thrummed against his wicked lips, with nails biting into his smooth flesh.

"Yes." A subtle groan escalated from her chest and rippled in her throat.

Her insides clamped around him tightly. It felt so damn good.

Each deliberate thrust chased his long seductive kisses that clung to her lips. Her legs wrapped his hips and his hand slotted under her buttocks, tiling her higher, penetrating her deeper.

This man made her body liquefy to molten desire, his touch burned into her wanton flesh, but it was the stormy emotion in his eyes that Lana couldn't decipher. She fell inside the intense dangerous gaze, taking her completely off guard.

Her limbs quaked and the spasms shuddered through her core. Marcus dropped his forehead to hers and gripped the flesh of her buttocks as he released. His warm mouth pressed the tip of her nose as he hovered over her used body.

"I missed you, beautiful," he added before settling on the bed beside her.

Lana curled up against his side with her ear resting on his heart. "Hmmmm," she purred. "I love the sound of your powerful steady heartbeat."

He twisted the lengths of her hair through his fingers. With one tug of the sheet, he covered her body with warmth and her eyelids fluttered shut.

13

Marcus waited until he was certain Lana was in a deep sleep.

He had trouble on his mind. It weighed down his shoulders like the ugliest motherfucker of hatred. Revenge was waiting to be dished out, McGrath style, and he needed to lay plans for retribution with the actual devil himself.

He hadn't always been the suave business man kitted out in tailored suits, with surplus cash to splash and business investments all over the world. Life before success was a rough ride, and even though it threw him more jabs and kicks than most, he had quickly learned how to survive.

Not only did he rise from the underworld, but he garnered loyal support from all walks of life. Carl Reed wasn't the only guy with cockroaches buried in his contacts list.

Marcus sought inside help and Malachi Kennedy, an old friend and mad man, who was his golden ticket. A twinge of guilt squeezed in his chest.

He didn't want to keep secrets from Lana, but she didn't need to know that Carl Reed would more than likely get out of jail without sentencing, and that Marcus was planning justice.

Carl would wish he'd never met her.

He would pray he'd never looked at her.

He would regret having ever wanted her.

He would weep for having breathed the same air as her.

He would pay for his crimes, one way or another.

Marcus slipped out of bed and sauntered to his office. It was easier to call Mal at night because the guy slept all day. Pouring a large whiskey, he sat deep into the office chair and hit speed dial on the desk phone.

"Well, well, well, Marcus. It's been a long time since I've heard from you," Mal answered with an Irish lilt that kissed the tip of his tongue.

"Thanks for taking my call, Mal. I need ears to the ground on the inside." Marcus got straight to the point. Time was ticking and he had zero patience left.

"Which cooler?"

"Maghaberry prison—in Ramand."

"And the reason?" asked Mal.

"Carl Reed. An 'ex' member of Verto. He murdered his own wife and he kidnapped my girl, Lana."

A throaty laugh gurgled down the connection. "Fuck off, McGrath. Don't talk shit. You have a girl? I don't believe ya. Old dogs don't settle." As Mal laughed, he wheezed.

"What the fuck is so funny?" Marcus's hackles rose, partly because he knew Mal was right, but mostly, because he wanted their relationship to last longer than the summer.

A wrench of uncertainty weighted his gut. Could he commit to her? This was unchartered waters and he felt an anchor heaving him under his usual calm surface.

"I know ya want ta settle with a good girl. It's just, guys

like us will always be chasing tits and ass. So, what's the point pretending?"

"You clearly haven't changed." Marcus necked the last drop of whiskey from his crystal cut tumbler.

"Nope." Mal sighed like he was blowing out smoke. "The reality is, I don't give a fuck about protocol or social expectations. I take care of 'me.' If ya wanna play happy fucking families, then I applaud ya. That life isn't for me, and I guarantee ya'll be back chasing skirts in a month when the novelty wears off." He hacked up saliva in a cough after planting a monster seed of doubt in Marcus's already wavering conscience.

"It's different with her." Marcus poured another large glug of whiskey. "I know it won't be easy. I wasn't sure if I wanted ties, but I've kinda fallen into it."

"Ya'll either break her heart or she'll fuck ya over."

Marcus curved his lips to the right. "I won't hurt her." *But could I be the guy who sticks with the same girl for eternity, buys her a wedding ring and fathers her kids? Do I even want to have kids and chuck more responsibility at my feet?*

"Sure, ya will. We all fuck up," Mal sneered. "We've got dicks that need attention, every, damn, day."

Marcus blasted air from his nostrils and shrugged off his comment. He knew Mal was right. Although that had been the truth before he met Lana, things had changed.

"You think you can help?" he asked bringing the conversation back to Carl.

"What's the plan?" Mal asked.

"I want to know everything about Carl Reed while he's inside. Who he talks to, what cell he's in and who pays him a visit. Then I'll decide what happens next." Marcus watched the golden liquid cling to the glass as he tilted it back and forth.

"Should be easy enough. You expecting more trouble?"

"The guy knows people. It won't surprise me if he gets out in the next week or so. I need to know the minute he's free, so we can take care of him. I have a feeling he'll be back for Lana."

14
———

Lana shot upright.

The room was shrouded in a soft haze, emanating light from the owl night light plugged in at the opposite side of the bedroom. Marcus had it delivered the night he left for Belfast, so she wouldn't feel so scared without him.

She rolled to the empty space where Marcus had been. Dropping off the bed, she bolted to the door like a skittish colt and peaked through the narrow slit. Her ears strained to detect his deep dulcet tones. Not a solitary sound. The house was deadly quiet.

She padded to the moonlit kitchen. The pale glow shifted shadows into threatening shapes. Her pulse jumped. He wasn't there.

Darting through the house, she finally heard his deep sexy voice behind the door to his office. She pressed the shell of her ear to the lacquered wood, hearing muffled footsteps like he was pacing.

"I'll admit, it hasn't been easy. Her head is messed up.

She's clingy as fuck." His voice was stern. "It's suffocating but I'll stick it out."

Lana clutched her stomach, dipping forward. *Clingy? Suffocating? Stick it out? What the hell...*

She sucked in a gust of air the exact moment her knees weakened. Leaning her shoulder into the wall for support, her palm flew up to cover her mouth, hoping to muffle her whimper but a shuddering gasp burst into the silence.

The door flew open. Marcus dragged his hands over his speckled jaw and trailed his fingers through his inky black hair. A heavy sigh tightened his features.

His bare chestnut coloured skin seemed darker in the dim light and taught muscles contracted like a shield locking into place.

"What are you doing?" He planted his feet in a wide stance and stared at her oversized tee and messy hair. "Are you okay?"

She stared at him blankly, mulling over jumbled words that would fit how she felt.

"Lana?" He leant forward.

She flinched, scooting back from his magnetic pull. His concerned gaze lingered on her twitching muscles and the quick rise and fall of her chest.

"What's wrong?" he added, resting his hands on his hips. "Nightmare?"

She turned away, her head dizzy, but his hand flew out and grabbed her elbow with a firmness that bordered on unyielding.

"Did you have a bad dream, beautiful?"

She opened her mouth to speak but the words stuck to her tongue, unable to flow. Pounding panic swirled in her belly and the words finally stuttered out, "I'm just an obligation. Clingy, Marcus?"

Marcus looked to the ceiling and let out a long puff of air from his nose. His grip softened until her arm fell away.

"Look, you didn't hear everything. I'll admit that's how I was feeling at one point. It's not an issue, Lana."

Her eyes stung. "Of course it's an issue, Marcus."

He threw his hands up in the air. "I knew it. I just knew this wouldn't fucking work."

Her brows snapped together. "Really? You don't think this will go anywhere?" Her voice pitched. "So you've just been biding your time before kicking me out on my clingy ass…" She sucked in a steadying breathe but her chin wobbled. "I can't believe this. Why couldn't you just be honest with me? I didn't ask to stay here."

"I never promised a happy fucking ending, Lana – but when have I not been honest?" His tone was clipped.

"I've been suffocating you, apparently. Keeping you away from all those other women you want to fuck. After all, that's what you're all about, Marcus. You're the owner of a sex swapping club. Your morals are fucked up." She swiped away a tear before it left her eye. "I thought you wanted to help me. To be my rock, Marcus."

His Adam's apple bobbed and his sultry look hardened. "*My* morals are fucked up?" His temper twitched his fists. "I met you in that fucking club, Lana. I got you off in my office while your boyfriend was fucking someone else. Or did you forget that? We can't keep arguing like this." His hands snapped to his nape, raising his elbows to the air and his fingers locked together. "Lana, I really want you in my life, but I don't think we should be together right now." He stepped back and exhaled quietly.

His statement reached out and slammed her in the chest. She scanned his impassive face, hoping and praying this wasn't the end. The rash reaction was wrong, and her accusation had scalded him more than she anticipated.

Although she was no longer held captive by Carl, her heart was imprisoned by the man before her. His gaze fell to the floor and his hands slotted into the pockets of his joggers.

Her mouth trembled but he still retreated into his office, leaving her all alone in the shadowy hallway.

"Marcus, please." She flew into the room like a demon was on her back. "We can talk about it. We have to talk this through."

He faced the window with his shoulders pulled back. "I'll arrange for my driver to collect you in the morning. Goodnight, Lana." His tone was like ice - business like.

"That's it?" Her voice cracked.

His silence was louder than words. She bit back a sob. The distance between them was cold and silent like no mans land after ceasefire. He didn't turn around to gift her with a forgiving smile or give her any subtle sign that he wanted her to stay.

The broadness of his silhouette was framed by the radiant glow of the crested moon making him appear almost unreal, untouchable.

He didn't want her anymore.

Whatever had sparked between them was destined to fizzle out. Marcus had given up too easily. He didn't fight for her, for them.

When the driver pulled up outside in the very early hours of the morning, Lana fled the Coach House like it was engulfed in flames, without looking back.

Marcus stood by the window in his office, watching the

car door slam shut and the tail lights vanish around the bend. He hoped she wouldn't take his heart from his chest as she left, but she did.

He had seamlessly slipped into autopilot and shut down his emotions. Her interrogation had made him realise they would never really work together.

No need to argue with fate, right? The internal fight was like a game of championship ping pong. Keep her or let her go? Emotions were heightened and a mix of doubt and desire had morphed into a mass of fucking crazy.

He had to break away from the intensity, from the woman who blurred the lines and gave him something important to fuck up.

Now, she was gone, and he was lost in a tornado of regret. He was used to making ruthless snap decisions in his work life, but his heart told him this decision was the worst mistake he had ever made.

Marcus was responsible for Verto Veneri – the buck stopped with him. The business trip had been a necessity even though Donna Marie was more than capable. It wasn't everyday a client was murdered.

Little did he realise Lana would get so damn jealous. The entire trip was focused on the club, nothing else. They scrutinised security options and even considered a ruthless membership weeding exercise.

Marcus and Donna Marie had thrashed out details of the pending merger with Luke Devereux, which would take the club to the next level and up the financial stakes.

As they refined the business proposal, Donna Marie was quick to point out that Marcus needed to be on top of his game, hinting that his focus had been elsewhere. It wasn't his fault that his mind kept wandering back to Lana's sexy giggle, or that he could still smell her sweet fragrance on his shirt.

Donna Marie was right. Marcus knew he needed to be one hundred percent available for the merger and Lana was a distraction. The reality only added to his already wavering doubt.

Then his stomach ached when he witnessed the distrust flash in Lana's eyes and he felt the hurt that cracked in her voice. It fueled his uncertainty.

He inhaled her pain and exhaled the reasons why he shouldn't be in a relationship. The persistent doubt sat heavily on his chest, telling him they had no future. Did he want her to leave? Fuck no, but was it the right thing to do —probably.

What he hadn't accounted for, was the maximum effort it had taken to set her free and let her walk away.

The Coach House became unappealing for the first time, ever. Her beautiful face and hair of spun gold haunted her vacant bedroom. Each empty room begged to echo with her soft sweet laugh.

She had completed his sanctuary and without her in it, it was more like a torturous prison, than a tranquil home.

He decided not to stay the night. After several whiskey's, he rang his driver to drop him off at St. Angelo airport, which catered to light aircraft and helicopters, just a few miles down the road.

His regular pilot had been on standby and was ready and waiting to fly Marcus to the main airport for a connecting flight.

Business was his sole priority, once again. A life-changing merger was on the table, and the finer details required his full and undivided attention. It was a deal he and Jamie had been building up to for months.

If successful, this final chess move would catapult them into the big league, expanding their bank balances from millions, to a potential billion.

One thing was certain, Carl Reed would pay for what he did to Lana. Marcus had made her a promise that he intended to keep. No matter what the cost.

15

The front door flew open. "Are you okay?" Lana's best friend, Amanda, launched into her neck and squeezed tightly. "I'm so glad you've come back. I've missed you," she cooed with annoying cheer.

Lana breathed into her shoulder, absorbing the contact. She inhaled the waft of cocoa butter mixed with the scent of Amanda's freshly laundered robe.

"I've missed you too." The words choked out amongst her best friend's mass of soft springy spirals.

Amanda clucked her tongue. "Come inside, you're shaking. Your clothes, and the stuff you brought from Rory's is over there." She pointed to a paltry cardboard box that sat like a rejected toy in the corner of the minute living room.

It was packed with a few odds and ends. The total sum of her relationship, not to mention her life, over the past few years. "You can take my bed, and I'll sleep on the sofa," Amanda said bossily.

She was a good friend, loyal and brutally honest, with a

huge heart. Amanda flicked the kettle on while Lana balanced on the edge of the armchair.

She sighed inwardly. The tiny apartment was beyond cramped. It would only be a matter of time before she got under her friend's feet.

"No way, Amanda, I'm not taking your bed," she said firmly, even though she was abso-fuckin-lutely exhausted and wanted to curl up under the duvet for eternity.

"Look..." Amanda said, dipping her hip and resting her hands on the angular bones like she was ready to dish out a lecture. "You're my guest, and my best friend. You've been through the mangle. I won't hear another word about it. You're sleeping on a proper mattress." She wagged her painted fingernail and shook her head causing her russet corkscrew curls to bounce wildly.

Lana forced a faint smiled. "Okay, just for a few nights, until I get sorted with my own place. Thanks, you're such a babe."

"Bestie?" Amanda's brow crept up mischievously.

"Yes. The best, bestie ever," she said softly.

Lana didn't have the energy to argue about the sleeping arrangements. Marcus hadn't called since she left his place a few hours ago.

In her heart she hoped he would order the driver to turn-around, but she was dropped off in the centre of Belfast without any hesitation. The bland dove grey sky and light drizzle had lowered her mood even more.

She tried to pretend Marcus didn't mean that much to her, but her foolish mind games were a sham.

Amanda strutted from the kitchenette to the sitting room in four strides. "You'll be back to normal in no time, Lan. The bruising on your face looks way better. The Arnica gel worked a treat. It just looks like you haven't washed your face."

"Seriously, was that meant to make me feel better?" She scowled.

Amanda's shoulders met her jaw line. "Umm, yeah?"

"So, not only do I feel like I've aged ten years, but I look like a homeless person too." Lana cocked her head. "Which technically, I am."

"At least you didn't break your shoulder, then you would look like Quasimodo."

Lana forced a sound that almost resembled a giggle but was more of a strained grunt.

"Lan, I'm here to look after you, warts and all. Have you told your parents?"

Lana exhaled slowly. "Yeah, I called them a few days ago. Mum wanted to fly over the minute I told her, but I played down the whole ordeal. The last thing I need is Hurricane Judy whirling through my life."

"Would you think about going over to stay with them in La Rochelle, to get away from it all?

"I guess it's an option, but I really need to organise my life here first. I'm homeless, manless and soon to be jobless. What a catch," she scoffed. "I need an apartment and a new career. I'm sick of pushing paper about all day. It's soul destroying. The majority of people in that place are like emotional vampires who suck every living aspiration and creative idea out of my personality. Maybe I'll go back to college and study photography." She half shrugged.

"You could do wedding photography," Amanda suggested. "That's popular."

"Hell no! I'd rather claw out my eyeballs. I like landscapes and season changes. I could travel the world and capture images of nature in all its glory." A twinge of excitement fluttered in her belly. "Or take foodie pictures. Freddy wants to open his own restaurant. I could take promo pictures."

"Who's that guy Freddy? He sounds hot!"

Lana hummed a laugh. "He's Marcus's personal chef. I hit it off with him the minute we met. You're not his type."

"I'm everyone's type." Amanda's grin stretched across her cheeks as she sauntered back to the kitchen and grabbed two mugs. "Is he your new best friend now?" She pouted.

"He's cool, but you're nuts. And nuts, trumps cool. Okay?"

Amanda puckered her lips and blew a kiss. "Good. What about Marcus? Where does he fit in now?"

Lana pulled her sleeves over her hands and crossed her arms. "It's over...before it really began."

"He saved you from a deranged asshole, stayed by your side and looked after you for nearly a week?" Amanda's brow creased. "That's not normal for a guy who doesn't give a fuck, Lana."

"I heard him on the phone to someone. He was talking about me and the exact description was, 'clingy as fuck and suffocating'. He was apparently, 'going to stick it out'."

"I'm sorry to hear that, Lan. He's a player after all, and guys like that never commit to feelings. It was only a matter of time. Just as well you got out now, before you fell for him."

Lana's eyes glittered with tears as she looked to the ceiling. "Bit late for that. Anyway, it doesn't matter how I feel. He's not interested in my baggage sitting on his playboy doorstep. I feel like such a fool. He was probably just waiting for me to feel better and then he was going to dump me."

A little piece of her fragile heart broke for the hundredth

time. Her subconscious scolded her for ploughing straight in with her eyes wide open.

He had taken her in and spun a fantasy out of false concern. Was it out of pity or even worse, misplaced duty? Either way, she fell into his illusion and dropped out the bottom with a colossal life changing thud.

Now, she was cut off. An insignificant number on his fuck list. At first, she had hoped he would call, to show that she meant *something* to him, but now, she accepted the cold hard truth.

Amanda rested her hand on Lana's shoulder, squeezing it gently.

"It'll be okay, Lan. I promise. I'm just thankful Marcus rescued you. If it wasn't for him…well, I dread to think." Amanda shuddered.

"Yeah, I know. I'll be forever grateful to him for saving me." She sighed. "What about Rory? No one can tell me anything. He doesn't want to see me."

"When Marcus called me from the hospital, he told me not to worry. He said that he had paid for the best legal team to step in and fight Rory's case and that you would be safe, no matter what. That's all he told me."

Lana scrunched her forehead. "Why is Marcus paying for a legal team…for Rory?"

Amanda raised her shoulders to her ears. "Your guess is as good as mine. It's all hush, hush. It happened in one of his hotels. The whole thing was kept out of the press. Perhaps he needs it to blow over quickly, so it doesn't affect business?"

The penny dropped. Of course, business came first for Marcus McGrath. "I'm going to head out in the next couple of days and browse the estate agents. I need to get an idea for what's out there."

Amanda handed her a mug of steamy hot tea. "Do you want some help?"

She shook her head. "No thanks. I have to do this on my own."

Amanda fell silent, her face contorted as though it pained her head as thoughts tumbled around searching for answers.

"Go on, Amanda, spit it out. What's on your mind?"

"How did you guys meet Marcus? Like, how does someone meet a rich handsome playboy like him? It's not as if he goes to the local pub after work."

Lana pressed her lips to the rim of her mug and blew gently. She wasn't prepared for the inevitable question. It was going to come out kicking and screaming at some point.

Amanda was a trusted friend, yet discussing the fact that she and Rory visited a club that permitted sex with strangers and traded partners for partners. It was a secret she dreaded to unravel.

She sucked in the warm liquid with a tentative slurp. "It's not important where I met him," she muttered, hoping to chase Amanda off the scent of her investigation.

Amanda cocked her head like a blood hound. "*Where* did you meet him, Lana Craig?"

"Okay. Have you ever heard of Verto Veneri?" Lana watched Amanda's expression carefully.

"Nope."

"Well..." She paused, nerves fluttering in her chest. "It's a special club. An invitation only kind of set up. For couples."

"Right...like dancing or knitting, or some boring married hobby to stave off the desire to fuck other people? Like a chastity belt for couples?" Amanda laughed and slapped her thigh, not realising how close to the truth she actually was.

"You're pretty close...Verto Veneri is all about long term couples exchanging their partners." Lana fell silent waiting for the truth to drop between the creaking cogs of Amanda's brain.

"For sex…" Lana added.

"Like a swinger's club…You went to a sex club. Lana Craig went to a sex club? Shut the fuck up. No way!" She gasped, holding her cheeks in the palms of her hands. "You dirty wee minx. I never thought you had it in you. I have just promoted you from best friend status, to a bloody Goddess on a pedestal. I'm so not worthy. In fact, I pale in excitement compared to you." Her words tumbled out all at once without pausing to take in air. "But how does Marcus fit in?" She stilled. "Don't tell me, he's secretly married. You bucked him senseless and his wife found out. This is mega gossip!"

His name slammed in her chest like a bullet, obliterating any chance of forgetting the unforgettable. The fleeting glimpse into their time together resurfaced and then dissipated, dropping her back down to earth with a thud.

"No, Marcus isn't married. He owns Verto Veneri and all the hotels it's based in. In fact, he owns hotels everywhere. Not all of them are privy to the secret club. He's made an absolute fortune from Verto alone." Lana rested her chin on her knuckles. "I met him the first, and only, night I went to the club."

"Did you shag him in the hotel, in some sort of steamy hot sex romp with other guys?"

"No!"

"Oh, come on."

"No, I didn't. I swear."

"Don't burst my bubble, Lan."

"I didn't have sex with anyone," Lana hissed, feeling a little overwhelmed by the nagging questions. "I was going to have sex with…" She jerked, shaking the unapologetic face of Carl out of her mind. "I met a guy and we sorta got on well but thankfully we didn't have sex. Someone was looking out for me, I guess, because the guy was Carl Reed."

Amanda gasped, her eyes swirling like a perfect storm. "You knew that asshole?"

"I asked him to have sex with me. I'd had way too much gin, met Marcus on the way to the hotel room, and then I left before anything happened with Carl." She crossed her arms, protecting herself from the memories. "So, to reiterate the answer to your question, I didn't have sex with anyone at the club. Rory, on the other hand, met Jacqueline and continued to see her behind my back, outside of the club. The rest is history."

Amanda flopped back in the chair. "And Marcus…he just showed up at your door?"

The tea stung her lips as she took small sips. "We had a connection, or I thought we did. Looks like he got what he wanted. No strings." Her eyes lowered.

Amanda reached forward and patted Lana's thigh. "It's pretty obvious you're crushed, Lan."

"I'm fine, honestly."

"You're so not."

"Look, he probably just felt guilty that I was abducted by a guy from his club. Maybe he was doing the right thing, so I wouldn't kick up a fuss and ruin his reputation."

"You can't fool me. It's written all over your face."

Lana sucked in a gust of air. "I thought we had something. I was kidding myself."

"He obviously wanted to have things his own way."

"Seems that way."

Amanda's nose scrunched up like she was about to suggest something unthinkable. "Maybe you should call him and get some closure?"

"No way!" Lana's voice shook.

Amanda's tight tendrils shook as she leant closer. "What have you got to lose, Lana. You're already miserable."

"My self-respect, my dignity, or how about my sanity?"

Amanda perched on the edge of her seat. "Do it, Lana. Woman the hell up and call him."

Lana gazed longingly at her mobile phone. Her knee bounced up and down. "What if he doesn't pick up?"

"PHONE him, Lana."

"But…."

Amanda snatched the phone. She scrolled through the contacts and quickly found Marcus's number. She selected call and dropped the ringing phone back in Lana's hand.

Marcus answered after one ring. "Lana, are you okay?" he barked with urgency.

She gulped back her nerves. "Yeah, I'm fine." Her mouth dried up like the desert, unsure what she wanted to say to him.

Silence.

Marcus cleared his throat. "The counsellor phoned. Your appointment is at one thirty, beautiful?" he announced. "Are you okay?"

Her heart lit up under the power of his words. "I'm feeling good. Talking about it won't change the fact it happened," she said with false confidence. "I'll pass on the counselling."

His sigh whispered through the connection. "Lana, you should consider it. Please."

"Can I see you? I think we should talk," she added through quivering breaths, ignoring his plea for pointless counselling.

"I've just arrived in Monaco," he said matter of factly. "Are you staying with your friend?"

Her stomach knotted. "Yeah. I'm going to Butler &

Walcott Estate Agency tomorrow to look for an apartment," she replied with a half-hearted shrug.

"Look, I'm wrapped up in business for a few weeks. I can reschedule a counsellor for you," he suggested, but it was more like a boss instructing an employee without any hint of desire to see her.

"Marcus, we should've talked it out properly." She winced. "I know I've been crazy lately, but I'm working on it, we can work on it together."

Silence.

"Marcus?" she demanded.

Finally, he spoke. "I don't want a relationship, Lana. I'm sorry."

Her scalp prickled. "Okay... fine... I just thought we could talk. Don't worry about it. Thanks for taking my call."

"Wait, Lana," he barked as she was about to cut him off. "Whatever you need, just let me know. Anything at all."

She quickly ended the call and slumped into the sofa, drawing her knees up and her palms close.

He couldn't give her what she really wanted—him.

16

Marcus left Northern Ireland to attend a rescheduled appointment in Monaco.

He reverted to business mode, trying to gauze up the gaping hole in his heart.

At the start of the year he had purchased a desirable and extravagant hotel on the Mediterranean coastline overlooking the yacht-lined harbour. All his hotels were given an internal facelift to meet his particular style, which had become legendary in the hotelier circle.

This trip was primarily business, although his brother Jamie was stopping in for a few nights, before flying to Italy to conduct his own business deals. When possible the two men met up, spending time together talking business, family matters and most importantly drinking and having sex with gorgeous women.

He brought forward a meeting to discuss decor ideas with a renowned interior designer. The consultation dragged on for a few hours, becoming tedious as the over dramatic and flamboyant, Cherie Monique, got lost in a whirlwind of inspiration.

He had people who could run through this shit with her, but it was best to deal with her directly. To take control. To keep himself busy.

Cherie had worked for him on a previous renovation - her ideas and final creation met with his approval. On this occasion, the French beauty had once again provided a vision that sat well with his unwavering brief, but today his mind was elsewhere. His thoughts stuck to the last conversation he had with Lana.

He was constantly on edge from the minute she stormed out of his life, so when her pretty face lit up the small screen on the mobile phone, his mind had raced with possibilities.

Her sexy husky voice held a whisper of hope. An all-consuming need to wrap himself around her in every possible way had burned through his soul. He wanted her more than he wanted the millions in his bank account.

A rampage of possibilities charged through his head like a stampede only to be halted by Mal's harsh warning. He ended up hurting Lana after all. However, it was better to end it sooner rather than later, before she actually meant those three little words.

Cherie clicked her fingers in front of his face, snapping him out of his reverie.

"Your brother, is he here?" she asked in a thick French accent.

Her blazing red hair was half knotted on top of her crown, the remaining tresses pouring down her back like streams of fresh blood.

Marcus grinned widely. "Why do you ask?"

Pouting her glossy lips, she waved a swatch of fabric with nonchalance, trying to hide her obvious flush. "I was just wondering if he was here. Perhaps he could join me for a drink this evening?"

He stretched back in a low leather armchair, in his already prosperous French hotel lobby. His lips curled to a rakish smile. "He's flying in later. We'll be in the bar this evening if you want to join us."

"Us?... Un ménage à trois?" She licked her lips, smiling with a delicious wickedness.

"Afraid not, Cherie. I don't share women with my brother. Ever," he replied with a husky timbre.

Her lips smacked apart and she shrugged. "Shame. I don't usually mix business with pleasure, Marcus, but you two are...irresistible, and together...it would be..." She couldn't finish the sentence and fanned her face with dramatic vigour instead.

He shook his head and puffed a blast of air down his nose. "Not gonna happen. I'll tell Jamie to keep an eye out for you." Marcus stood.

Cherie dropped the swatches on the table and daintily lifted to meet him face on. He leant in and kissed her cheek lightly, then the other. A polite 'au revoir', rather than a sensual invite.

JAMIE'S FLIGHT LANDED ON TIME. HE ARRIVED AT THE HOTEL in high spirits and was ready to party.

He barged into Marcus's suite like a rogue bowling ball, searched out his brother and brought him to the carpet in a headlock. The two wrestled and punched playfully until Marcus pinned him to the floor like a savage bear.

"I've got you hooked up with Cherie tonight." Marcus chuckled, hoisting Jamie off the camel coloured carpet.

Jamie unbuttoned his gleaming white shirt that hugged his

torso. "She had better not be a stalker, or I'll shave your eyebrows off when you're sleeping."

Marcus grunted. "I could still have sex with more women than you, even with no eyebrows."

"I don't count how many women I've been with. That's just pointless."

Marcus slapped Jamie on the back. "Or you can't count that high."

Jamie bounced on his toes, jabbing Marcus lightly on the arm. "I can count right up to a billion, big brother, and that's exactly where the pounds will hit once you sort out this deal with Devereux."

They ambled over to a built-in bar in the corner of the luxurious suite. Its mirrored shelves were miraculously blemish free and reflected the puffy clouds hiding the blue sky.

"I'm heading out to New York soon. The deal is pretty much done." Marcus forced a smile.

Not even a billion-pound bank balance could fill the emptiness he hid inside his black heart. Jamie grabbed a bottle of beer, yanked off the cap and handed it to his brother.

"I'm finalising business with Emilio Falcone and the other Italians. This will be the biggest deal I've closed to date." Jamie's eyes sparkled.

Marcus patted his little brother on the bicep, squeezing his brawny muscle. Jamie was his world. The kid brother who had followed him around like a bad smell and turned out to be his closest and best friend.

"I knew you could score it, Jamie. You're fucking ruthless. I'm really proud of you. I know dad is too."

"Uh shucks, dickhead. That girl has brought out your softy side." Jamie launched into Marcus and hugged him playfully. "What's the story with you and Lana?"

The sound of her name spliced through Marcus's head like a sniper's bullet. His gaze dropped and he took the beer without saying a word.

"Well? Are you going back to Belfast to see her?" Jamie persisted.

His blood crashed against his muscles like hot oil. "I don't have time for her. So just leave it. Don't even think about lecturing me either. The whole shit just pisses me off."

"She had it rough, Marcus." Jamie shrugged. "It's obvious you really like her."

"I wanted it to work but the whole thing fell apart the second I left her side. I fucked up." His mouth twisted in a snarl.

"What did you do?"

"I was talking to Mal on the phone and she overheard me telling him she was clingy."

Jamie shook his head. "Shit, mate. There's no coming back from that."

"I went to Verto Veneri to help smooth things over with a few clients and organise more security. Some of them were unsettled after the murder and kicking up about protection. I was only gone for a few hours, and when I got back Lana freaked the freak out. She was jealous that I'd spent time with Donna Marie, and she was pissed off that I didn't return her calls. Then she overheard me on the phone with Mal, telling him she was clingy." His head lowered as Jamie sucked in a burst of air through his teeth. "I didn't think she'd hear for fuck sake. It wasn't meant the way it sounded. I know why she's that way, but still, it was hard to deal with."

Jamie palmed his forehead. "You called her clingy, that's worse than ignoring her phone calls. Is it any wonder she's that way. You're her hero, Marcus."

"Well maybe I don't want to be a hero. Maybe I just want to fuck and move on, as always."

Jamie shrugged. "Your call, bro."

Marcus slipped off his shoes and popped open the first three buttons of his shirt. "Exactly. It would've ended badly anyway. I would've hurt her."

Jamie pulled up his sleeves, so they ended before his elbows. "That's her risk to take, if you're willing to try. How do you know you haven't already messed with her head?"

Marcus shrugged. "Look, I need to focus on business, that's the priority here."

"If you say so. Seems like she's under your skin. I've never seen you like this before."

Marcus tilted the beer bottle to his mouth. "She's all I think about, and it's driving me insane."

"It's called love, mate."

"Fuck off, Jamie."

Jamie smirked and tapped his brother on the cheek with his palm. "Fine. I'll jump in the shower, and then we can head downstairs to meet the ladies."

ONCE FRESHENED UP, MARCUS CHANGED INTO DARK DENIM jeans and a black fitted shirt that moulded to his rock-hard physique. They took the lift from the penthouse suite down to the hotel lobby and sauntered into the crowded bar.

Jamie sat to his left soaking up the attention, laid on thick by Cherie Monique. He didn't even have to say a word and she would willingly drop to her knees and suck him off.

Each seductive word that rolled off her tongue reminded Marcus of Lana's silky loose hair and vivid ocean blue eyes. His cock strained against his zipper while his heart shrank.

His self-preservation coping strategy was whiskey. The more tumblers of amber liquid he sank, the less he cared. Or so he tried to convince himself.

"Excuse me, is anyone sitting here?" asked a well put together young woman, with mid length chestnut hair and false fluttery lashes.

"Not yet," Marcus said casually, swilling the whiskey in his glass.

"I'm Jenny. Nice to meet you," she sang in an English accent, smiling up at him from the bar stool, making herself comfortable.

She bit her lower lip, smiling coyly. This woman was plastered in desperation, eager to be the woman Marcus brought back to his room for something more than a drink.

Maybe that's just what he needed. Someone else to fill the void. Dirty rebound sex.

He held out his hand. "Marcus."

Her delicate hand clasped his.

No connection.

Zero.

Her perfume was cheap with a sweetness that would become annoying after a few long minutes. Her perky breasts protruded upwards in a slinky green dress, heaving with anticipation.

Suddenly, he found himself imagining his cock wedged between them, thrusting up and down, spurting over her throat.

He didn't really want her. It was just a ploy, a contrived trick to push away all thoughts of Lana with her silky soft skin...her arousing giggle...and those entrancing blue eyes that saw straight into his soul.

For fuck sake. Forget about her already.

His decision was final.

Jenny offered mildly interesting conversation. Her dress clung to her hour glass figure like it was stuck down with glue and her big tits were begging to be fucked.

"Fancy joining me for a drink upstairs?" Marcus asked huskily, playing the game.

She looked up under spidery lashes. "Sure." If this girl had a tail, she would be wagging it like crazy.

Everything about the situation was wrong, right down to Jenny's hungry kiss in the lift and her grappling fingers that tugged off his shirt as they crashed into the suite. Her greedy hands caressed every ripped muscle on his smooth bare chest and her tongue flickered along his warm flesh.

"You're so hot," she panted, pulling away to peel the dress from her round shoulders, exposing her surgically enhanced breasts that stayed in place like two big balloons.

"Like what you see?" she purred, shimming her bounty side to side.

I just need to fuck.

He shoved her half naked body against the mirrored bar, smudging the perfect finish, caging her in place with his arms at either side of her writhing body.

His lips savagely kissed hers, an aggressive impulsive interaction with no enjoyable thrill. His rough stubble grazed the delicate skin around her mouth. Jenny moaned and mewled, pleasure seeking, enjoying his punishing lips.

Flicking open his eyes he glimpsed at their entwined reflection in the mirrors, seeing a naked woman laid out for the fucking. A stranger. A random woman.

There was no buzz. Just a body to use for sex. His mind recoiled at the futility of the charade. Her fingers fumbled with the buttons to his jeans, and the warmth of her inviting hands felt good against his thick shaft.

Even in the throes of passion with a beautiful woman, his

body was encoded to think of Lana. His cock sprang from his boxer briefs thinking about her, he rolled on a condom while thinking of her, his hard shaft thrust into warm wet flesh thinking about Lana. Only his Lana.

She was unforgettable.

His whole performance was a sham. He was present in body but not in mind. He didn't revel in the guttural gasps spilling from the woman who he relentlessly pounded.

He continued to thrust into her until she shattered with a fierce orgasm, legs wrapped around his hips, but he didn't have a happy ending. There was no satisfactory release to their coupling.

"That was awesome." Jenny grinned, collecting her breath and fixing her dress. "I'm up for more. How about I suck that big dick of yours?" She glanced at his unsatisfied cock.

Marcus ripped off the empty condom and threw it in the bin.

Get the fuck out.

He pulled up his trousers, strode behind the bar with his bare torso on show, and poured a super-sized whiskey.

"I've got a business meeting first thing. I'm going to crash now. Order whatever you want at the bar downstairs, and I'll pick up the tab. Nice to meet you," he said firmly.

Jenny nodded meekly, the understanding she had just been used for sex flashed across her face. She stumbled awkwardly towards the exit with her heels in one hand and her bag in the other.

"Yeah, it was fun," she replied looking over her shoulder with a hopeful gaze.

Marcus focused on the mirrors. He knew he was being an ass, but he wanted her fucking gone, to pretend the ordeal hadn't happened.

Once the door clicked shut, all his pent-up guilt crashed

into his gut a thousand times over. Overwhelming betrayal stuck in his throat.

He just had mindless sex with a stranger, it was his choice. On reflection, he should have just stabbed himself in the heart a few times instead because nothing felt as bad as the emptiness and remorse he kindled in his broken heart.

To top it all off, he couldn't even finish the job for himself. A complete waste of time. What should have been a dirty, fun fuck, taking her over and over, was just like a routine trip to the dentist.

Christ, he'd had sex with plenty of women in the past and enjoyed every minute of it, but tonight his skin crawled with disgust rather than sexual adrenaline. The brutal reality of being with a woman who wasn't Lana hit him tenfold.

Were all woman set to disappoint from now on? Substandard shells, that failed to arouse him. Was he forever void of the thrill and excitement without her?

Not only had Lana stolen his heart, but she had stolen the pleasure of casual sex too, casting a spell on his heart and his cock for eternity.

Marcus continued to torture himself. While he wished Lana was curled up beside him, he scrolled through the list of contacts on his phone until her name appeared. He wanted to call her back—and say what? No, she was better off without him. They needed space and enough time to think everything through.

But he fucking missed her.

Gulping down the last dregs of whiskey, he sank behind the bar, sliding down the wall. He was lost in denial and drowning under the surface of his stupid ass decision to let her leave.

Fumbling in his jeans, he palmed his dick, fantasising about Lana. He swept his finger across the images of her pretty face and her bare alabaster skin amidst his clean sheets, captured on his mobile phone.

There on the floor, he revisited her writhing body and recalled her sensual taste. He stroked his hard length and brought himself the gratification he needed, spurting come all over his jeans.

He lay in the ashes of his regret and drank the remains of his resolve, knowing perfectly well that Lana was the only one to fix him.

17

"Sign." The monosyllabic prison officer pushed forward a pen.

Carl scribbled his name.

"Here." The officer slammed down a transparent plastic bag. "Your possessions."

Carl grabbed the few items that were snatched away on the day of his arrest, returning his gold watch to his wrist.

He swivelled on his heels, away from the prison officer and clapped his hands with a slow, appreciative pace. "There he is, my hero!" He spread his hand across his heart and faked a loved up grin.

"How does it feel to be a free man, Carl?" asked the hero.

"Fucking amazing, Paul. You really are the best. No wonder you're the head of the Law Society." Carl patted the suited man on his back. Paul was shaped like a barrel and stank of designer cologne. "If anyone could get me out, it would be you."

"Isn't that what lifelong friends are for." They shook hands. "Try and stay out of trouble. Your 'get out of jail free' cards are limited now that the police have you on their books."

Carl shrugged on a jacket. "Don't worry about me, Paul. I have everything under control." Carl smoothed down his sleeves, buckled his leather belt and smiled curtly.

He winked at the ruddy faced man whose top lip was hidden behind a wiry black moustache. Paul's bushy brow perked up.

"I'll see you at the next meeting. We can talk about that certain 'thing' you promised me." His lip twitched with menacing excitement.

Carl's dark eyes gleamed. "Of course. It's a done deal." He nodded and slid into the car waiting at the roadside.

"Now, if you'll excuse me, I have some unfinished business to take care of."

Carl inhaled the fresh clean air of freedom. Paul left a bottle of champagne in the back of the town car, ready for Carl to celebrate his release. He supped the fresh nectar, slapping his lips loudly.

Nothing felt as good, as deliverance tasted. Apart from revenge. That was a dish best served cold—deathly cold.

18

It was much cooler in the afternoons now that summer was creeping behind autumn.

Thankfully, the typical Northern Ireland drizzle held off for an hour, so Lana tugged up her hood and left behind Amanda's gaudy lemon umbrella. Grey clouds masked the sun and made everything look cold and dreary, the days lacked colour.

She trudged along the damp footpath, searching for the Estate Agent her mother recommended. She hoped the perfect cheap and cheerful rental would fall into her lap without too much effort.

Even though Amanda had given up her bed, Lana found the nights long and lonely. She mostly lay awake wondering if Marcus was touching another woman and begging her untrustworthy eyelids not to close and welcome sleep.

Thoughts of Marcus consumed her, every damn minute. It was bordering on ridiculous. Obsessive, and she knew it. But the second she dozed off, his powerful maleness evaporated and he was quickly replaced with the stale breath of Carl who persistently seeped into her sub conscious, choking her screams.

Every time the memories snuck into her dreams, she drowned in fear. Exasperation clawed her lungs as she tried in vain to run. Her body lay paralysed, her screams muffled.

The nightmares intensified, even waking Amanda during the night. Perhaps counselling really would help her deal with the aftermath, but she wasn't ready to open that trunk of emotions.

The door chimed when she stepped inside the small premises that displayed an array of expensive city rentals. A pretty brunette looked up through purple frames.

"Good afternoon, I'm Sinead. How can I help you today?" She lifted her hand and waved.

Lana strolled over to the seat in front of Sinead's cluttered desk. "I'm looking for a cheap one-bedroom city rental."

Sinead cocked an eyebrow. "I have quite a few listed, but the rent is really high. Do you have a budget in mind?

"The cheapest you have, please."

If Lana went back to college, she would have to get a part-time job to help fund the course and pay her bills, so the cheapest and smallest apartment would be necessary.

Sinead batted aside her sleek hair that hung like curtains over her ears. "Well, you won't find anything in the city centre on a tight budget. The further out you go, the less the monthly cost. How about I pull together some potential properties in the surrounding areas and schedule you in for some viewings through the week?"

It's not what she wanted. On a low income it would be all she could manage. Lana had no choice other than scaling down and focusing on the long-term goal.

"Perfect. Thank you." She gave a tight smile and dropped

into the spongy chair opposite the perky girl whose fingers blurred as she typed.

"Your full name and contact number please?" she asked.

Lana scribbled her details on a house shaped notepad and handed it to Sinead whose eyes were fixated on the barely visible bruising that marred her cheek.

She tapped her pen on the counter. "Did you get yourself in some sort of trouble…" She looked down to the details on the quirky page. "Lana?"

"A crazy night out with the girls. Too much gin." She faked a smirk.

"Oh, I hear ya, loud and clear. Just the other week I barrelled down the stairs in my mate's house." She shook her head regretfully. "I only had ten shots. Omigod! I nearly ruptured my spleen. And that bone just above my..." She pointed to her bottom and mouthed the word ass. "It's been sore ever since. I've decided that five shots are my limit before I go out, any more than that and I walk like a puppet."

Lana sighed with relief when a buzz from her pocket saved her from the jaws of too much information.

"If you'll excuse me." She nodded to her phone and stood, edging away from Sinead's big ears.

Freddy's name glowed on the small screen. "Hey!" She listened avidly as he launched into a conversation about a new hot guy he wanted to tap.

"Oh goodness, listen to me babbling on, how are you feeling, honey?" He finally asked. "How's the face?"

Lana chuckled, she was more than happy to hear the sordid details of Freddy's most recent hook up.

"The bruises have faded," she all but whispered. "I'm out hunting for an apartment just now. Can't kick Amanda out of her bed for much longer. It's been nearly a week."

She glanced back to Sinead who was pretending not to

listen. "Would you like to call round and catch up?" she asked.

"Sure thing, I need to talk to you about something anyway."

Lana nervously ruffled a few pages on a plastic stand near the door, wondering if she was about to hear news of Marcus. "That sounds ominous...?"

"Oh, honey, I haven't heard from 'he who not be named,'" he joked.

She exhaled in a gust, not realising she had held her breath. "Oh, right. I'll text you Amanda's address. Call round about 7 p.m. Can't wait to see you again, Freddy." She ended the call, smiling inwardly at the thought of seeing his refreshingly happy face.

The desk phone rang. "Good afternoon, Butler and Walcott."

Lana returned to her seat, waiting for a list of rentals to check out through the week.

"Uh huh, sure." Sinead nodded. "Oh right, yeah she just walked..." Sinead's head bobbed back, her eyes cut to Lana.

"I understand, Mr. Butler. Of course."

Sinead set down the receiver, clearing her throat.

"Good news, Lana Craig. One of our landlords needs his apartment occupied immediately. He's prepared to accept a low rental for the right tenant. Looks like it's your lucky day, the luxury penthouse apartment is slap bang in the heart of the city."

"Really?"

"Can you commit to a one-year lease?"

"How much are we talking?"

"One hundred pounds."

"Per week?" Lana gasped.

"Per month, Lana." Sinead smirked. "Bargain, huh?"

Lana's hand fanned her breastbone. "And I can have it? Don't you need to see references?"

Sinead fiddled with her pen. "If I was you, I'd take it. Offers like this don't come around that often. My boss assures me it's fully legit. He knows the owner very well."

An unsettling feeling tingled through her body. "Who is the owner?"

"I'm bound by discretion, Lana. Do you want it or not?"

"Do I have time to think about it?"

"Sure. Call me before the end of the day."

"And which building is the apartment in?"

"The penthouse in The Square."

"The penthouse..."

FREDDY THREW HIS LONG ARMS AROUND LANA'S NECK, pulling her into a tight hug. He was doused in fresh aftershave reminding her of a summer breeze at the north coast.

His slender legs were poured into a pair of stone grey skinny jeans with a snug pale pink tee clinging to his athletic physique.

"Honey, you look so much better, nothing a little concealer wouldn't help with." He cackled.

His honeyed eyes twinkled while he fiddled with strands of her tousled locks. Lana's mouth curved upward, she had become very fond of the lovable Freddy and his cheeky chappy banter.

She grabbed his arm, tugging him into the small living space. "Amanda is out this evening, it's just us. What's your poison, sweet cheeks?"

Freddy tapped his mouth with his manicured fingernail and hummed. "I love it when you call me sweet cheeks. I'm very proud of my ultra-firm Gluteus Maximus. I brought a bottle of red and white. Let's go for the white tonight."

They settled into the sunken sofa that creaked suspiciously under their weight.

"Amanda hates this thing." She patted the worn fabric. "She's not sure how long it will last before someone gets a spring up the ass." Lana waggled her brows.

Freddy rolled his eyes upwards. "Good Lord. Spare me! The last thing I need right now is to become a human kebab!"

She was thankful to let his happy vibes stamp over her anger. She was hurt and upset that even a blind man on a horse could have seen her blatant stupidity ride into town.

How could she actually believe that she would be the one to turn the bachelor into a one-woman man?

Lana twiddled the tips of her hair and the words trickled out with a mind of their own, "What's he up to?"

Freddy shrugged. "There's a massive business deal on the table, but I don't know anything else."

Marcus and Freddy were tight, their relationship surpassed employer and employee after they quickly bonded over their mutual appreciation of good food. Freddy was eternally loyal and knew where to draw the line with personal information.

"He's been out of town the whole time."

"Partying, I suppose." She grimaced.

Her life was upside down, hanging by a thread. Taking time off work had only left her feeling lonely and depressed. She felt trapped in a glass room with no way in and no way out, and passers could peer in at the wounded spectacle.

She popped open the pale Chardonnay and filled the only two wine glasses in the apartment. Freddy received the tall stemmed glass with a boyish grin.

"How are you holding up?" A defined eyebrow arched and his eyes were sympathetic.

Lana sighed. "I have good days and bad days. The bad are spent in bed, afraid to leave the house, and the good, well, let's just say, I think about Marcus in ways I shouldn't. I can't believe Carl murdered his wife. I hope that sick pig gets what he deserves." Her eyes narrowed to slits. "Being stuck here makes it worse. I'm trapped. I need to get my own place, start searching for another job and move the fuck on with my so-called life. I'm thinking about going to college to take up photography."

"You like taking photographs?" His forehead wrinkled as he nodded in thought. "Have you considered taking pornographic images? There is a definite market for that sort of stuff. The internet is crammed with it." He shot her a playful grin with a twist of seriousness.

"Freddy!" She groaned and rolled her eyes to the ceiling. "I don't think taking photos of people, clothed or unclothed, floats my boat. I prefer nature."

"Lana the hippy. I never had you pegged as tree hugger." He smirked.

Freddy set his drink down on the end table and clapped his hands, baring pearly white teeth.

"Well, all that aside, I have the perfect idea, honey," he sang. "I got a call from none other than the sexy Jamie McGrath. He's heading to the south of Italy tomorrow. His chef, Ronan, has taken ill, appendicitis or genital warts or something gruesome like that. Anyway, he asked me to take over for a few weeks. He has a really important deal on the table too and wants everything to be perfect."

Lana's smile faded. "Oh, that sounds wonderful, Freddy. You're so lucky, what an opportunity!"

He grabbed her hand. "I want you to come with me. You

need a break, Lana, and I could do with help in the kitchen. When we aren't needed we can party in the sun. Jamie always has guests, so with you there to help, it would be fun, and you'll get paid too."

Lana shuffled to the edge of the sofa. "Really? Jamie wouldn't mind if I tagged along?" *He wouldn't think there's a physco stalker in the midst?*

"Honey, I wouldn't be here if he cared. And don't worry, I asked him about Marcus. Apparently, they're in Monaco together at the minute, and then Marcus is going to Madrid, and then off to New York to finalise some mega deal. He won't be in Italy for a few months, by that stage you'll be back here and shacked up in a new pad."

Lana sighed, was it relief or disappointment that pinched her gut? She needed time to heal both physically and mentally, having a few weeks in Italy would be just the ticket, and now was the perfect time.

"I may have found a swanky city apartment already. If I don't sign the contract, I'll lose out on a once in a life time offer."

Freddy's head cocked. "Really, do you have a bundle of cash stuffed in this sofa?"

"It's a penthouse. The owner wants someone to take out a year's lease, immediately, and they're prepared to take low rent for the right tenant."

"Holy shit balls!"

"It seems a little weird."

"Why?"

"The day I walk into the estate agents, some guy needs his penthouse rented at a reduced rate? Tell me that isn't suspicious?"

"Maybe it's the hand of Karma, dishing you some good vibes for once."

"I'd feel happier if I knew who owned it." She crossed her arms.

"Does it matter, it's not as if the landlord is going to live with you?" Freddy pursed his lips. "Come on, honey, sign the lease. Then, it will be waiting for you when you get back from Italy," he coaxed.

She leapt forward, pulling him into her chest. "Thanks, Freddy. I'm so freakin' excited! When do we leave?"

He clanked their glasses together and took a sip of the chilled wine, slapping his lips together after he swallowed.

"That's a crisp white. Marcus sends me bottles from all over the world to pair up with my dishes. This one is French," he rambled, blissfully unaware that the mention of Marcus pumped a barrel full of pain into her heart, until it was full to the brim and ready to explode like an incendiary device.

"We would need to leave soon. Jamie is entertaining business associates in two days. Oh, Lana, he has a gorgeous villa on the southern coast of Italy. The views are breath taking. People like us could only dream of owning a property like it. But on the plus side, we get to stay in the villa free of charge."

"Won't we be in the way?" she asked.

Freddy chuckled. "You need to see this place to understand. Don't worry, we definitely *won't* get in the way, and the Amalfi coast is the perfect place to take photos."

Lana set down her glass and slapped her hands together. "You're amazing. Let's do this." She grinned.

This was the best news she'd had in days. Italy had always been top of her list for holiday destinations. It felt a little odd going to Jamie McGrath's villa though.

She met him briefly, when she was drugged up to the eyeballs and half naked. *Great first impression that was.* She winced. As long as Marcus was on the other side of the world then the awkwardness would settle.

"How about we hit the town tonight to celebrate. Go on a pub crawl in the Cathedral Quarter?" Freddy chirped, locking his fingers in prayer position.

Her shoulders sagged. "I'm not really in the mood to go out tonight."

"You have to step into the world at some point, honey." He pointed out, shaking his head as she grunted loudly.

"Fine." She scowled. "You can be my date." A smile tugged at her lips as she staved a laugh.

19

Lana and Freddy stumbled along the uneven cobbled street towards the third pub on Freddy's list.

They had already shared a bottle of white wine, a bottle of Prosecco and slammed a few shots.

Before leaving Amanda's flat, she threw on a pair of skinny jeans and a fine knit jumper, keeping her heel height low, pre-empting aching feet from standing all night.

Freddy grabbed her bicep. "This one here. The Krooked Krow. They have live music."

He threw his arm around her shoulder with a comforting squeeze and together they staggered into the open-air pub. To the right was a long wooden bar with fairy lights strewn across the top like a Christmas cabin, and to the left were benches and tables filled with raucous party goers.

The alcohol gave her a merry buzz. Freedom from the gloomy cloud that followed her every step like an insensitive ghost. A musical duo played acoustic guitars and the bearded guy belted out husky vocals.

"Think I'll go for another shot," she shouted, pushing her way through the crowd towards the bar.

Freddy nodded. "Me too. I'll get these ones," he shouted.

"No way, I'll get them." She grappled with the money in her jeans pocket, nudging her elbow into a fleshy waist.

A tall man in a light blue denim shirt swung around. "Hey!"

His eyes were like ice and his expression stern, but his features were chiselled and perfectly proportioned on his attractive face.

Lana looked up, taking a pregnant pause to study his face. As she stared, his brow softened, and his lip curled.

"Sorry. I was trying to get cash out of my pocket." She leant in, standing on tip toes so he could hear her.

The crowd moved as more people tried to reach the bar, shunting Lana face first into the stranger's chest. She tried to step back. "Oh, I'm so sorry!"

His firm grip locked her in place, holding her waist, pressing her body firmly into his hard chest.

"No worries. If you were a guy I'd punch you in the face, but as you're a hot chick, I'll just stand here and enjoy the view," he said with a rakish grin.

Lana and the stranger were forced together by hordes of thirsty people, face to face, but even though he was good looking, she just wasn't interested. Let's face it, he wasn't in Marcus McGrath's league, not even in the same stratosphere.

"I'm hoping that's not your boyfriend buying those drinks?" he asked, gazing down at her.

Lana giggled awkwardly. "No, he's my mate."

As soon as the words left her mouth, tall dark and handsome planted his lips to hers. The taste of beer and cigarette smoke seeped into her mouth, hitting her nostrils.

Ripples of terror scattered across her chest, gripping her lungs, squeezing tightly. That familiar smell, the one aroma that reminded her of Carl Reed was back.

The music swirled while her fists clenched. Mustering an inner strength, she gave him a forceful shove. *How dare he kiss her without permission? How dare any man kiss her.*

Pleading for a solitary breath to fill her tight lungs, she struggled to stand. The shooting pains in her ribcage ricocheted into her gut causing a gush of bile to burn her throat.

"It wasn't that bad, for fuck sake," he sneered.

A warmth spread across her back as the friendly arms of Freddy enveloped her, his hand gently stroked her hair.

"Lana. I'm here. It's okay," he said softly into her ear.

"What's wrong with her? It was only a kiss." His lips slashed into a thin white line.

Freddy straightened and slid in front of Lana.

"Back off, dickwad. Did you ask her permission before sticking your ugly lips on her?"

The guys face reddened and his knuckles whitened around his beer bottle. Lana tugged at Freddy's jacket, a silent plea for him to back off. The stranger could pulverise him with one punch and there was no way she could deal with more violence.

"Run along home and play with your toys. You guys clearly aren't ready to play with the adults," he snapped.

Freddy turned back and focused on Lana as she gasped for air while a thundering pulse filled her skull.

"C'mon, honey, let's get you home."

"S…Sorry F…F…Freddy," she stuttered.

Her heart crashed inside her chest, trying its hardest to break free.

"Oh, honey, it's okay. Just think about Italy. The warm sun, fine food, tasty wine and plenty of time to relax. A holiday is just what doctor Freddy prescribes."

Her breathing began to regulate, but her mind was racing

with memories of the hideous ordeal with Carl. Anger slid through her veins like a venomous snake.

She was fed up being the victim and fed up with men thinking they could rule her body, her mind...and her heart.

20

Carl ordered the driver to stop at the street corner.

His newly appointed house was only a short walk from the local shops. Paul had organised a new house for Carl, under a pseudo name and was efficient enough to find one in the same area as his old one.

The car pulled up outside the small deli. The same little corner shop that Carl frequented on a regular basis. It started off as a place to purchase his favourite cheeses and thin slices of prosciutto, until a particular shop assistant sprinkled him with possibilities.

She had caught his attention like a defenceless little bird with wide innocent eyes and a puffed out chest. She was a far contrast from Lana with her sinful curves, wicked tight dress and cherry red lips but behind the young eyes lurked a desire to please, and that look had flashed freely when he had gifted her with a roguish smile.

The shop assistant repositioned a log of pastrami in the refrigerated glass counter. She wore a large hessian apron and her honey coloured hair twisted on her crown with a fine net covering lose strands.

Carl stood by the potted chutneys, beside towering mahogany shelves that were stacked with olives and jars of pulses. He studied her fine neck and dimpled chin.

The potent smell of mature cheddar filled the warm air and made him think back to Paris, when he treated his traitor wife for their wedding anniversary.

With his eyes focused on her delicate hands, he smirked as they trembled with nerves. A swell of pride gave him cause to flex his biceps.

He didn't know whether the rush of endorphins was lust or an overwhelming sense of superiority, knowing he had the power to turn her insides to jelly.

He craved to unpin her golden tresses, to let them flow over her narrow shoulders. Her hair was her best feature, it didn't matter that she wore thick black glasses or that her mouth was a little crooked.

None of her imperfections mattered when she had glossy blonde hair, like all his leading ladies.

He loved golden locks. So sexy and perfect.

It angered him when the little shop girl wore it up.

"Hey." He nudged up his chin when she finally got the nerve to look up at him.

The girl blushed. "Hey," she replied with a flutter of her lashes and a silly grin stretching wide.

"You work in here every day?" He stepped to the glass counter and rested his hands on the surface.

"Feels like it. I get Sunday and Monday as my weekend." She chewed her bottom lip.

The corner of his mouth hitched up a fraction as his eyes traced the knotted mass on her head. "I'll see you around then, sweetheart." He winked.

"Wait!" She gasped breathlessly. "I'm Jessie." Her eyes sparkled and her lips parted, waiting for his name.

A sly grin formed on his handsome face. "Ed, I'm Ed Carrel. Nice to meet you, Jessie."

She threaded her fingers around the ties of her apron and looked up at him under her pale lashes. The glint in her eyes was magnified by her round lenses.

Right now, his priority was punishment. The McGrath men snatched away his girl. They stole what was rightfully his.

They robbed him of his chance to have Lana as his girlfriend. And the bitch went with them.

She left him again.

Maybe he was wrong, maybe she wasn't worth all the hassle, maybe Jessie was the one for him.

That was a minor detail now because the McGrath brothers would pay for having the audacity to steel from him.

He had connections, old and new, and his plan was coming together perfectly.

21

"Holy crap, Freddy. This place is surreal." Lana gawped at Villa Veronica.

A remote romantic villa that spread in a vast circumference, high up on the cliffs of the coast, nestled between the towns of Positano and Amalfi.

Wheeling in their suitcases from the blazing heat, they stepped inside the spacious cylindrical hallway, designed with four tall white pillars. The wheels chugged over an ornate polished tiled floor leading to an expansive living space, quadruple the size of Amanda's whole apartment.

Lana dropped her luggage, walking dreamily through the open room. Framed pictures of thoroughbred horses lined the chalky walls.

Some stood alone in all their splendid glory and others were accompanied by Jamie McGrath. Her eyes quickly darted to the next photograph, then the next, until her search was cruelly rewarded.

Grinning widely, Jamie stood beside his big brother, Marcus. His startlingly handsome face blasted her with a devastating blow. Her head dropped and her eyes quickly left his perfect face. Her heart fractured, splintering her soul.

She continued to tour the impressive villa, marvelling at the interior design that combined traditional Italian features with sleek modernistic finishes.

Passing through a seamless opening created by sliding doors, she gasped as stifling heat burned her skin. Dramatic mountainous terrain housed a mass of colourful dwellings, stretching along the coastline to meet the calm sapphire ocean.

"Welcome. I will take all your luggage to your rooms." Greeted a lean older gentleman, sporting beige chinos and a cream linen shirt, who quietly appeared behind them as if by magic.

Freddy shook the man's hand. "Thanks, Alberto. Good to see you again."

The sun glowed, an intense burning ball of orange flames, illuminating the homes that snuggled into the hillside. Beyond an intricately designed wrought iron balcony, the sea glistened as the sunlight kissed its wide flat surface like a tender lover.

This place was straight out of a magazine. One of those posh glossies that only the rich housewives bought for their coffee tables.

The journey from Naples had been relatively short, but now she was dog-tired. Their flight left Dublin airport at a respectable time of ten o'clock in the morning, but Lana had lay awake for hours after another vivid nightmare.

Waking in a cold sweat, she proceeded to toss and turn like the princess and the pea, only a tiny green pea was more innocent than the reality of Carl Reed.

Jamie arranged a private car to collect them at Naples airport - his helicopter was undergoing a safety inspection and wasn't ready on time. The chauffeur driven car had been a godsend with its air conditioning and chilled drinks compartment.

Alberto removed their luggage and Lana continued her inspection of the majestic villa. A sunken infinity pool created the illusion of its tranquil water blending with the ocean.

Wooden loungers lined exposed stone, part of the mountain hugging this little piece of paradise.

"There you are. Good flight?" The sound of a husky male voice bellowed from behind.

It was similar to Marcus's husky Northern Irish accent, only this voice had a roughness of speech.

Jamie McGrath wrapped his arms around Freddy and slapped his back with a loud clap. The two dodged heads, making sure not to clash with the peak of Jamie's black cap.

"Thanks so much for helping me out at short notice. Marcus is a tight arse when it comes to his chef."

Freddy lifted onto his toes and dropped back down again. "No worries, Jamie. Just glad to be out here again. When do you need us to start?"

"Alberto will brief you on the business end. I have a few associates calling tomorrow afternoon, it won't be an all-day affair. Tonight, it's just us, so let's chill. How does pizza and beer sound, mate?" He glanced over his shoulder to Lana and raised his brows. "It's the only thing I know how to make. My chef always has batches of tomato sauce in the freezer."

"I'd be more than happy to make up some authentic Italian pizza." Freddy beamed.

Jamie's cheek dimpled, and he chuckled in a low rumble. "I'll make them, I wouldn't ask you to cook after traveling all this way. I'm not that much of a dick, no matter what my brother tells you." He patted Freddy hard on the shoulder.

"Marcus was gifted with the art of cooking, I on the other hand burn bread, but I can make a mean pizza. Just remind me to take it out of the oven!" His voice boomed in the stillness of the evening.

Jamie strolled towards Lana with his flip flops clapping his heels. He wore loose grey sports shorts and a white polo and sported a half smile on his pink full lips. He stretched out his hand.

"Well, Lana, it's good to see you again, love. You look well considering. How have you been?"

She met his dark hazel eyes and her hand grasped his. "I'm on the mend, Jamie. Thanks for asking, and thanks for letting me come out here. I've never been to Italy before, so this is a real treat."

Jamie squeezed her fingers. "No worries, love. Marcus will be glad to hear you're doing well."

Her head tilted backward, her brow furrowed. "Why would he be glad to hear that?" she spluttered.

Jamie's super sexy dimple indented his stubbled cheek and an impish smile spread across his handsome face. "You're a strong woman, Lana. Hats off to you. That Reed creep will get what's coming to him. Karma will dish out some real nasty shit for him." He brushed a light kiss on her cheek and ignored her question.

No sparks.

No inappropriate feelings crossed her mind. Yet she longed for him to hold her, to feel a connection to Marcus in whatever way she could.

She leant into him and wrapped herself around his muscular form. "Thank you for everything. For saving me. I vaguely remember, but I do know you were there." She sighed into the crook of his neck, inhaling his clean soapy scent.

A wolfish snarl ghosted his face as their embrace fell away. "I'd kill that bastard in a heartbeat, love, for what he did to you, but I'm second in line for that task."

She gulped. "Who would be first?"

Jamie's hard expression softened. "Marcus, of course."

Before Lana could question his comment or wrap her head around the possibility that Marcus might actually care, Jamie stood back.

"Right, let's get dinner sorted. Alberto fired up the pizza oven a few hours ago." He nodded over to an outside kitchen area, under a pretty pergola adorned with bright yellow lemons. "It should be the perfect temperature now." Jamie rubbed her shoulder like a brother to a sister.

Together, Freddy and Jamie made the most delicious pizza. Freddy couldn't help lending a hand, throwing on some anchovies when Jamie wasn't looking. Lana opted for a simple margarita with fresh basil, happily washing it down with a cool bottle of beer.

They sat on spongey armchairs, surrounding a large circular table that could double as a sunbed. She was in awe of her surroundings and Jamie's wealthy lifestyle. To think, this was how rich people actually lived—how Marcus lived.

Jamie chatted about the history of his villa and how he renamed it after his beautiful mother Veronica. Being set high amongst the mountain, gazing towards the heavens helped him to feel close to her. He was only nine when she died, but he kept her memory alive.

He was light hearted and ever so charming, with a cockiness that would sizzle the heart strings of both men and woman. The cute dimple on his cheek gave him an adorable edge.

No doubt, he knew how to manipulate his appearance to get exactly what he wanted. If he was anything like his sinful brother, then he would certainly use his striking looks to his advantage. Lana, on the other hand, could only see the similarities to Marcus, wishing it was him before her instead.

After three beers, she plucked up the courage to mention him again. "So, how *is* your brother? What has he been up to?" she asked, then sucked her lips between her teeth, waiting patiently.

Jamie swilled the remaining beer in his bottle and raised his shoulders to his jaw. "He's okay, I guess. Doing business in a few places, you know. Keeping busy as always. The guy's a machine."

Lana swallowed the lump in her throat. "I'm sure he enjoys having a different woman in every country." She blurted out with ragged breathes, regretting the words as they crackled in the still humid air.

Letting out a sharp puff of air, her eyes darted to the ocean beyond as a pang of jealousy stabbed her insides.

Jamie's back straightened.

After a brief silence he cleared his throat. "He doesn't have much interest in the ladies, he's too busy right now securing a merger. He needs to focus on that." He paused as if he was trying to send her subliminal secrets, then he flashed a devilish grin. "Business before beauties." He winked. "Suppose that's what happens when you get older. Life turns into a snooze fest." He smirked and clanked bottles with Freddy.

"Have you heard from Rory?" he asked, seamlessly changing the subject.

"He's being kept on remand. He won't speak to me. I don't know much else. I can only hope he didn't kill that poor girl." She shook her head woefully.

Jamie scrunched his face. "We don't think he killed her, but getting the evidence is proving tough."

"How do you know he didn't kill her?" Freddy asked, lunging forward. "What do you know that we don't?"

"I don't really know that much either. I only know snippets. Let's just wait and see what turns up," Jamie's words rushed out in a raspy tone.

"Right, I'm calling it a night. Need some sleep before the shit goes down tomorrow. The Italians drive a hard bargain." Jamie stood, nodding to them both. "Thanks again for coming out to help. It means a lot having you guys out here. People I can trust."

He shook Freddy's hand and brushed his lips on Lana's knuckles before retiring to the villa for the evening. He was the ultimate charmer, courteously deflecting their inquisitive questions.

"You know that guy is cut throat in business. Marcus described him as quote on quote." He wiggled matching fingers on both hands like bunny ears. "He's not just the king shark, he's the mother fucking ocean, unpredictable and ruthless."

"He seems so down to earth and friendly." She wondered if they would've got on well as family. Then she pinched herself for letting such foolish hopeful thoughts play out in her head.

Freddy nodded with a dreamy sigh. "And he's totally sexy. The guy is sex on legs."

He was, she agreed whole heartedly, but he wasn't Marcus. "Does he have a girlfriend?"

Freddy snatched his beer bottle away from his pursed lips, interrupting his sip. "Good god, woman, you're not going after the brother, are you?"

Lana inhaled sharply. "Hell no." She ducked down and quickly looked over her shoulder. "I'm just asking out of curiosity, you eejit."

"Oh phew." He fanned his face theatrically. "Jamie is a true McGrath, through and through. Says he's too young to settle down and gets off on all the stunners constantly hurling themselves at his feet. All he has to do is walk into a room and they swarm like he's shark bait. Apparently, he'll settle down at some point in his life." He shrugged. "But seriously, looking like he does, why the hell would he?"

Lana knocked back her beer. "Just like Marcus then. Breaking hearts wherever they go," she said mournfully.

Freddy and Lana sank two more chilled beers, relaxing in the serenity of Villa Veronica. She followed Freddy to the lower levels, where they set up camp in separate bedrooms.

Her room was elegantly decorated in muted pastels and minimal furniture. It was a simplistically styled room, yet it had all the luxuries she would expect of a five-star accommodation, including a walk-in wardrobe complete with a silk robe and slippers.

The adjoining bathroom mirrored the size of the airy bedroom, with a kidney shaped bath positioned aside dual aspect windows with stunning coastline views when submerged in a bubbly cocoon.

It didn't take her long to drift off to sleep. Steamy dreams of Marcus soon faded, inviting the haunting face of Carl to relentlessly attack again. She awoke on top of damp sheets with her pulse thumping in her throat. The villa was shrouded in a peaceful silence.

Carl's in prison.
She's safe.

"Wakey, wakey sleepy head," cooed Freddy as he sprawled across her bed on his stomach and rested his jaw on the heel of his palm. "Busy day today, honey. Some big wigs are coming over for lunch. We have to get cracking with prep."

Lana hummed into the pillow. "Just five more minutes," she pleaded.

He jumped off the bed and grappled with the sheet wrapped around her waist like a bungee cord. "No rest for the wicked." He paused. "I'll get the shower running for you."

She groaned and tugged a feathery pillow into her chest. "Okay, Freddy," she muttered. "I'm getting up now." Her eyes closed again.

Freddy sprung forward and pinged the elastic on her shorts. "Oh no you don't, missy. You need to get up, get dressed, and prepare yourself for the mega rich and sexy as hell men that will be here soon!"

Her eyes peeled open. "Sexy. Rich. Men?" Her voice cracked. "Why didn't you just say that?" She rolled to the edge of the mattress, letting her feet drop to the floor. "Let's get to business, chef."

After a quick shower, a dusting of bronzer and a coat of mascara, Lana pulled on a loose spaghetti strap maxi dress that Freddy choose from her limited outfits.

They spent the morning prepping delicacies in the large vaulted kitchen, fitted with high tech modern appliances, stainless steel counters and multiple encased ovens. Lana was in awe of the impressive room, right down to the elaborate grey and white palazzo floor tiles.

Meanwhile, Alberto, the house keeper, arranged the seating arrangements and replenished the bar, which already housed enough alcohol to sink a small yacht. The kitchen was a hustle of activity, Lana and Freddy worked alongside one another in perfect harmony.

He took the lead, having all the experience and know how, whereas, Lana was happy to follow his orders and learn from the best.

He was a skilled experimental chef. Having spent a few years at culinary school, he then travelled the globe to learn about cultural cuisine. His long-term goal was to develop his own menus and style of restaurant, not caring for Michelin stars. He told Lana he wanted to make food his way and watch the customers marvel at his taste sensations.

Alberto marched into the kitchen, tapping a black strapped watch on his golden wrist. "The guests are here. The servers will be ready to collect starters in five minutes, chef." His Italian lilt was thick and his face stern.

Alberto was the epitome of professionalism. He took his job very seriously, which is why he had been on Jamie's payroll for many years.

"We're good to go, Alberto." Freddy beamed with pride.

Lana crossed her legs at the ankles. "I'll be back in a sec. I just need to pee."

She darted out of the kitchen, bounding down the corridor like a happy puppy. The door slammed shut behind her with a bang. Any minute now the servers would expect plated mains of lobster ravioli drizzled with citrus butter and a side of wilted spinach sprinkled with parmesan shavings, to present to the hungry guests.

Catching a glimpse of her flushed cheeks and high-top knot hair do, she actually grinned. She looked happy. A revelation to crack open her gloom. The dark clouds floating above her head were starting to break, and rays of sunlight were flooding her with a fresh start.

Even though she looked dishevelled, she felt like there was a reason to get out of bed. There was a new and improved life waiting to be snatched up with both hands.

Freddy was right, Italy was the perfect remedy for her damaged soul.

Racing back to the kitchen, she rounded the corner and crashed face first into a hard chest. Her palms stretched across the smooth fabric that hid taught pectorals.

Firm hands clamped her waist. The fresh citrus scent was an interesting choice, mingled with a hint of spearmint. Her eyes flicked up and she tilted her head to meet the stranger's striking face.

"Are you okay, bella signora?" The deep dulcet tones of his Italian accent scattered tingles from her scalp to her spine.

His mysterious granite eyes darkened to black, set amidst high chiselled cheekbones that lead to full wet lips. A furrowed brow waited for her to answer.

The words wedged in her throat. "I'm sorry," she mumbled. "I'm needed urgently in the kitchen." She slid her palms down his cornflower blue shirt feeling each curve on the way down.

A pink flush of realisation spread over her cheeks and her hands dropped away from his warmth.

There was something super sexy about a well-dressed man and this guy ticked all the boxes. He was pristine, bordering on pretty and his wolffish smirk hinted sinner rather than saint.

Thick russet waves tumbled over his forehead, teasing the back of his collar and his olive skin glowed with a natural depth of mystery. He released her from his steadying grip and nodded respectfully.

"It was a pleasure bumping into you, bella signora." He cleared his throat and winked. "That means pretty lady."

Lana's toes curled right into her sandals. "And you." She spun around and clopped back to the kitchen. The noise of her sandals echoed off the tiled floor in direct competition with her quicken heartbeat.

Her insides clenched with a beguiling burn. He wasn't Marcus, nor did he cast a captivating spell, but nonetheless, he was fascinating and Italian.

In reality, it didn't matter one iota if he was hung like a horse or as hot as sin because the cracks in her heart were too deep to repair. Any possibilities of a holiday affair were too farfetched after Marcus dropped her fragile heart into the flames.

Back in the kitchen, Alberto clapped his hands, geeing up the service as they skilfully stacked plates in their palms and on their forearms.

Freddy peered up from the stove. "What's wrong, honey? You look a little flustered."

She fanned her face with a napkin. "I literally just bumped into a tall, dark and handsome Italian."

He dabbed his forehead with a cloth. "Really? He must be one of the guests. Do you think you'd jump his bones?"

"No!" The idea wasn't absurd. She wasn't ready to jump into bed with anyone, let alone a guy who looked like he swaggered out of a glossy magazine, as if by magic, like the universe was offering him up on a plate, with a side order of 'fuck me hard'.

"It's okay, honey. You're allowed to fancy other men. It's inevitable."

Her head tilted while she sprayed disinfectant on the steel counter top. "He took me by surprise, that's all."

Freddy wiped up the wet cleaning fluid and removed all traces of the perfect lunch he created. "He's clearly got you all hot and bothered." He looked up at her rosy cheeks and flashed a mischievous smirk that gleamed in his eyes like amber tree sap in the sunshine.

Her arms covered her chest. "It's not like that. He stopped me from falling over when I crashed into him. It was more awkward than steamy."

Freddy tapped his cheek. "Hmm. Let's get tidied up, and then we'll investigate."

Jamie was on the terrace, surrounded by smartly dressed men who chatted in fluent Italian. With the mysterious dark ocean as his backdrop, his presence exuded power like Poseidon, god of the sea.

Lana wondered if Marcus was bilingual too. Those unwanted thoughts kept springing up out of nowhere, just to remind her of what she didn't have.

Freddy and Lana hid a few yards away, lingering with intent behind a broad pillar. The aim was covert surveillance with the task of observing the men as they talked business. They took turns, peering around the white column.

"Look. There he is," she whispered, standing on her tip toes, stretching out her neck. "That's the guy." Lana pointed to the dark-haired male beside Jamie.

"Hellooooo. He's edible. Like sugary candyfloss on a big, long, thick stick." Freddy sighed with a dreamy expression.

He angled back around to face her with their sides pinned to the plaster, face to face.

"Let's head out this afternoon. Jamie owns a hotel nearby with a roof top bar and an amazing resident DJ." His hands formed prayer position, pleading to the fun girl lurking inside her.

She squeezed his arm, letting out a shrill burst of excitement. "Okay. I think I'm ready to party again. I feel really good today."

A husky voice came from the other side of the pillar. A twinkling pair of grey eyes came into view.

"I'd love to go with you, bella signora." The handsome Italian stranger moved into their hiding place. An impish smirk danced on his freshly shaved face.

Lana gulped. Clearly their attempt at discretion failed on an epic level. Her cheeks went from pale, to pink, in zero to thirty seconds.

"Are you going to Sunrise?" he asked with a silky timbre.

Freddy reached out his hand, sensing Lana's inability to string words together. "I'm Freddy, and this is Lana."

He reciprocated the hand shake with his free hand, the other held a crystal tumbler filled with an amber liquid, ice and lime, smelling oddly of burnt sugar.

"Emilio Falcone, pleased you meet you." His perfectly neat eyebrow arched. "I'd like to escort you to Sunrise as my guests, if you don't mind the company?"

Freddy subtly nudged her side with his elbow, clearing his throat suggestively.

"Sure," she muttered, instantly feeling like an idiot.

"Bene." Emilio took a sip of his drink. "My business is almost finished here. I will be ready to leave in twenty minutes. Does that suit you?" he asked, leisurely assessing her from top to toe.

She swallowed loudly and cursed herself for the odd gulping noise that sounded louder than it should have.

"Sure." She shrugged lightly and fumbled with the straps on her dress.

His rosy lips twitched. "Are you always this sure, bella signora?" A wicked smile brought the corners of his mouth up to meet his twinkling dark eyes.

His perfect white teeth gleamed amidst his clean-shaven mocha cheeks.

Her stomach spun like a rinse cycle and she couldn't tell if she was going to be sick or faint with the rising heat. "Only when it suits, Mr. Falcone." She almost panted.

Emilio nodded in appreciation. He turned on his heels and sauntered back to the gathering with a hand in his pocket like he was on the catwalk.

Freddy gave her a sideways glance. "Wow! That's one sexy guy. Quick, let's get ready. I stink of cooked food."

She fully agreed with Freddy's assessment of Emilio, even though her heart was elsewhere, her mind was telling her to move Marcus to the left and get on with the rest of her life.

They parted ways in the lower levels. Lana made a quick dash to her room with a pang of guilt swelling in her belly. She planned to get dolled up for an afternoon of partying and unsavoury behaviour—as recommended by Freddy.

She rummaged through her suitcase, desperate to find an outfit for the swanky roof top bar, in the company of Mr. Sexy Falcone. She wasn't going to over think the situation. Emilio oozed sex appeal and gave the distinct impression that he was a player, much like the last man she made love to.

Marcus was on her mind, his face emblazoned in her memory. They had furious and thrilling sex, but after the desire had subsided and they lay side by side, they entwined on a deeper level—beyond the physical.

His touch had softened to appreciation. Like a foolish school girl, she was certain he felt something more than lust. It was actually quite tragic how she'd misjudged the whole dynamic. The intensity was a mirage, the desire was a lie, and the tenderness was just a mind game.

After tossing away multiple garments, she finally found a

citrus yellow dress that hugged her body like it was painted onto her skin and ending just above the knee. The best choice of a disastrous bunch.

Its saving grace was the low-cut material that left her back the main source of unprotected flesh. A sexy understated approach that didn't scream out 'rebound sex required'.

Emilio blew a long whistle when Lana finally joined them. She had skimmed her long lashes with mascara and dusted bronzer over the caramel freckles that kissed the bridge of her nose. Her golden hair tumbled softly over her shoulders, curling at the ends.

Freddy was ready and waiting by the door. His navy chinos hung loosely at the hips and his flamingo pink shirt was neatly tucked in at his slender waist.

"Is your driver here?" Jamie asked Emilio as Lana pranced closer.

"Sì. Are you sure you will not join us?" They shook hands.

Jamie nodded to his right, indicating to the remaining men who gathered at the bar. "These guys are having a few more drinks. Maybe later, Falcone. Once again it was a pleasure doing business with you. We will seal the deal tomorrow evening, now that you're happy with the terms."

"Sì. Tomorrow evening will be a big celebration. The money will be transferred once the contracts are signed. Send my regards to your brother. I hope to see him in the near future. I hear he is going after Devereux?" Emilio widened his stance and lifted his palms to alternative armpits with his thumbs pointing upwards.

Jamie nodded with confidence. "They've been in discussions for some time now. It's a mutual merger, Marcus is ironing out the agreement before signing on the dotted line."

Emilio slapped Jamie on his taught bicep. "As long as he knows who he's getting into bed with, my friend."

Lana inched closer. Jamie's business-like demeanour softened as if he understood her inquisitive behaviour.

"You behave yourself, love. If you're stuck for a ride home, please call me. I'll arrange for one of my guys to collect you." He winked like it was second nature, then shoved his hands in his pockets and casually strolled back to his guests.

"Shall we?" Emilio held out his elbow, beckoning Lana to latch on.

She gazed up at him, wondering if his kisses were more delicious than Marcus's.

22

A warm breeze caressed her bare shoulders, sprinkling chills over her skin.

Emilio's lustful eyes bore into her with a smouldering intensity that made her stomach churn. He was undeniably handsome, envied by men and desired by woman.

Yet, his exceptional manners and stunning looks didn't project the same red-hot passion that overwhelmed her when Marcus was near. With one lazy smile, Marcus could cast a spell over her body and mind, fuelling her veins with flames of desire.

The upbeat music swallowed her reservations. Emilio pressed his palms to the curve of her lower back and held her close to his firm physique. The thumping bass thrummed between their entwined bodies sending vibrations straight to her core.

Emilio's hands drifted over the thin fabric of her dress and gripped her hips with a pleasant pressure. She willingly snaked her arms around his thick neck. Her searching fingers traced the groves of his muscular shoulders. She consciously forced herself to relax in the moment and accept it for what it was—light-hearted fun.

She swayed against him. Her thick long tresses bounced playfully when he spun her under his arm in a controlled manoeuvre.

"Una donna così bella," he whispered with a husky timbre. "A *very* beautiful woman," he repeated as his dark, seductive gaze wandered from her face to her chest. "You are like the goddess of the fiery sun with the power to bring a man to his knees."

Her encased heart twanged, just a fraction. His zesty masculine scent was both alluring and sensual, stirring a glimmer of heat between her legs.

"You would look stunning in a red dress, to match your inner fire." He thumbed her cheeks, drawing the pad over her wet lips.

"Maybe." She swallowed hard.

"Hmm," he purred with a sexy smoulder. "I could drown in your ocean blue eyes, bella, but it's your Northern Irish accent that drives me wild."

She sucked in a gust of air as his groin nudged her hip. Emilio was on the charm offensive and her insides were fighting a battle.

Her heart was telling her to stay away, but the sexy sizzle that tore through her bloodstream, begged her to taste him.

"What's it like, where you live?" he asked.

Her lips quirked. "We have long winters and short summers, but there's a million different shades of green wherever you look. It's lush and picturesque."

"I'd like to go there sometime. How long will you be in Italy?"

Their eyes locked, and she chewed the inside of her

mouth, feeling her heartbeat race. "A few weeks, at most. I'm helping Freddy in the kitchen."

"Will you be my date tomorrow night at Jamie's soiree? And maybe you can give me a tour of your emerald island?" He gifted her with a sexy smoulder.

Lana nodded once, outwardly smiling, but inside the idea of going on a date made her organs pause and her pulse thrum.

They continued to grind seductively into each other. She closed her eyes briefly and gave in to a fleeting thought, where Marcus danced with her instead.

Staving a sigh, she forced a wide smile just as Emilio dipped her backwards at the hip and traced his fingertips down the soft curve of her throat, pausing at her breastbone. She giggled as their bodies crashed back together. The alcohol was making her head light and her inhibitions were slowly melting away.

Looking upward under dark lashes, she pouted. "How about another drink?"

His eyes blazed, and he quickly cupped her cheeks. "Of course, whatever you want, bella," he said in perfect English with a sexy Italian lilt.

With his full lips only inches from hers, she hesitated. His intent stare focused solely on her parted lips.

She swallowed hard and took a step back. With a teasing flick of her hair she flashed a playful grin.

She wasn't going to make it easy for him. After a little more Dutch courage, she might just give in to his requests and let herself unravel at his touch. Anything to banish the disruptive thoughts of the man she couldn't have.

Carpe Diem.

Emilio's bronzed arm draped her narrow shoulders. He

ushered her through the heaving crowd. The sensation of his skin against hers was pleasant.

She noted the wandering gaze of the ladies as he sauntered past, their lustful eyes searched for an opening, so they could step in and swoop him away.

Bikini clad women paced the rooftop club, elegantly carrying trays of drinks high in the sky. Men hung out in groups around the edges watching the ladies dance for attention, silently selecting their prey for the evening.

Is that all Lana was tonight? Did she care?

The bar was only a few metres away, when she stopped dead in her tracks.

Marcus.

Her breathing hitched. Her hands fisted as Marcus sauntered away from the bar. He wore knee length denim shorts and a snug white polo that set off the sun kissed skin on his toned arms.

A petite sable haired beauty, bursting out of a bikini top and squeezed into tight denim hot pants, trotted to his side. Her arms wrapped his hips and her pert breasts pressed into his chest.

Lana's sandals stuck to the floor. In a loud sharp gasp, she sucked a mass of air into her lungs. The arm hugging her shoulders slipped to her waist.

"Have you forgotten something?" Emilio asked in ignorance of her struggle to breath.

Her chest tightened and her startled gaze never wavered.

A whirlpool of anger stirred in her belly and her body trembled. Heat scorched under her flesh and melted away all rationality.

Her heart pounded so hard that she was sure her ribs would crack. The pulse magnified in her head like a galloping horse.

His eyes were shaded with black aviator sunglasses and his gorgeous lips curved slightly at the corners. Then he slapped the bitch's ass playfully, before she scampered off.

In a frenzy of maddening jealousy, Lana spun around to face her date. Standing on tip toes, she urgently pulled Emilio's head down and crushed her mouth to his.

He immediately responded, intensifying her needy kiss with a hunger of his own. Their tongues clashed and their lips welded together.

Emilio tasted of amaretto and aniseed, a sumptuous combination but not enough to capture her in a dizzying spell.

The deafening music vibrated through her bones and the chatter of party goers echoed in her skull. The crowd clapped as the saxophonist belted out a haunting dance riff and her exasperation peaked.

Was he watching?

Did he feel the same unbearable jealousy?

Her chest heaved against Emilio's rippled muscles, but there was no sizzling passion. Her adrenaline was soaring because Marcus was merely yards away. She was putting on a show, purely for the attention of Marcus McGrath.

Suddenly, she sensed his rapid approach, feeling the pull of his magnetism. The only man for Lana Craig was standing right behind her.

She broke the wet kiss with a gasp after Emilio hummed inside her mouth, his need more powerful than her own. Sliding his hands down her arms, he kissed her forehead while she caught her breath.

Emilio cleared his throat. "Thought you were in New York, McGrath?"

Lana's world spun out of control as they turned and met Marcus's molten green eyes with golden sparks of fire. His intense gaze ignited flames in her soul sending a flurry of electrifying tingles over her skin.

She swallowed hard, trembling under the weight of his intent stare. His nostrils flared and his fists contracted. Her gaze flicked to the lounge area behind him. His perfectly proportioned date was draped over a sun bed like a lazy kitten.

Lana licked her lips and took a deep breath. "Marcus." She nodded curtly.

He was met with her profile as she turned to Emilio. "If you'll excuse me, I need to freshen up."

She feigned a smile and almost stumbled back.

"Lana, how are you?" asked Marcus in a sultry low voice.

"I'm great," she lied, keeping her eyes low to prevent falling into his sexy allure for the millionth time.

"Seems so. Do you have a minute?"

She inhaled his familiar musky scent, and her stomach instantly clenched. "As I said, I need to use the washroom. You should run back to your date," she said breathlessly.

As if he sensed the suffocating tension, Emilio slid his hand across the arch of her back and nudged her closer to his hip. "Everything okay, baby?" He nuzzled her hair.

Marcus lunged forward and grabbed his arm, forcefully yanking it away from her bare skin. "She's not your fucking baby, Emilio," he hissed.

Her pulse thrummed in her throat. "And I'm not yours either. I'm not interested in dragging up the past, so if you'll excuse me." Her voice shook and her heart lurched as she inched away from the two men.

His fiery gaze locked with hers. His green eyes scorched

with a fury that both scared and delighted her. The world abruptly stopped on its axis, floating off course.

People faded from existence with only Marcus present in that very moment. He broke their intense trance, as always, the one in control. His eyes cut to Emilio.

"Make sure your driver delivers her back to the villa safely," he snarled.

He gave her one last look, pausing for a heartbeat, and then swivelled on his heels and marched towards the exit. The petite woman chased after him at haste.

Freddy bounced to her side, with a look of concern on his sweet face. "Let's get out of here, Lana," he said quickly, nudging her poker straight back.

Her face paled. "Will he be staying at the villa?" She spoke directly into his ear.

Freddy shook his head, resting his hand on his hip. "He might be staying here, Sunrise is their hotel after all. But after what just went down, I'll expect him at the villa."

Her eyes widened. "What do mean, nothing went down, Freddy." She hauled him away from Emilio.

"Marcus was soooooo angry." He slotted his hands on his hips.

"He was only angry because I declined a pointless conversation."

Freddy blasted air from his lips. "Ya think?"

"Yes. He dumped me, remember?" She wanted to cry but swallowed back the hurt instead.

"Honey, he was one bulging vein away from turning into the Hulk." He shimmied side to side as a cracking tune surrounded them.

Emilio moved closer and twirled his fingers through the lengths of her hair.

"My driver is waiting outside, shall we go now?" he half

asked, half ordered. "Freddy, we will take you back to Veronica," he added.

Lana looked into his unknown grey eyes that were full of anger, yet his stance displayed perfect restraint. "Yes, I'd like to go back. I'm sorry to cut the evening short."

The night was ruined, as was she.

Sandwiched between Freddy and Emilio in the back of the sleek black Maserati, Lana stared out at the stunning Amalfi coastline. Mt. Vesuvius depicted her current mood. Calm on the outside yet a fiery molten mess on the inside.

Emilio rested his hand on her thigh and squeezed gently. The atmosphere around them was cool from the air-conditioning but the feel of his manly touch warmed her insides with a surprising curiosity.

"You were his once?" he asked.

She sighed lightly. "I don't believe I was ever actually his. We had a moment once upon a time, but that's all it was."

Freddy whipped his head around. "Eh, Lana? I don't think that fire is out *just* yet. I saw the look on his face when you were kissing studdly here." His head bobbed sideward gesturing towards Emilio.

Lana let out a short blast of air. "Too late, Freddy. Anyway, Marcus was happy enough with his date before he caught sight of me."

Freddy slid back in the leather seat. "Smoke screens, Lana, smoke screens."

Emilio's warm breath caressed the shell of her ear, and he rained kisses along her jaw.

She automatically turned into him and met his wet lips to savour hers.

"He had his chance, baby, now it's my turn." The rumble of his sexy masculine voice reached through the refreshing air and landed on her skin with a rush of prickles.

She sucked in her lower lip as the pads of his fingers grazed her cheek with affectionate tenderness.

23

Carl sat in his new accommodation with a glock in one hand and a vodka on ice in the other.

"No one gets the better of me," he spat with venom dripping off his tongue like a poisonous snake.

He had chosen a new outfit from the expensive fashion boutique on the Lisburn Road. A pretty little blonde thing had served him.

She fell foul to his handsome features and suave stature. With a slight touch of his arm she had shamelessly giggled and flirted. He was pumped full of bravado and feeling on top of the fucking world.

Together they selected a black fitted shirt with white stitched seam and black trousers, completing the perfect revenge ensemble that would mask blood spatters. He told her he was trying to win back his ex and had big plans...but left out the part that he was going to blow a hole in a few guys first.

His mission was clear. Take out the fuckers who stole from him and those who helped them do it. Donna Marie was on his hit list.

The smutty woman who ran Verto Veneri for Marcus Fucking McGrath. She stone walled him, investigated him and more than likely offered to testify against him.

But Marcus was the son of a bitch who took Lana. His medalling put him in prison with the sicko's.

That being said, Carl's time behind bars had proven to be very rewarding. Never in his wildest dreams would he have ever imagined that he could make alliances with the tough guys in remand.

But he did. He shook hands with the low lifes who offered him a wing of protection in exchange for a hefty financial reward wired straight to their accounts. And low and behold, his protection became a reality.

They gave him information to help him take on those cocky McGrath brother's, and he knew exactly where to start.

24

The chauffeur driven car pulled up outside Villa Veronica. Emilio held back deliberately waiting for the driver to open the door.

An orange glow from the setting sun kissed the darkened car interior, bringing humid air with it. Emilio reached his hand out and assisted her exit.

Standing tall, he fluttered tiny kisses along her shoulder, initiating a shower of goose bumps down her spine. She smiled inwardly.

"Come back with me tonight?" he growled into the crook of her neck.

His tongue traced the curve of her jugular. She laughed nervously when a low grunt reverberated from his throat.

The idea of using Emilio to get a reaction from Marcus was a childish game, nevertheless she toyed with the idea. Emilio's offer was tempting, but her heart was wrapped around Marcus. Emilio was just a sexy distraction.

"Not tonight, Emilio. I'm tired." She leant into him and placed a light kiss on his cheek.

He trailed his fingers from the parting at her forehead,

down a strand of hair and tucked it neatly behind her ear. "Of course, baby. But as I said earlier, it's my chance with you now."

His lips parted and he waited a breath away. She was caged in his arms and tight against his hard body. She held her breath, anticipating his touch.

He tilted in and seared her lips with a hard scorching kiss. Cupping her buttocks with his hands he squeezed her hips into his hardness. She had to admit, the guy sure knew how to kiss.

Freddy cleared his throat. "Excuse me, can I *please* get out of the car," he called from inside the Maserati.

Their lips smacked apart. "See you tomorrow," she muttered through open fingers as they padded her swollen lips.

He winked. "Buona notte, Lana. Good night." A wicked grin stretched his cheeks.

The villa was eerily quiet. Lana kicked off her heels and padded along the cold floor. Jamie was nowhere to be seen. Probably upstairs in his private quarters, entertaining. Lana bid Freddy goodnight with a quick cuddle.

Climbing into bed, alone, she knew she had made the right decision. She cursed the inevitable nightmares, ready and waiting in the wings of sleep.

A stiff ache in her shoulder niggled like an old war wound. Reluctantly, she closed her eyes and thought of Marcus. With his handsome face brought all the feelings she desperately tried to suppress.

She pummelled the pillow, puffing up the feathers. The luxury mattress held no comfort. She flipped from lying on her back to her side, tucked up her knees then stretched out her legs, but it didn't matter because mindless jealousy bubbled inside her veins and twisted her stomach in knots.

How dare Marcus flaunt around like a playboy when she had been trudging through the past few weeks like an empty shell.

There was no way in hell she could speak to him, let alone forgive him.

Her heavy lids closed.

Carl's hideous mouth opens wide. The stale stench of tobacco torments her with its wicked wispy fingers.

Acid burns her tender gullet. His snake like tongue whips her prickled flesh.

She can't move.

She can't get away.

She can't fight back.

He's on top of her, overpowering, suffocating, pinning her to the mattress. His fingers knead the plump flesh of her breasts, harder and harder.

Her throat closes, straining to scream.

She tries to hit out, but she was lifeless.

She tries to yell, but nothing comes out.

Her eyes pinged open and her breathing was hard and fast. The shorts and camisole set that she slept in were wringing with sweat, even though the room was like a refrigerator.

Rolling to the edge of the bed, she propped herself up on her elbow and breathed deeply. She slid off the bed and stood on shaky legs. The latch on the patio door was stiff but she managed to crank it open. An inviting subtle breeze cooled her clammy flesh.

Her throat was prickly and her lips dry. She peeled off the damp clothes and covered her trembling body with a short silk robe, belted by a ribbon.

Dashing upstairs to the kitchen, she swiped a bottle of ice-cold Pellegrino and pressed it to her forehead. The crisp freshness was an instant relief. The villa was lit by the full round moon, yet every corner was swamped with shadows.

An unsettling feeling tingled over her scalp. She hated the shadows, just as much as she hated Carl. Trotting back to her room, along the dimly lit corridor, she unscrewed the cap and sipped the fizzy water.

A hand gripped her elbow, spinning her around. Her jaw dropped to ready a scream, but a whisper halted its escape. "It's me, Lana."

A familiar masculine scent wafted in the air and settled her nerves. Pressing her back to the wall, Marcus pushed his commanding body into hers.

The bottle thudded to the floor, blasting them with flashes of water bullets. She gasped loudly as his fingers tightened around her forearms. He yanked them above her head and secured them with one hand by the wrists.

Unsettled hair hung over his forehead and his lips glistened with moisture. Marcus held her captive, his dark gaze lingering on her lips.

Quick puffs of air expelled down his nose and his nostrils flared. His presence was consuming and authoritative, not threatening. Her insides quickly responded to his touch, melting beneath her fear.

With only her rapid heartbeat thudding in her ears, a shuddered breath left her lungs. Her initial swarm of panic and terror drifted away, replaced with the overwhelming hunger that Marcus always initiated.

Using his free hand, he finally stroked the curvature of her jaw with the pads of his fingers. His warm alcohol breath agitated the strands of hair that tumbled over her face.

He didn't utter a word. Only short sharp breathes gave away his true intentions. She wanted to yell at him for scaring her half to death, but the irresistible magnetism that drew them together sparked a current of hunger, connecting them with an invisible force.

His brawny torso was silky and smooth leading to a pair of loose sports shorts that rested on his angular hips. An obvious arousal strained against the jersey fabric.

His roaming hand slid further, manipulating her covered breasts. He tugged the delicate ribbon that held the robe in place and let it fall away.

Her skin was exposed in a position of surrender. She inhaled sharply as the swell of her need grew tenfold when his gaze drifted down her trembling curves.

"Marcus?" she mumbled, teetering on insanity. "What are you doing?"

A soft groan escaped her throat as his teeth grazed her collar bone. With her hands still above her head, he shunted her legs open with a bent knee. He leisurely licked the hollow of her neck in one sweep, invoking a pleasurable shiver.

His wicked mouth ventured lower and his teeth latched on to her pebbled nipple. When he pulled away, a seductive pop sent sparks of excitement through every muscle.

Teasing wet sweeps, trailed between her breasts, tracing the quick pulsing beat in her throat. In a short few seconds her heart was going to spontaneously combust.

Quickly locating her folds, he inhaled sharply, finding it wet and ready. His middle finger hesitated at the entrance to her sex, waiting, teasing an intrusion that would give her exactly what she craved.

Their breath mingled and their lips barely touched. Marcus's dark pensive gaze held her prisoner. "Stay away from Emilio," he commanded with a low rasp.

Her heart lurched. "Why are saying that?"

His gaze dawdled on her heaving breasts, then oh so slowly reached her inquisitive eyes. "I miss you." His words clung to the heated air. "I can't even enjoy fucking other women without thinking of this sexy body."

Her heartbeat hesitated. "You've been with other women – already."

The pressure around her wrists grew. "One woman, who failed to do anything for me."

That familiar unwanted feeling of jealousy ripped through her body like the tremors of an earthquake. An involuntary shake started at her head and rocketed through her bones.

"So soon," she choked out.

Her lungs ached when a gust of bitter air filled them full, but it was her shattered heart that crumpled, accepting the cold hard truth. Marcus didn't love her.

He ran straight into the arms of another woman. The man had lived up to his playboy status like she dared to believe he would. And here she was, falling back into his arms like a mindless fool.

"I regret every second I was with her," he gritted out, digging his fingers deeper into her wrists and dragging his probing hand away from between her quivering legs.

"I don't believe you."

"One woman, one fuck, zero enjoyment." His eyes glowed with an intensity that pierced through her barriers.

He wasn't smiling or bragging. No sign of contentment in

his revelation. A remorsefulness weighed the creases on his brow and a flash of his penance swallowed her whole.

Lost in a dizzying torture, she jutted her head closer, wanting but waiting. A burning need to have him all to herself blazed through her soul.

She needed him, despite the consequences, aside from his thoughtlessness. His warmth and power were the tonic for her soul. The medicine to soothe and remedy her broken heart.

The soft fleshy warmth of his lips melted away the tightness in her chest when they finally met her needy mouth. She sighed through her nose, savouring his seductive taste and letting his teeth tug at her defences.

He cupped her chin with a firm pressure, pressing the pad of his thumb into her cheek to deepen his scorching kiss. The prickles on his cheeks scratched wildly as the angle varied.

Giving in to him, she danced with the devil and let him singe her heart with a lust like none other. She propelled her hips into his groin.

"Marcus," she murmured gutturally.

His breathing was ragged and his grip unyielding, until he freed her wrists, and her hands dropped to his shoulders. She rocked into him, draping her arms around his neck. His probing fingers slid down her silky skin, over her fleshy soft belly and back down to her thighs.

"Lana," he growled. "Stay the fuck away from Emilio."

"What if I don't want to?" she panted. *What if you could feel the same crippling jealousy that I do?*

His eyes blazed and his mouth continued to punish. The tip of his finger entered her warm wet entrance. She sucked in loud gust as it pushed deeper inside.

Her forehead fell to his smooth bare chest and she inhaled his manly scent. Her erotic groan echoed down the empty corridor, filling their ears with naughty deeds that were hidden in the threatening shadows.

Her heavy-lidded eyes turned navy with lust, like the deepest darkest ocean. She soared with pleasure, floating in a world where they could be together.

The cold dark reality welcomed her back when Marcus slowly removed his wet fingers, leaving her empty inside. With his forehead brushing hers, he drove his hardness into her groin and pressed his mouth over her parted lips again.

The kiss blazed through her core, setting her soul on fire. She matched his hunger, teasing the soft short hair at his nape, holding him close without wanting to let go.

He broke their feral kiss and pushed back. Lana whimpered at the loss of his all-consuming heat. Her redundant arms flopped to her sides and the robe skimmed her goose bumped flesh.

"Stay away from him," he growled.

Grappling with her robe, she covered her vulnerability. "Why should I stay away from him, Marcus?" She gave him an uncertain look. "You're allowed to do whatever the hell you want. You've been off fucking your way around the world. We weren't in a relationship – I get that. Just like now."

His jaw tensed. "Like I said, it was meaningless sex with one woman." He held up his index finger, emphasising the amount. "That prick, Emilio, is no good for you, Lana," he bit out.

Those words weren't exactly the declaration of jealousy she had hoped for. Tilting her head, a half laugh bubbled in her throat. "And you are?" She hugged her chest with self-protection.

Marcus sighed, his eyes lifting to the ceiling. The creases on his forehead deepened. "I don't know."

She tipped forward and her brows snapped together. "What the hell was *this* then? Did you not hit lucky with your little girlfriend at Sunrise, so you thought you'd take your chances with me?" She extended her hands outwards. "Fuck you, Marcus!" Her voice cracked.

With a powerful shunt, he forced her back into the wall, caging her vibrating body. An unknown look shadowed his eyes.

"I don't have a girlfriend. I've never had one and never been interested in having one. She propositioned me. I wasn't in the mood. I'm never in the fucking mood since you left. I don't repeatedly fuck the same girl to save complications." He swept a strand of her hair away from her face, sliding the curled tip behind her shoulder.

Her eyes narrowed, spearing him with whatever strength she had left. "Yeah, Marcus, I understand perfectly. I'll see whoever the hell I want. In fact, I'm meeting up with Emilio at Jamie's party. I actually really like him. He's fucking hot and just my type," she lied with conviction. She wanted to hurt him. To make him suffer like she had.

Marcus's eyes turned to slits. The air around them filled with electricity, a storm was brewing under the calm exterior of Marcus McGrath. Fighting the hypnotic pull between their two bodies, he stepped back, leaving an empty void.

"Fine," he snarled.

An ache of guilt squeezed her stomach. "Yeah, fine." She was poking his fire with a plastic stick and watching it melt under the heat of his glare.

Rubbing a hand down his face, he sighed heavily. "I've had too much to drink. This was a bad idea."

"What the hell, Marcus? What was a bad idea? Scaring me half to death, getting me off in the hall or telling me to stay away from Emilio? Or was it that you fucked someone else or the fact you're a damn hypocrite!" She tugged the seams of her robe tightly across her chest.

The silence was so loud. His chest expanded, and his nostrils flared. Words were left unsaid as an internal battle commenced, and his dangerous gaze burned.

"Goodnight." He nodded.

She reached out to touch his arm as he took a step to leave, but her fingers grasped the empty space between them. He turned away.

"Marcus," she called breathlessly. "Why did you bring me back to the Coach House if you didn't want a girlfriend?" His gaze fell straight ahead as he sauntered away.

"You always break the rules, Lana." A subtle laugh rumbled in his chest. "You're the exception to all the fucking rules."

He strode into the shadows, and she accepted their encounter for what it was—Marcus McGrath's drunken game. She wanted to call him back, to tell him that she didn't really want Emilio, that it was a stupid idea just to get a rise out of him.

Instead, she let him walk away because that's what she knew best. It was better to watch him leave than to let him hurt her all over again.

Lana trudged back to her room with a heavy heart. A man like Marcus does as he pleases and takes what he wants. So why wasn't he in New York shaking hands on a life changing business deal?

She flopped into bed, leaving the sheet to the side. His presence had overwhelmed her and shattered the anger that she had placed at his feet.

He had given up too easily, and now, fucked another woman too quickly. His flippancy had bruised her heart and created invisible wounds that only her soul could see.

They were worn as a constant reminder that she wasn't what he really wanted. The painful marks remained, darkening as each day passed. They deserved to heal. Not split open by a flimsy promise of something more.

He was playing a cruel game and Lana wasn't prepared for the attack.

Tiny kisses flutter over her warm skin. She's held captive by his long heated kisses that leisurely cling to her lips. Jeez, she loves how this man could turn her on with a flick of his tongue or a curve of his wicked mouth.

She willingly gives in to his possessive commands, displaying her quaking body to him. He grunts with obvious desire when she submits. He tugs her nipples and kneads her creamy breasts like they're the best treat he's ever devoured.

His beautiful chiselled features morph into another. Carl clamps his teeth down hard on her tender flesh leaving a stingy welt. The pain burns like acid.

He taunts her with words she doesn't want to hear. His slimy tongue slathers her skin leaving his repulsive scent. That hideous smell of stale tobacco permeates her senses. It triggers her fear.

No, please. Let me go.

She struggles but her body is paralysed. It's always rooted to the same spot. She is powerless. She can't move.

He has won.

He has control.

Gentle fingertips brushed her cheek, smoothing away sweat laden strands that clung to her neck.

"Shhh, beautiful. You're safe. It's okay. I'll never let anyone hurt you." Powerful arms snaked her waist, pulling her closer, immediately comforting her distress. "I promise to keep you safe."

Half asleep in a dreamy daze, she blinked open her eyes to the softly lit room, feeling the heat from his body enveloping her from behind. A familiar heady scent pacified her torment.

"Marcus?" she stuttered with heavy eyelids.

Turning into him, a wave of relaxation washed over her like heat from the summer sun. She became hypnotised by his beating heart. Instantly, his strength calmed her blind panic and brought her senses back to the room.

They lay together in silence. Her racing rhythm changed from a gallop to a canter. His deep exhale caressed her shoulder.

She was safe in his embrace and a peacefulness surrounded her fearful heart. For tonight she would sleep beside him, permitting his powerful presence.

Gazillions of stars could burn out all at once and the oceans could dry up into mounds of salt, but none of that would matter if she was lying in the arms of Marcus McGrath.

Lana drifted off into a heavenly dream, where she dreamt that Marcus showered her with kisses and they made love under the bright blue sky, only to wake hours later, completely alone and unsatisfied.

Rolling over, she noticed an indentation in the pillow next to hers. Pressing her nose to the cotton, she inhaled the male aroma that never failed to make her stomach flip.

Marcus had left her alone, again.

25

The next morning Marcus kept out of sight until noon.

He kicked back on the grand terrace like a king observing his land, lying on the sun lounger with a bottle of beer and a phone pressed to his ear.

"Thanks for the update. I really appreciate all the hours you've put in, Arthur. I'll ensure the remaining funds are transferred into your account today. Let me know if you hear anything else."

Jamie strolled onto the terrace wearing nothing but bright red ass hugging shorts, his toned muscular torso was on show with a detailed wolf tattoo on his brawny bicep. He was an exhibitionist, much like his brother, only Jamie had a brazen streak.

"Wee brother, I see you've stopped working out?" Marcus roared playfully.

"I can lift more than you, old man!" He threw a low punch at his brother's shoulder, ducking with nimble agility as Marcus sat upright and tried to grab his fist. "If you weren't my bro, I'd kick the crap out of you."

Marcus hummed in the back of his throat. "You know I'd have to let you win. It wouldn't be a fair fight, you punch like a little girl." He smirked.

"You wouldn't need to let me win, I'd have no bother knocking you flat on your back," Jamie replied with an air of confidence bordering on arrogance.

Jamie grabbed another bottle of beer from the cooler and chucked it at Marcus. "What brought you out to Italy?" He winked, lying back on a padded sun lounger.

Marcus took a sip. "Since when did I need a reason to see you?"

Jamie spluttered out a breath of air. "Bullshit, Marcus. We were in Monaco a few days ago. You've got it bad for Lana. Never thought I'd see the day when you fell for a woman."

"Whatever, shit-head." Marcus trailed his aviators from his eyes and slotted them above his forehead.

"Did you come out here to get her back or play about a bit more?" Jamie quizzed, running his palm over his washboard abs.

"I want her back. You told me she was here, in the villa, and a switch flicked in my head. The next thing, I was on the first flight to Naples." He tipped the bottle to his lips and swallowed a thirsty glug of beer. "The plan was to stay the hell away from her. It didn't work out, as you can see."

Jamie scratched the damp label at the side of his beer bottle, peeling it from the moist glass. "And now you've seen her. So…?"

Marcus shrugged. "Yeah, I saw her alright - with her juicy red lips all over that son of a bitch, Emilio. I wanted to kill dead things – but it didn't work out between us and I don't know if it ever will."

"My big brother is doubting himself? Pinch me. Am I

dreaming this shit or have you turned into a pussy?" Jamie chuckled.

Marcus glared at his brother. "I became her anchor, it was suffocating…but, it made me feel fucking alive knowing I was all she needed. You know me well enough to know it won't work, Jamie."

Jamie slammed his glass on the table and bolted upright. "Fuck sake, Marcus. Keeping yourself away from her won't stop bad things happening.

What exactly are you trying to achieve by denying yourself happiness. You're torturing each other for what fucking purpose, mate?" His tone was hard and direct.

Marcus slid his bare feet off the side of the lounger, drawing himself upright. "You don't understand, Jamie." He scolded, rubbing the back of his neck.

Jamie's eyes narrowed under his scrunched brow. "Dad and I lost her too, Marcus. You're not the only one," he snapped gruffly.

"She was driving that night because of me, Jamie. If I hadn't pleaded for her to come back…she would still be alive." Marcus stroked the top of his head, ruffling his hair into place.

"We've told you before. It. Wasn't. Your. Fault. It was Johnston's fault for drinking, and it was his fault for ploughing through a red light and smashing into her."

Jamie stood, walked to his brother and dropped down beside him, nudging shoulders. "It was his fault, mate. Not yours. Do you really think mum would want you to deny yourself happiness?"

Marcus let out a long breath, shaking his head slowly. He never considered sticking with the same girl, until Lana blew into his office like a refreshing summer breeze.

His heart whispered the suggestion of love, and his mind

battled with a mash of fear and denial. Her name had been woven into the fibres of his flesh, her taste seared onto his tongue. Her laugh danced in his mind like a love song on repeat and he couldn't pause his crazy emotions.

He hadn't planned a trip to Italy, and he certainly didn't expect to find her kissing a good looking Italian guy when he got there. Although what was really unexpected, was the ugly jealousy that drove him to the bottom of a whiskey bottle, that made him hunt her down and forced him to wait in the shadows just to steal just a kiss.

It was a huge fucking mistake. A dirty and divine catastrophe because Lana confirmed, after everything, that she wanted someone else.

"I just got off the phone with Arthur, they've got evidence to clear Rory. They found a cigarette butt in Rory's house. It matched Carl's DNA, the same DNA that was found on Jacqueline's neck. His nails broke the skin and the cocky fucker left his mark. He pretended to be the concierge, stole one of the uniforms and gave Rory and Jacqueline a complimentary bottle of champagne, laced with a strong sedative. A few hours later, he was spotted by one of the guests going back to the room. He strangled Jacqueline when she was out cold, probably to frame Rory so he could get to Lana." He ran his finger down the neck of the frosted beer. "He would've killed Lana when he was finished with her."

"Sick bastard." Jamie tilted his head and took a slug of beer. "He'll rot in hell!"

The mobile phone buzzed on the table. "Arthur?"

His face dropped. "Are you fucking kidding me? Right, change of plan. Get in touch with Mal. We need eyes on the bastard urgently."

He ended the call and tossed the phone on the lounger.

Marcus dragged his palms down his face. "Don't breathe a word of this to Lana, Jamie."

"About?"

"Carl's out."

"What the fuck. How the hell could they let him out?"

"I told you, Jamie, he has people in his pocket…but so do I," he growled.

Jamie lifted another couple of beers from the cooler and handed one to Marcus. "I'll keep my ear to the ground. I know you'll sort it out like you always do. Are you going to tell Lana that Rory is off the hook, at least?"

Marcus jumped up. He was antsy and angry. How the fuck did that sick fuck get out of prison so soon. He marched to the wrought iron railing that sat between the terrace and the sprawling ocean, stretching across to Mt. Vesuvius. The sun heated his golden skin and fury scalded his organs.

"I don't know how to let her in without fucking it up and getting both of us burned in the process."

"Well, you better be careful because Falcone has her in his sights, and the last thing I need is you busting up my deal."

"I know. I told her to stay away from him." He shook his head. "But she's into him for fuck sake."

Jamie rested his elbows on his knees and chuckled. "She's so not into him, dickhead. I'll bet you a mill she'd drop him like a dirty dick if you told her how you felt. Let Falcone sign on the dotted line, in blood, before you declare your undying love." His laugh rumbled. "I can tell she wants you - it's pretty damn obvious."

"Falcone better keep his hands to himself or I'll bust his face." Marcus grimaced, shaking his head to banish the memory of her insides squeezing his fingers.

"Look, Marcus, please don't fuck up this deal. I've been

working on these guys for months now. All you have to do is wait until the contract is signed. I'll even escort her to your bedroom after the deal's done," Jamie pleaded. "Then you can talk to her and make her understand that she has your nuts in the palm of her hands." Jamie kicked back his feet and stretched out under the sun. "I'm sure she'll understand why you pushed her away."

"I don't know if I can watch that asshole, Falcone, put his hands on her." Marcus's eyes narrowed.

Jamie crossed his ankles and raised his bottle in the air. "Marcus, it's only for few hours." He clucked his tongue. "Good luck! Can't say I'll be delighted about you joining the other side and becoming a boring brother. You're supposed to be my wingman, but I know Lana means something to you. I guess it leaves more pussy for me." He snickered with a wolfish grin dimpling his cheek. "What about the merger with Devereux?"

Marcus strode back to the lounger. "Like I said, I flew straight to Italy when I heard she touched down in Naples airport. Devereux is in New York. He can wait a day or so until I get what's mine."

Jamie's eyebrows shot up. "You held back on the merger to come out here? You really are crazy about her or just pure fucking crazy!"

Marcus's mood was up and down. One minute his head was screaming about revenge, the next his heart was exploding for Lana, and now his gut was twisted at the thought of Carl on the loose.

"And Dad? Is the carer going to bring him out here?" he asked Jamie, trying to pull himself together with a mental slap. If anything could do that, it was thoughts of his father.

"Sure is. Rebecca is worth her weight in gold. I was going to fly him over yesterday, but I'll get the deal closed first. I'll send for him in a few days. I want Becks to fly with him, but she has an appointment of her own to attend. I wouldn't trust him flying on his own. Not after the last time," Jamie said with a solemn tone.

"Heard from Cherie Monique lately?" Marcus grinned playfully.

Jamie pulled his hands behind his head. "I owe you for that hook up, brother. Her sexy mate arrived minutes after you left with the English girl. How could I say no to both of them? They kept me entertained for most of the night."

Marcus shook his head. Although he was proud of his brother's wily ways, he was ready to give it all up for Lana. He wasn't interested in meaningless sex anymore.

What he wanted ran deeper. He was bored with the long shameless list of female faces without names.

It was Lana who teased his feelings to the surface, and now he was going to win her back.

26

Carl's plan was becoming his reality.

He had gone over the details in his head multiple times. He didn't need to ask the guys behind bars for her location. He knew it already. Paul was a magpie for information as well the king chess piece with the law.

Donna Marie didn't have golden hair, and that made her repulsive. Her payback would be fitting, something symbolic.

After this little visit, he was primed and ready to seek the most satisfying revenge of all. To finish Marcus McGrath.

The guy was a cocky asshole who was finally in reach. Carl was going to piss on his parade by whipping up a cataclysmic nightmare, with an ending that he'd never wake up from.

Carl stood in front of the mirror, hung over the mantle of the unfamiliar home that he barged into twenty-three minutes ago. His pleased gaze lingered on the subtle smirk that danced happily on his lips.

"Please don't kill me, Carl," Donna Marie sobbed.

He swivelled around to the pathetic creature, bound and

bloody on her living room carpet. "I go by the name of Ed Carrel nowadays. Not that it matters to you. Not after tonight, sweetheart."

His gaze floated back to the perfect reflection. The cocky grin, dazzling eyes and silvery flecked hair that was professionally coiffured and set with spray.

A smattering of blood trickled down his temple. He clucked his tongue and muttered under his breath. "You can't even bleed without fucking it up, Donna Marie."

He wiped the red stain from his skin and tossed the tissue to the floor. He knew he was a lady killer, ironically in more ways than one.

That power alone gave him the ultimate feeling of satisfaction. So much so, he was getting off on the vibes of his power. His phone buzzed and he snapped out of his self-appraisal.

"Good evening. Do you have what I need on McGrath?" he chirped.

"Sure do. You ready to end this, Carl, once and for all?"

"I was born ready. I'll teach those motherfuckers that they messed with the wrong guy. I'm a bit tied up at the minute. I'll call you back soon."

27

The staff at Villa Veronica busied themselves all afternoon in preparation for Jamie's intimate soiree for his business associates.

Freddy worked his magic concocting delicate Italian canapés and entrees. He gave Lana the task of putting together elegant Puccia bread chips which she eagerly prepared with feminine finesse.

She synchronised her iPod to the wireless speaker, freeing her playlist, a mixture of current chart hits amplified around the high ceilings.

"What's happening between you and Emilio?" asked Freddy, gently placing a beef Carpaccio canapé on an ornate oval platter.

Lana's cheeks warmed. The very thought of Emilio made her stomach flip, in an unusual way. Good or bad? She wasn't sure. "He's a nice guy, kinda hot too."

Freddy let out a loud puff of air. "Well I know he's *hot,* Lana, but I want to know the deets…size of full erection, six pack, kissing abilities, etcetera, etcetera." He listed his requirements for an in-depth integration.

The right side of his mouth crept up into a wicked grin.

She giggled, twirling a dish cloth in the air and whipping him on the back side with a slap.

"I haven't played with his dick yet, you horn dog!" Her voice reverberated through the room under the blanket of music.

Freddy rubbed his buttocks. "You said 'yet', does that mean you intend to unleash the beast at some stage?" He waggled his eyebrows.

"I'm not ready." She ran her nails over her arm nervously recalling the ease at which she granted Marcus permission to touch her.

"Take it slow. You don't have to do anything with him if it doesn't feel right." He patted her reassuringly.

She exhaled slowly. "I know, I need to get over what happened and move on from Marcus. Easier said than done now that he's here, right under my nose."

"I'm sure Emilio could help you move on." Freddy winked. "I bet he's packing some luggage in those skinny trousers."

"Jeez." She contorted her face in a look of disgust and pain.

"Like the Lough Ness monster cock, hidden in the depths ready to surface."

Lana held a slight smirk, her eyes giving away her laughter. "You're as bad as Amanda. What is it with you guys and monster sized cocks? I don't know if I'll do anything with him, I'll play it cool and see how it pans out."

His smile faded. "I guess he's just not Marcus."

She fumbled with the messy bun at her nape, winding a loose strand around the base. "He ordered me to stay away from Emilio." Her pulse thrummed.

Freddy's eyebrows lifted. "He's so into you, Lana."

"Why the hell did he come here to flaunt other women in my face? Could he really be that cruel?" she snapped.

Freddy's mouth formed a firm line. "He's been known to flit from country to country on a whim, following business deals and chasing up loose ends. I don't think he came here to flaunt anything in your face, honey. There must be a reason for his visit."

Her heart sank. If he wanted her back, then he would have come right out and said it. *Marcus always takes whatever the hell he wants.*

"I had another nightmare," she announced. "Marcus came into my room and held me until I fell asleep again. I let him stay."

Freddy's brow scrunched up. "Did he just hold you?"

"Eh, in bed, yeah…and when I woke up the next morning he was gone." She blew out her cheeks, releasing a confused sigh.

"Honey, I'll stick my neck out here and say that Marcus came here for you." Freddy wrapped his arm around her neck, pulling her in for a hug. "I've known him for a long time now. The guy's got a commitment phobia, but I've never known him to chase any woman."

"He hasn't come near me all morning."

"Play it cool. If he hasn't laid his cards on the table after tonight, then let it go, hon. Now, let's get the food sorted or Jamie will turf me out on my ass."

Working as the dream team, they pulled together a splendid entrée of oven roasted Salmon with a Kumquat pesto, finished to Freddy's high standard. However, it was the red and black sesame encrusted fresh tuna, perfectly pink on the inside, served with a Riesling reduction and jasmine infused long grain rice, that made him sigh with contentment.

"Wow, it all looks so tasty. You're a gastronomic prodigy." Lana popped a piece of fish in her mouth and let out a soft groan. "Delish! Let's get ready while they eat."

A tingle rushed down her spine. Her eyes flicked to the doorway to find Marcus. Their eyes met across the room, and her deep breath stuck in her lungs.

His hair was slicked back from a dip in the pool and his white tee clung to his broad shoulders like the fabric didn't want to let go of him. His sexy lop-sided smile made her stomach twist and her insides burn. Each confident stride brought him before Freddy.

"You've gone and done it this time." His hand rested on Freddy's shoulder.

"Marcus?" Freddy's eyes bugged.

"You cooked up a storm the other day. Jamie's guests were really impressed with *his* chef."

"Oh!" Freddy threaded the dish cloth between his fingers.

Marcus cleared his throat. "Look, mate." His grip tightened. "I know we've got a good thing going on, but I'm going to have to let you go."

Freddy's palm flew to his mouth and he clutched the dish cloth to his heart. "You're way too talented to cook for one miserable bachelor," Marcus continued.

"No! I don't mind working for you, honestly!" Freddy looked like he was going to cry—like an ugly sort of cry with scrunched eyes and snot.

"Marcus, please don't." Lana stepped closer.

There was a hint of mischief in his eyes, as his gaze cut to her. "I'm not cutting him loose, beautiful." He winked and her heart flipped hysterically, shooting sparks into her muscles.

She drew in a steadying breath as his gaze wandered down to her breasts and settled for a few seconds before returning to Freddy.

"Marcus, I really need the money, plus, I really enjoy working for you," Freddy urged, still hugging the soiled cloth like a kid's comforter.

He chuckled softly and a slow sly grin spread across his cheeks. "Freddy, I want to fund your new venture."

Freddy's brows nearly sprang off his face and hit the ceiling. "New... venture?"

"Yeah, your new restaurant. Wherever in the world you want to open it, I'll fund it."

The cloth fell to his feet. "Are you serious?"

Lana's heart doubled, the swell of emotion made her dizzy. Marcus deserved a prize blow job if he was hers...*he's not. So just stop with the dirty thoughts.* Her thighs pressed tighter.

"A talent like yours shouldn't be hidden. The world needs to taste your food."

Freddy gulped back a lump in his throat. "Really? Why would you do that, Marcus?"

"I've watched you grow these past few years. The food you create up is pure genius. I like you, mate. I want to do this for you. No strings."

And there it was, those hideous, non-committal words that flowed easily from the mouth of Marcus McGrath—'no strings'.

Her fingers fumbled with the edges of her apron while Freddy launched into Marcus's chest and hugged him like a cute Koala.

"Omigod. I know you're serious. If I've learnt anything during my time working for you, it's that you're true to your word. How will I ever repay you?" Freddy beamed.

"Just make it work for yourself. Go after your dream, like I'm going after mine." His eyes settled on Lana.

"That's very kind of you, Marcus." She swallowed hard, feeling the weight of his heated stare.

"What's your dream?" he asked, leaning closer to her.

"I...uh..." *I want you.*

"She wants to be a photographer," Freddy blurted out with excitement bubbling on his tongue.

"Uh, yeah. I'm enrolling in a course when I get back to Belfast," she confirmed.

Marcus nodded in approval.

"And you—what's your dream?" she dared to ask in a soft whisper.

His emerald eyes sparkled. "When Jamie shakes on his Italian deal then everyone will know what that is. And believe me, I'll do anything to succeed."

"Business. Of course." Her hip leant into the counter for support.

"For now. Jamie has been working on this deal for some time. I won't jeopardise his efforts."

His body radiated a sexual heat, suffocating her composure. Freddy stepped away, sensing the thick atmosphere wrapping around their two bodies.

"Thanks for last night...I mean, thanks for helping me get back to sleep." She managed to stay calm even thought her stomach churned.

"I got used to you falling asleep beside me," he admitted with an emotion flaring in his eyes that she couldn't read.

"Yeah...I guess you just got bored."

"No, Lana."

"Sure."

"Lana." His expression hardened. "I wanted to be there for you. It's just..."

"Forget it. I understand. It was too much, too soon," she interrupted, shaking her head.

His nostrils flared. "No, you don't understand," he growled. "I'm consumed with anger. That bastard, Carl, needs to be put in a box. I was trying to protect…" his words drifted to a halt.

Her eyes bugged, panic swirled in her gut like an old arch enemy. Her hands trembled. She reached out to the counter to steady herself. Short sharp bursts of air escaped her lungs, and the room started to spin.

Her frightened trance was wrapped in his tight protective embrace. Her rapid heartbeat found his slow and steady rhythm.

"I'm sorry, beautiful." The words rumbled in his chest. The hot air from his nose warmed her scalp and soothed her distress.

She held onto him, willing herself to be strong but loosing herself in his strength.

"It's okay. Everything is okay." His palm caressed her back and his lips pressed down onto the crown of her head.

After a few settled heart beats, his arms slackened and he pulled away. Coldness crept over her skin when his body heat retreated.

His phone buzzed. Retrieving it from his jeans, he answered the call and muttered a few quick words before slotting the phone back into his pocket.

His expression fell blank but his face paled and the pulse in his throat bounced. "I have something urgent to take care of. Freddy, can you get Lana a glass of water."

"Of course." Freddy trotted to the fridge.

"You okay?" he asked flicking out his wrist and checking the time.

A warning beacon flared like a bright red firework. She was taking up his precious time. She straightened her spine and rolled her shoulder.

"Yes, I'm fine." A forced smile barely twitched her lips.

"We'll talk later, beautiful." With one step, he leant in and pressed his lips to her temple with a quick peck.

Her stupid heart leapt, even though it was more like a friendly gesture. He turned away and marched out of the kitchen with his phone screen glowing.

She inhaled with an unsteady stutter.

"You okay, honey?" Freddy handed her a tumbler of water, placing it in her shaky hand.

She sipped slowly. "Can you believe it? He's giving you the money to set up your own restaurant."

Freddy slapped his palms to his temple. "My head is spinning."

"Mine too."

28

After spending an hour or two relaxing by the infinity pool, Lana wandered through the cool corridors back to her bedroom.

She spent the morning thinking about her situation. *Did Marcus know she was here? Was she an unexpected ex who he knew would fall at his feet?*

He was playing a wicked game of tease and she was adamant he wouldn't win.

A large cream box sat on the edge of her bed, wrapped with a thick white ribbon. Her fingertips lightly brushed the shiny opalescence material before she released the flouncy bow.

Hidden beneath crisp white tissue paper, nestled ruby red silk. Pinching the fabric, she raised the garment to eye level, allowing the most beautiful dress to ripple out of the box.

A white card dropped to the floor with the words, 'A beautiful dress for a beautiful woman', handwritten in black ink.

The thought of a gift from an Italian lover sprinkled chills down her spine, quickly turning to a head whirling panic.

What if it didn't fit? Over the past few weeks, sadness had trimmed her shapely silhouette.

What if Emilio bought the wrong size? *Ugh, what a disaster.*

She lay the dress on the bed and stepped back, falling into the realms of darkness yet again.

The black dress splayed out on the bed, the matching shoes beneath. *Someone is in the house, creeping up the old wooden stairs.*

It can't be Rory, he needs help. She's the only one who can help him. Her bones are on ice, her spine stiff with fear.

There's nowhere to hide, no way to get out. Too late to think. Get behind the door.

His eyes are dark and his smile sinister…

The galloping tempo of her pulse thrummed in her veins. Her knees buckled and she slumped to the hard floor. The walls blurred and spun like the Waltzer at the village fate. Stingy bile burned her gullet, and her hands splayed in the tiles, barely holding her up.

She half crawled, half heaved her body towards the adjoining bathroom, reaching the toilet just in time. A jet of yellow liquid sprayed the clean white bowl.

She begged to inhale deeply into her tight chest. It felt like a sharp set of claws had latched onto her lungs and were squeezing her to a slow death.

Fear pulled her under the surface of a thick black pool. *What the hell was happening? Was she having a heart attack? Was she going to die?* Her limbs were weak and her mind on high alert, fearing her lungs would refuse to work.

She gripped the toilet seat until her knuckles whitened. A steady breath slowly passed through her nostrils and finally a controlled inhalation gusted past her lips until each deliberate breath satisfied her lungs.

Climbing up the wash basin, she hunched over the sink. Her legs were shaky, and her face was ghostly pale. It took the last ounce of effort to peel off her dress and scramble into the shower cubicle. The water blasted from above and drenched her sweat laden skin.

She pressed her palms to the steamy glass and lowered her head, savouring in the freedom of breathing. She was angry that Carl had the power to terrorise her even though he was in prison. That ordeal was in the past now, and that's where he belonged.

She rounded her shoulders and directed her head under the powerful jets. The water pelted her skull with a satisfying pressure.

Her weary muscles relaxed and her crazed thoughts calmed. She gulped back her fear and let her imagination flow. In her thoughts Emilio's solid arms tugged her close, his full pink lips trailed kisses along her neck, his hard cock nudged his zipper.

The thought of his presence wasn't comforting. It didn't soothe or settle her. She didn't need a hero anyway. She just had to move on from Marcus, however difficult that may be.

Lana squeezed her eyes shut and considered the options with Emilio. While her soapy hands slid from her navel to her breasts, her mind wandered.

With a pinch, she rolled a nipple between her finger and thumb, invoking a soft groan. She quickly hunted the pressure building between her thighs and invited his face into her fantasy. Not Emilio's, but Marcus's.

The naughty sensation of her swirling fingers was heightened by her lustful imagination. Under the warm jets, she happily indulged in the memory of his sinful mouth and pretended her hands were his.

Marcus continued to haunt her daydreams and now he was blocking her alone time and storming her fantasy of being with another man.

Every heart beat trebled in speed as her excitement intensified. The very thought of Marcus and his divinely chiselled body brought her to a quick and powerful climax.

He was trouble.

He was playing a game.

He had his chance and blew it.

Emilio's thoughtfulness squeezed her heart. He gifted her a red dress to bring out her inner fire, and that's exactly what it would do.

She chose to wear the dress because she loved it, not because she wanted to please Emilio. The truth was, she still craved a response from Marcus that echoed her need for him.

The coconut moisturiser gave her skin a subtle sheen and its delicate tropical aroma reminded her of the balmy summer nights back home. Standing in front of the mirrored closet doors, she held her breath as the fabric poured over her figure like a layer of strawberry syrup.

She secured the golden clasp at her nape and fixed her full breasts into the discreet stitched in cups.

The exquisite halter dress fitted her shape like a second skin. Fine stitching and soft material suggested expense and luxury, probably costing more than six months' rent. She was impressed by Emilio's perceptive and stylish eye.

A stuttered breath filled her thankful lungs and devilish plans to flaunt herself in front of Marcus flooded her mind. Thick golden hair cascaded down her back in a mass of tumbling waves. She was primped to perfection with matching scarlet lips and thick black lashes.

Tonight, she would give Emilio a chance. He might be the perfect remedy to help her forget Carl Reed and Marcus McGrath.

She sauntered away from her sexy reflection with a confident swing to her step and a knowing smile on her curved lips.

Lana was ready for her date with Emilio Falcone.

29

Alberto clapped his hands with authority, demanding more effort from his staff.

On the extensive balcony there was a wide rectangular table covered in fresh pressed linen, scattered with twinkling tea lights and silver candelabras.

Freshly clipped Bluebells and fragrant Jasmines nestled amongst the dancing flames and tied the overall style together with simple elegance. Dotted around the enchanting terrace, were large glass cylinders housing tall candles that oozed an aroma of zingy lemons.

The smartly dressed staff bustled through the kitchen and upper rooms, efficiently tending to each guest.

Freddy had briefed Lana on the importance of the evening. Jamie had to wrap up a mega business deal with the Italians. The likeminded men threw millions about like pocket change.

After months of ironing out the finer details, Falcone Construction was finally signing the dotted line to work alongside McGrath Industries. The deal would save the brothers millions.

Emilio was wealthy, one of the super rich. In Lana's eyes that didn't make him anymore attractive. Stripped of all his money and flashy materialistic items, he was just a man. A hot-blooded, sexy Italian male.

She smiled inwardly. Her hands rested on the wrought iron ledge as she gazed out to the mysterious dark ocean.

A gentle breeze caressed the loose tendrils teasing the curve of her lower back. A flurry of prickles cascaded down her spine as a large hand brushed down her arm.

Marcus.

If at all possible, her heart quadrupled, yet she remained adamant in her mission to move on, to stand tall and show zero emotion.

"You're so beautiful." He paused by her side. His smouldering gaze locked her side profile.

Giving him a sideward glance, she eyed his fresh, white shirt that hugged every inch of his muscular chest with a few buttons casually left open. His heady musky scent drifted through the breeze and caressed her senses like an affectionate lover.

His torso dipped, twisting a little to meet her gaze. "Come on, beautiful. Let me see those amazing blue eyes," he said with a sultry timbre.

She smiled lightly, feeling the pull of his words like a lasso. He nudged her waist lightly with his elbow. "Lana…"

She turned into him and held her breath. His hot gaze lowered to her parted red lips. The green of his eyes twinkled wildly when her light sigh escaped with a soft groan.

She automatically titled into him, but a gap of mere inches kept them apart. Her body was deceiving her resolve. It gave into the invisible force tugging them together.

"Did you come here for business?" she asked softly,

letting the words drift off as she lost herself in his devastatingly handsome face.

His sinful mouth curved upwards in that ever-so-sexy grin. His long fingers trailed away a loose tendril that caught in her lashes.

"We need to talk." His hand retreated and her heart paused at the loss of contact.

"Now?" Helplessly, she tilted forward a fraction.

"Lana...I..." He paused, as if he wanted to say something important, then he cleared his throat.

"Hey, Lana!" Her trance was interrupted by Emilio's Italian accent.

Her head flicked around to find Emilio by the door with his arms crossed and his hip dipped, leaning into the frame.

"We'll talk later, when we're alone," Marcus growled. His mouth moved a breath away from her forehead.

"Why can't we talk now, Marcus?" she whispered, captivated by the only man who could extract her heart and cut it wide open.

Marcus inhaled slowly, sucking in the tropical scent that emanated from her warm skin.

Tonight, he was going to take her back.

No bullshit.

He would win her heart, when the time was right. There was so much he had to say and so much needed to admit.

But worst of all, he had to tell her that Donna Marie was found dead with every hair on her head shaved off. His stomach twisted. That bastard, Reed, was at it again. It had to be him.

"I need to take care of business..." He stopped abruptly,

burning his gaze into her face, trying to implant the words rather than say them out loud. "I have to help my brother wrap up his deal and then we'll talk." He looked down to his chunky gold watch.

Half an hour, tops. Any longer than that and he'd blow the fucking deal to smithereens.

Her eyes ripped away from his face. "Right. Business," she muttered. "I'll leave you to it."

Emilio cleared his throat loudly. "Hey, baby. Let's get a drink," he called with cool impatience in his voice.

His greedy gaze lowered to the minimal fabric hugging her plump breasts and his eyes darkened to a shade of green like sodden moss.

"Enjoy your evening, Marcus. Please excuse me, my date is waiting." She daintily batted her eyelashes and forced a sweet smile.

His gaze lingered on the sway of her hips as she sashayed towards Emilio with sexy confidence.

Marcus remembered every curve, every dimple, every inch of her bountiful figure. The smoking hot dress had the desired effect, making his dick throb.

Each sacred section of her flesh was branded onto his brain, scorched into his mind for eternity, creating an erotic map of her sexy body that was stored in his memory bank.

Lana was perfect. A rarity he never knew existed. The calm to his wild, the serenity to his storm and tonight he was going to explain everything. As soon as Falcone signed the contract.

Patience wasn't a quality he would claim to have. His stomach clenched with frustration. He wanted to halt her retreat and kiss her juicy red lips until she breathed in all the air from his lungs.

Marcus was used to getting what he wanted, no matter the

cost. But this time he couldn't fuck up his brothers long awaited plans. Truthfully, business was just business at the end of the day.

He couldn't give two fucks if Emilio bailed on the deal like a churlish schoolgirl, but Jamie was family, he was blood. He wasn't going to be a selfish prick. Lana would understand, and if she didn't, he'd damn well make her.

He stood in silence, a deep anger rose like hackles. He watched her peachy ass swagger over to Emilio's side. Emilio's beige chinos clung to the large bulge between his legs, and he wore a girly pink shirt, unbuttoned at the neck with dark tufts sprouting from his tanned chest.

He slotted her hand in his and tugged her close. She crashed into his washboard abs and giggled quietly.

Marcus chewed the inside of his mouth and stuffed his hands in his jeans. He hated that she laughed for him. He detested that she wanted him and he loathed that his fucking lips landed on her cheek.

He reiterated the reason why he was waiting.

Half an hour—for Jamie.

His stomach knotted and a pain in his chest magnified how much of an idiot he'd been. He stormed past Emilio's show of affection and didn't look back.

"Jamie." He grabbed his brother's elbow. "Get it sorted now. Before I kill Emilio and ruin the deal."

"Jeez, Marcus. Settle down. He's only arrived. I've got it covered." Jamie patted his brother's shoulder. "Maria has the contract. She's on her way."

"You look sensational, Lana." Emilio's eyes twinkled. "Let me see that sexy ass." He raised his hand and spun her underneath his arm in slow motion.

The dress gave her an air of sexual confidence, a feeling she had lacked for too long. He nodded in acceptance, sporting a sly smile that gave away the unsavoury acts he was clearly imagining.

She placed her hand in the crook of his arm. His long legs took one step for every two of hers. The bar was occupied by a group of males lined up on bar stools, communicating flamboyantly with their hands.

Without asking her choice of drink, Emilio ordered a flute of champagne and pointed to a bottle of scotch on a high glass shelf.

His quick decision to supply her with champagne niggled in her belly. She liked gin and champagne gave her a death like hangover. She brushed his misdemeanour aside and plastered a fake smile over her uncertainty.

"The McGrath boys certainly know how to make a fine scotch." He winked with a devilish glint in his eyes.

Leaning forward, his lips paused at her ear lobe. "I'd like to see that dress on my bedroom floor," he said thickly. His cinnamon breath sparked a subtle shiver.

His Italian accent was super sexy and his masculine citrus smell was fresh and inviting. She peeked up at him through her thick lashes.

"Play your cards right and you can tear it off me later," she said throatily, in a half attempt to coax herself into the idea of taking the evening one step further.

Emilio hummed into his glass and gulped down the liquid with urgency.

"I'd like nothing more than to tear that dress apart right now, Lana." He nodded to the bar man for another drink.

Her attention snapped to a tall brunette who strutted along the terrace and positioned herself between Jamie and Marcus. Her glossy dark hair poured down her spine like melted chocolate, splaying over her bare shoulders.

She wore, what could only be described as a bandage. The bright white material wrapped her enhanced breasts and finished just below her pert ass cheeks. She handed Jamie a Manila envelope and then traced her lacquered nails down his wide bicep.

Her heart skidded to a halt as the slender woman sidled towards Marcus and rested her palms on his pecs.

Her fragile heart bounced against her ribs. Dizzying, short breathes begged acceptance into her tightened lungs. Marcus's hands floated to the woman's waist and he flashed a sly grin. He gifted the woman with a devastatingly sexy smile, as if he knew her.

His chiselled features were like a priceless painting, revealing lust, desire and truth. Fragments of her cracked heart turned to ashes in her chest. Tiny black blobs traced her vision as she stared in shock.

Was she the reason Marcus came to Italy?

Emilio's fresh scent stirred her attention away from the visual horror show as he encroached her space.

"About that dress, bella signora…I'd like to rip it apart at the seams." His gold pinky ring clanked against his glass tumbler and he sank the contents in one long gulp.

She had nothing to lose. "Let's go then," she mumbled, swallowing back the aching lump in her throat.

Emilio cinched her waist and almost pushed her towards the exit. She looked back over her shoulder with a wilted gaze. Marcus was tearing Lana apart, organ by organ, limb by limb.

Emilio shoved her backwards until she was caged

between his arms with her back against the cool plaster. Daring hands glided over the fabric of her tight dress.

The hairs on her neck pricked with a rush of nerves. His starved mouth crashed onto her trembling lips. She opened her mouth to his hungry tongue and wrapped her arms around his sinewy neck, holding herself in place before her legs gave way.

His scorching kiss could wet the panties of any girl, but Lana's knees quaked because she had finally realised Marcus was a player and they would never reach relationship status.

Breaking their hurried kiss, Emilio's smoky eyes ate up her heaving breasts, mistaking it for lust. "We go to my place," he panted.

"Ummm...okay." She hesitated, dazed by the punishing scene that had brought her entire world crashing down around her. "What about the party?" she mumbled.

"Later, baby. Later."

His wet lips trailed along her collar bone. There were no electrifying sparks or tingles of dark desire. Adrenaline was keeping this one-sided charade alive, that, and her need to lose herself in another man, to feel something other than heart break and rejection.

Emilio lifted his chin. His fingers reoriented the angle of her face, bringing her gaze in line with his. A roguish smile revealed perfect white teeth.

"That dress is such a turn on, baby, but I need to see you naked. Take it off when we get in the car," he ordered throatily.

Her fingers twirled through his thick locks. "I'm sure it cost you a fortune? Can I wear it until we get to your place?" She almost smiled. The idea of taking it off for his pleasure was a daunting prospect.

Emilio frowned. "Baby, I would never choose a dress like

this for you." His pupils dilated and his eyes turned as black as coal.

Her eyelids pinged wide. "You didn't buy it for me?"

"I would never buy a dress that attracts other men to my woman." His mouth moved to the soft fleshy pad of her ear and he suckled gently. A sprinkle of heavenly heat raced over her skin and she inhaled in a gust of air.

"I'm not yours." She panted.

The lobe popped out of his mouth and a sexy growl rumbled in her ear. "You will be."

Lana adored the dress, it was gloriously seductive. It fitted her figure with so much accuracy that it could have been created just for her, but Emilio hadn't bought the dress for her.

The hairs on her scalp lifted at the root and an uncomfortable sensation jarred her muscles. *Who bought it then?* Obviously, it wasn't from Marcus. He had other ideas for the evening.

The guy couldn't help himself. Perhaps Freddy bought it for her, he wasn't short of a few pounds. Marcus paid him well and he did have impeccable taste.

The smile on Emilio's lips drifted away, and the intensity of his wicked gaze swathed her mind. His lust was inviting, and his evident desire pushed into her thigh.

As his juicy lips devoured her, a surge of guilt twisted her gut. He just wasn't Marcus. Admittedly, he was an Italian god, but he wasn't meant for her, nor she for him.

A little voice of reason popped into her thoughts. Her best friend Amanda would tell her to go for it. Lana wasn't going to marry the guy, she was just planning a night of mind-blowing sex. Isn't that how her journey started—the path of consensual sex with a stranger?

Emilio grabbed her hand, tugging her out the front door

and down to the pebbled driveway, where several pricy sports cars were parked facing the exit. She hoisted up her dress at the thigh and dropped into the passenger seat of the blood red Lotus.

"You don't have a driver?" she asked, sliding the seat belt over her chest.

"I just bought this little beauty." He winked.

Emilio pushed the start button and revved the engine to a mechanical purr. His grin matched that of an excited school boy until he turned to face her.

"Now, what about that dress. Off. Now!" His eyes blackened.

Her heart pounded hysterically.

Marcus would never commit, he proved that once and for all. She wanted to take the bull by the horns and have some fun. To put the past behind her.

She slowly unhooked the clasp and pulled the halter away from her breasts. His intake of air was loud and raspy. With a tentative tug she wiggled the remainder past her belly and angled her hips to the roof, so she could slip it under her buttocks.

It was no easy feat in the cramped passenger seat, but Lana managed to finally nudge it over her knees and let the dress rest on her stilettos. Emilio grunted with approval as she turned on her hip to face him. Her full breasts were on display and a lacy triangle covered her black mound.

"You are so sexy. I'm going to enjoy fucking you." He continued to rev the engine, with his hands wrapped tightly on the steering wheel like he was holding himself back.

In a heartbeat he lunged forward and smashed his mouth over hers. A sweet taste of amaretto and alcohol swirled between them. His tongue traced the inner rim of her top lip with a scorching passion.

The reality jolted her heart and her pulse raced through her body at high speed.

Lana wasn't ready to move on.

Just as she readied herself to retreat, Emilio's lips smacked loudly as they were brutally ripped away. His body was yanked backwards, and he was violently pulled from the driver's seat.

Her breathing became erratic, and she watched him tumble helplessly to the ground.

30

Marcus stood over Emilio with his palms balled into fists.

His eyes cut to Lana. Her fingertips immediately brushed her swollen lips.

Emilio scrambled to a stand and swept a hand through his dishevelled locks. "What the fuck, McGrath?" he growled, preparing himself for warfare.

Ignoring Emilio, Marcus glared at her as she tried to cover herself with the flowing red material. It caught on her pointed heel and she tugged vigorously in the confined space. His chest heaved with blinding fury.

"Get out of the fucking car, Lana," he roared.

His fists clenched and contracted as he marched around to the passenger door. Lana gulped, her throat tightened. The car door flung open and Marcus grabbed her arm with an unforgiving pressure. He heaved her out of the bucket seat and held her tightly until she could stand for herself.

"What are you doing, Marcus?" she blasted.

Her naked body trembled, and her chest expanded as she breathed with short sharp blasts.

His nostril flared and his jaw locked tightly. He stared in silence, dragging his eyes from her bare breasts to the black lace thong. In one swift movement, he tore off his polo shirt and chucked it towards her.

His chest was on show, each rippling muscle contracted with a ferocity that sent an unexpected thrill though her muscles. A bright moon lit up the villa from behind and cast shards of cool silvery light across the still sea.

Warm air ruffled her wavy hair and prickled her unprotected skin. The weighted silence between them was fuelled with unsaid words.

"Put it on and get in the fucking villa. This asshole has been drinking alcohol. He's not driving you anywhere." Marcus's voice cracked through the quietness.

She snatched the shirt and blanked out his angry glare with the fabric as it passed over her face. At first she thought he was jealous, but she quickly realised he was just pissed that the guy was going to drive after drinking alcohol.

Emilio rounded the car. "Stand the fuck back, Falcone!" Marcus shouted over his shoulder when his shoes crunched over the gravel towards them.

A tear rolled down her pale cheek. "I didn't think he drank that much?" She gulped.

His face furrowed into a deep-set frown, a look she had never seen before, a darkness behind his uncompromising glare.

"Even if he had one sip..." He held his finger up in front of his face. "Just one - that's more than enough to put your life at risk. He's not allowed to put you in danger. Deal or no fucking deal with my brother." His breathing deepened, and his eyes cut to Emilio who lowered his head.

"Is this who you want, Lana. A prick who would risk your life?" He lunged forward and seized her wrists.

She choked back tears, staving the urge to burst into sobs. "N...No, Marcus. I..." Feeling utterly overwhelmed she violently shrugged off his hands, shoving him away.

"Stay away from me, you head fuck!" she yelled. With the large polo shirt covering her decency she hurried back to the villa.

"Lana!" he shouted, but she continued to run, as best as she could in sky high heels.

Voices echoed in the corridor. She quickly yanked off the heels and scampered up the staircase that flanked the main entrance hall.

It curved the cylindrical wall, taking her to the upper level. Finding herself on a long white mezzanine, she was gifted with multiple exits to retreat behind.

She chose to run to the very end, so she could hide in the farthest room. Pushing down the handle, she gently cracked open double doors.

Inside was the most enchanting room she had ever set eyes on. A glass domed ceiling with long windows lead to a rapid incline, giving the impression that the whole room floated in the sky.

It was built into the mountain and the entire left side of the room was bare rock that dropped into a crystal blue water lagoon. She wandered into the magical space with her jaw slack and her heart heavy.

The door slammed shut behind her.

"Lana," Marcus called with a stern tone.

She spun around to face him. Each shallow breath made her lips quiver. "Go away, Marcus. Please, just leave me alone," she pleaded.

He stepped forward closing the distance between them. "Please, Lana, we need to talk. I've blown the fuck out Jamie's deal now anyway," he said in a low rasp.

Lana sighed loudly and wiped her tear streaked cheeks with the back of her hand. Her heart was pumping so fast that she could feel it in her throat.

"There's nothing to talk about!" she snapped.

Marcus slowly shook his head. "I don't know how to do this, Lana. I feel like I'm under water and you're the only one who can reach in and pull me out," he finally admitted.

"Do what, Marcus?" Her voice cracked.

"I can't stop thinking about you. I need to hear your voice, savour your taste, feel your skin. I've never felt this way before."

"Are you being serious right now, Marcus? The guy who walked away and then flaunted women in my face?" she murmured through gritted teeth.

He stepped closer and she backed away. "I wasn't flaunting women in your face?" His brow creased.

"Yeah, you were. At Sunrise and then downstairs. I'm not an eejit, Marcus. I knew what you were like when I let myself fall for you."

The gold fleck in his eyes lit up like fire. "Lana, I want to try…us, together. No matter what it takes. It was wrong to let you go, I knew it from the second you walked out the door."

Her jaw slackened and her teary eyes blinked wide. "I don't believe you."

"It's true."

"Then why didn't you come after me?" she stammered.

He stepped closer again, and this time she stood tall without retreating. "Truthfully, I couldn't handle it. I got scared, if that's actually fucking possible." He half laughed. "I'm in control of every single part of my life. That's a constant, but then you wandered in to my world and tipped it upside down." He rubbed his hands over his face and scratched his coarse jaw.

"He took you because of the club. I had to protect you. Taking you back to my place was the only way, but it messed with my head. You slotted into my life like you were meant to be there. I shouldn't have said those things to Mal…" his words trailed off.

She hugged herself tightly, protecting her heart. "I was intense, I get that. I was in a bad place and you let me leave. You totally cut me off. I stupidly thought we had something." She looked away from his troubled face. "Just leave me alone, Marcus."

His handsome features hardened in momentary defeat. "We do have something, beautiful. Something real. I feel it, Lana. No bullshit," he insisted.

She swallowed hard.

"I'm sorry I bailed on you, beautiful."

Silence swallowed them. Even though she was riddled with hurt and rejection, Lana couldn't fathom why she desperately wanted him to hold her.

"It was a dick move. I should've listened to my heart and not my head. I thought you would be stronger without me."

Her breathing hitched under the weight of his confession. "Are you serious? I told you I loved you, Marcus. You pretended like it didn't happen."

In one stride, he was inches from her melting heart. "Lana..."

She blinked wildly. "The time we spent together…was it just out of misplaced duty?" she dared to ask.

"I was trying to protect you, like I've tried to do from the second we met. Then it all went to shit. I doubted being the right guy for you. But you have to understand, when I put my lips to yours for the first time, something changed inside me."

She fell into his hard chest and pressed her damp cheek to his smooth skin. His arms wrapped her shoulders and he grabbed the hair at her nape, yanking her head back. "Do you want Falcone?" he growled.

Her breathing stuttered. "No...I saw you hitting on the girl on the terrace," she whimpered with a flush of foolishness on her rosy cheeks.

His teeth grazed the dip of her jugular. "Maria is Jamie's solicitor. The girl has been after him for ages. He doesn't mix business with pleasure, ever. I was playing along with her silly game. It was only brotherly banter. I'm sorry."

Her lips lifted at the corners as his eyes flicked up to meet hers. "I thought Emilio bought me the beautiful dress I was wearing earlier. If I'm honest, a part of me liked his attention," she admitted, hating how desperate it sounded.

His chin nudged upwards ever so slightly. "Did you like it? The dress?"

"Yes. Turns out he didn't buy it for me." She shrugged with a puzzled look on her face.

Marcus ran his fingers along her jaw and stopped at her chin, holding her gaze. "I know he didn't buy it." He brushed his lips across the tip of her nose.

"How?" she whispered.

"I couldn't mess up the deal with Falcone. I knew he'd take it badly if I barged in and stole you from under his nose. So, I had to bide my time. Then the night I was in your bedroom, I saw what little clothes you had. I wanted to make you happy." He paused. "And I wanted to see this sexy ass without being able to undress you." He cupped her buttocks and squeezed.

Scrunching her brows together, she said, "*You* bought it for me? It must have cost a fortune."

"It was only a few thousand, a mere fraction of what your worth. Of what you mean to me."

Her redundant broken heart jump started in her chest with

each intoxicating kiss that fused the lonely pieces back together again. She melted into his strong protective embrace, and her soul relinquished to his seductive allure, happily dancing to the beat of his heart that played a melody just for her.

"I've missed you so much, but…how do I know you won't cut me loose again? How can I trust you?" she mumbled as her lips clung to his.

"I can only promise you that I won't run from this anymore."

He thumbed her cheeks, taking her mouth with a tender kiss that was filled with promise, not like the passionate kisses she had come to expect from him. This one meant more to her than his words.

Their lips slowly separated. Her breathing became ragged shallow breathes. His arms held her close like he couldn't let go. Holding her cheek to his taught pec, Lana listened to his words rumble in his chest.

"This is what I should have done when you were leaving. I should have held on to you and never let go."

"I needed that, more than anything," she muttered, suddenly realising she had fallen in love with him.

She stared into his green gaze, quietly understanding why she couldn't move on from him. Marcus McGrath had the power to crush her heart, yet it was his.

He thumbed her chin. "It's okay, I feel it too, Lana." His voice was resolute. "We're on the same page."

Together they stood in silence, the seconds drifting into minutes. They were cloaked in the pale glow of the bright moon, lit up under its all-seeing contemplation.

She nuzzled her face into the crook of his neck, absorbing the feel of his skin next to hers. Then, she peeked up at him, fluttering her lashes.

His eyes were filled with emotion, a hot, raw intensity. "Christ, Lana, seeing you in those fucking hot little panties… let's just say, I'm showing a monumental amount of restraint right now." His sly grin sparked an intense throbbing heat between her legs. "But first, we need to talk."

Every molecule and every cell in her body ached for him. They had been apart for what felt like a century, a loss that rivalled death.

Her senses were consumed with his sensual smell, bare torso and sexy smile. Talking was the last thing on her mind. With a feather light touch, she fluttered kisses along his prickly jaw.

"We need to talk about it, beautiful," he persisted between long lingering kisses.

"Not yet," she panted.

She impishly pulled away from him. A crafty smile teased her stained lips. Taking a step back, she slowly lifted his polo shirt up and over her breasts and dangled it off her forefinger. It sank to the floor with a quiet swoosh.

He grabbed her hips and dug his fingers into her flesh, stuffing his nose into her hair and inhaling. "I missed this perfect body so much."

The tender kiss that followed welded their hearts together. A kiss of promise, a kiss of desire, a kiss of love.

Her thighs hugged his hips and he carried her to a lounger. Laying her back on the pillows. He gazed down at her with a heart stopping grin.

Maintaining eye contact, he knelt to worship her. She scooted back, dropping her knees wide at his command.

He licked from her navel to the seam of her wet panties and shoved his hands under her buttocks. She tilted her pelvis into his face as he breathed in her sweet musky aroma like it was his favourite scent.

"You're so fucking amazing, Lana. I could stay between your legs all night." His voice was rugged as he yanked off her panties and tossed them away.

He smoothed his palms across the silky flesh of her buttocks and buried his head in her heat. A low groan filled the serenity when he slid his tongue inside her.

"That feels so damn good," she said in a breathy gasp.

She was wet and greedy. Her internal muscles squeezed around his probing fingers and her hips bucked.

He wanted to talk, that's what she had craved for so long, but now, she just craved his touch more than his words.

His wicked lips latched onto her swollen bundle of nerves and he sucked, hard and fast before pulling away with a tug of his teeth. Her fingers had carefully threaded his hair before his demanding tongue circled and licked, but now her nails dug into his scalp and her fingers curled firmly.

A rippling sigh flew from her throat with each spasm, followed by a throaty moan. He gazed up, locking his dark gaze with her flushed face.

Lifting, he opened his mouth to speak, "Lana, we need to talk..."

She pressed her forefinger to his mouth. "There's a time to talk and that's after." Her tongue darted across her lips, and he urgently released the buttons of his jeans.

He freed his hard cock and quickly rolled a condom down his throbbing shaft. She let out a gasp, welcoming the sheathed crown as it nudged her opening, inching deep inside.

Her muscles contracted with the intensity, struggling to take his fullness as it stretched her wide. With gentle leisurely thrusts, he built up an excruciating arousal. Their lips found each other's in a deep sensual kiss.

Marcus growled into her open mouth. "You feel so good. So, fucking good."

With an upward shunt of her hips, he drove into her with an unforgiving force. Her raspy groans filled the silence, joined by the slapping of flesh to flesh.

The hedonistic pleasure swirled in her core, spreading like volts of electrical waves through each nerve ending. The intimacy of his skin to hers, coupled with the delightful rhythm and husky sound of his excitement, sent her into oblivion. She panted his name, unravelling in his eyes.

Her insides spasmed around his cock as her orgasm detonated like a grenade. The feel of his body on top of her was fucking amazing.

He grunted and growled, then released with a shudder like the pleasure tore through every muscle in his body.

Admittedly, it wasn't going to be easy. He was a renowned playboy who naturally flirted with woman. The man was charming and untouchable. Until now.

And now, she wanted Marcus McGrath all to herself.

31

Carl inhaled the excitement of his pending revenge.

"I'll show every last fucker who messes with Carl Reed that I'm the one in control. I'm the big guy around here." He spoke with an air of calmness as he lit up a cigar and drew the smoke into his mouth.

He gazed at his preened reflection with self-adoration pouring from his eyes. A wink preceded the release of thick white smoke that swirled past his lips. He puffed out his chest and pulled back his shoulders.

He pulled open his jacket and checked on the small black gun that sat snugly in his inside pocket. Patting his full pocket, he chuckled with a smug look on his face. Holding the cigar in his teeth, he hit dial.

The call was connected after three rings. "I'm ready, Kye. I'll take the route as planned and meet you there. Don't be late. I hate people who make me wait."

He terminated the call and slipped the mobile phone into his trouser pocket.

"Don't worry, sweetheart. I'll be back in a day or two for a victory party!"

He turned to face his new fascination. The little deli girl was writhing on the bedroom floor. Her limbs were tightened together with cable ties and her mouth stuffed full of a rolled-up sock.

He lifted his trousers at the knee and bent down to her side. She thrashed from side to side like a trapped animal in the jaws of its killer.

Carl stroked her hair tenderly. "I won't be long. Don't go anywhere." A low cackle brought tears to her eyes.

Her pretty little face was crimson and the lenses of her glasses had become smudged. With the pad of his forefinger he pushed the frames back up the bridge of her nose.

"Don't cry, sweetheart. You should be happy that I picked you." He smiled slyly.

Rising to a stand, he watched her pointless struggle. The black frames that shielded her watery eyes slid back down her nose and hung loosely.

As she whipped her head back and forth they slipped off and fell to the floor.

In one step, he stomped on the flimsy plastic, crunching the glass beneath his shiny shoe. "You don't need those ugly things. How about I give you something to take the edge off?"

He didn't get the same exhilarating thrill that he felt when Lana was paralysed beneath him. This little blonde didn't have the same look in her motionless gaze.

Horror spilled from her watery eyes, whereas the lovely Lana had grit. Carl hummed in the back of his throat, considering all the things he would do to Lana when he found her again.

Carl jumped into his silver Jaguar, switched on the neon lights and reversed without checking if the road was clear.

Hitting the main road, the car blazed along the empty lanes towards the International airport.

His eyes flicked to the rear-view mirror. His brows were neatly trimmed, and his eyes had darkened with a perilous glint. The roads were eerily quiet for a Sunday evening, allowing him to gather more speed.

He knew exactly where he needed to be—Italy.

32

Her cheeks were flushed and her body ached with satisfaction.

Melting into his naked torso, she trailed her fingertips over every curve of every muscle on his stomach. "What did you want to talk about?" She finally asked as her heart beat steadied.

Marcus lifted her chin with his knuckles. His eyes were unreadable, emotions hidden behind a swirl of dark green.

"Rory's off the hook. Carl framed him. Arthur was able to get the evidence we needed."

Her trembling hands reached out for his at the mention of Carl's name. "Who is Arthur?" she asked, linking her fingers with his.

He pressed his lips to her temple in a sweet, caring gesture. How she had missed the softness in his eyes and the feeling of his protection.

"Arthur is my PI, he's been with me for years. He's the best private investigator in the business," he said proudly, dragging her over his body so she lay on top of him.

Her brows pulled together and her mouth twisted. "You paid a PI to help Rory?"

A flash of pain turned the softness in his face to tight and firm. He dragged his eyes away from her searching gaze.

"Look, Lana, everything that happened was my fault." She spread her legs so they dangled at either side of his thighs and pushed herself up to sitting.

"We knew something wasn't right at the club." He continued. "Arthur is paid to know everything about everyone who joins. Obviously, we missed the fact Carl Reed was a fucking lunatic. When Jacqueline was murdered, Arthur got on the case straight away. He knew something didn't add up. It hasn't been easy gathering evidence on someone like him. It's taken longer than it should have." He rubbed the back of his neck. "I didn't tell you about Rory that night at Coach House because I wanted to keep you safe, but mostly, I just wanted to keep you away from him." He squeezed her thigh. "You were mine to protect."

Lana grinned at him. "I was never really his."

"When I first heard about her murder, I just assumed their sex antics went too far. Turns out Carl blindsided us. I had no idea he would take you, honestly. No fucking idea, beautiful. I'm to blame for all of this mess," he said angrily. The pads of his fingers deepened into her flesh, and he took forced deep breaths.

Lana tipped her torso onto his chest and nestled her cheek onto his shoulder. "None of this was your fault. It wasn't your fault he came after me, and it definitely wasn't your fault he abducted me." She sucked in a shuddered gust of air as she accepted the hideous memory. "Marcus, I chose to join Verto Veneri. I was the one who left Carl high and dry. I was the one who thought I could help Rory."

"Did you know I blocked your keycard that night?"

Her head flew up and her lips twisted. "Did you?" She smirked. "I'm glad you were looking out for me. What an epic mistake that could've been."

Her hair fell over bare skin, the ends brushed his smooth chest, but his loud gulp came from sadness rather than pleasure.

"I knew you weren't going to die after we found you at the harbour, but it felt like someone slammed me in the heart with a sledge hammer. I couldn't handle the surge of feelings that exploded in my heart. It was like nothing I'd ever experienced before."

His finger traced her bare thigh, shooting goose bumps over her skin.

"And then I started to doubt that we had a future. My track record isn't that honourable, you know. Guess I fooled myself into thinking I could forget about the unforgettable. I underestimated the power you have over me." His nose nuzzled her hair. "I'm supposed to be in New York right now, expanding the club."

Her brows snapped together, and her mouth formed an 'O' shape. "Then why are you here?"

His eyes were dark and serious. "Do you really have to ask that?"

"You're a business man, it's your priority."

"It normally is, but you come before everything, Lana. I've even fucked up Jamie's deal now." He sighed loudly, like he just sunk the biggest deal of the century. "I don't give a fuck about Falcone. It's Jamie I need to smooth things over with."

A thick silence of acceptance stole their words.

"What do you want from me, Marcus?" Lana finally whispered, her lips inches from his.

"I just want you," he said hoarsely. "All of you. With me.

Everywhere I go."

Her stomach twisted. *Could this really be true. Could the womaniser actually want to settle down? Was he ready?*

"What if it doesn't work out—if you decide to bail again? I won't give you another chance, Marcus."

He exhaled slowly. "Guess you'll have to take a chance on me, beautiful." Sweeping the ends of her hair away from her breasts, he said, "I can't let any other guy have these." A subtle curve of his mouth lifted to an impish grin as his nails traced her inner thigh.

Lana licked her dry lips. "And you want to repeatedly have sex with me…the same woman?"

"Yes."

"Like a relationship?"

"If wanting to make love, to just you, is a relationship—then, yes, Lana, that's exactly what I want."

She was hesitant to believe his confession, but the yearning to accept it was stronger than the possibilities of her heart being ripped from her chest again. A teasing grin lightly touched her lips.

"I'll have to think about it."

He crushed his mouth down onto hers, humming into her mouth. "Not an option," he growled. "I'm not taking 'no' for an answer." He pressed his forehead to hers and chuckled.

Lana peeled herself off his chest. The adrenaline pulsing through her body was sparked like an electrical current. Slowly and seductively, she caressed her swollen breasts, pinching a nipple and watching his eyes widen.

His cock stood proud and the darker flesh on the tip glistened with a creamy liquid. Stretching forward his fingers slipped into her wet folds.

"Hmmm, Lana. You're always so ready for me," he said

huskily as he pushed her to the side and rolled her flat on her back.

Her legs widened allowing his fingers to quickly locate her entrance. The need to have him inside her again was unbearable. "Please, Marcus, fuck me," she begged.

Marcus removed his fingers leaving her empty. He arched over her curvaceous naked body. He united his lips with hers, twirling and swirling his tongue in her mouth, ravaging her.

Lana shivered with red hot desire, sighing lightly with every brush of his skin against hers. She skimmed her hands down his ribs, revelling in the feel of his golden soft skin.

Suddenly, he swooped her up in his arms and strode towards the pool.

"What are you doing?" she squealed, kicking her legs playfully.

He carried her effortlessly, following the steps into the water and sending ripples across the glassy surface. He skilfully slipped away his arm from her knees and dropped her legs.

She splashed into silvery water right up to her waist. Her mouth formed an oval shape and she sucked in a gust of air as the cool liquid surrounded her sizzling skin.

"It's that cute giggle I'd die for." Marcus gave her a serious look. His face was soft, but his tentative gaze homed in on her smile.

Stepping back from his intense stare, she cupped her hands and collected a reservoir of water. She tossed it towards him, sending a blast of cold water over his muscular chest.

Marcus roared with laughter from deep in his chest, and his contemplation quickly switched to a sexy playful smile. He propelled a spray of water with both hands and doused her torso. Sopping wet strands of hair clung together like rat tails and her brown nipples poked out like pebbles.

With a powerful lunge, he came close enough to see the moon's reflection sparkle in her eyes. He grinned wickedly, deftly nipping each hard nub between his fingers and thumb. A bolt of pleasurable pain catapulted to her core, gifting her with an unexpected shiver.

Eying her reaction, he chuckled and dove backwards. His entire masculine form was encased in water and his head dropped beneath the surface. Within a few seconds he rose from the depths.

His fingers combed through his glossy black hair until it was slicked back from his forehead. He pressed his palms to his face and wiped the water droplets from his eyes. Her heart thrummed with excitement.

Wading towards him, she pressed her body into his and smoothed her hands over his brawny biceps. He was sexy as hell and ready for her all over again.

"Wrap your legs around me," he ordered.

She locked her arms around his thick powerful neck and hoisted herself up, hugging him with her inner thighs. Marcus held her round bottom in place.

His throbbing cock pressed into her like a hard rod. She inhaled deeply, preparing for his glorious cock to fill her with a prize that both completed and demolished her at once.

Loosening her grip ever so slightly, Lana slid down slowly and orientated herself over his shaft. In one sweep he lifted her ass and let it hover in the buoyant water.

He cupped her ass and held her in place, holding her high above his erection, away from what she needed, what she craved. "Please," she panted.

He paused for a heartbeat and held her at the tip of his hardness. "You let him kiss you," he growled.

"It meant nothing." She gasped with frustration, feeling the need tingle between her legs.

"He got to see those." His eyes dropped her breasts.

Her teeth grazed his lower lip and tugged. "That's all."

Marcus waded towards the tiled ledge with her legs still wrapped around his body like a sea urchin, minus his bulging cock. When the water all but lapped at his ankles, he released his hold.

She gazed into his serious face, his eyes tinged with gold like shamrocks in a field of corn, quickly turned dark with desire.

"All fours, now," he commanded.

Without hesitation, Lana crouched down and obliged. Lifting her ass in the air, her knees dug into the tiny mosaic squares underneath.

Her insides vibrated with delicious anticipation as he jogged to his deserted jeans, collected a condom from the pocket and tore the foil packet, ready to slide it down his cock.

The door flew open.

Marcus froze.

Her shrill scream was muffled by the deafening bang that rocketed through the peaceful serenity and ended with Marcus slumping to his knees, hugging his right side.

A deep breath stilled in her lungs and the burning lust vanished from her veins, replaced with heart stopping terror. Carl Reed stood at the entrance with a smirk plastered across his face.

Her wide eyes darted back to the surreal image of Marcus. In slow motion, she watched the air leave his lungs. His shocked gaze dragged up from the bloodied wound, resting on her quivering lip.

Each of his forced inhalations slowed, becoming shallow.

"Marcus?" The words almost failed to leave her throat.

Her heart hung in the eerie silence that followed, her

hearing strained to detect his short gasps. The momentary disbelief dissipated into the reality.

Scrambling towards him on hands and knees, the racing pulse thrummed in her skull, dulling the rumble of Carl's cruel laugh. "Marcus," she cried.

Marcus's eyes glazed under lowered brows, staring at her like he was taking a snapshot of her face to keep with him for eternity. Swaying sideward, his eyelids squeezed shut.

As he slumped to the tiles, she bounced forward to protect his head from crashing to the hard surface.

"Nooooo! Stay with me, Marcus. Please don't leave me. Please. Stay with me. Stay with me," she begged through wild breathes.

Strangled sobs choked in her throat, turning each stuttered breath into a whimper. Her shaky palms carefully allowed his head to rest on the ground. Shuffling back to assess the damage, her hands flew to his naked chest, then joined his face, staining his pale cheeks with a flash of red.

Her guts flipped in shock. Dropping her gaze, she watched the swirls of water blend with bright red blood. A trail of devastation trickled along the ridges of the tiles, draining towards the pool.

She didn't hear Carl yell profanities at her as he stomped across the room like the champion prize winner, nor did she give a second thought to her vulnerable nakedness.

"I love you. I love you. Please, Marcus," she chanted.

A puff of air left from his lungs, but his eyes stayed shut. Her hands slid over his icy torso in search for a bullet hole. Slipping and gliding through the crimson mess, her quest abruptly ended. She was hauled away from his body.

Her bloodied hair swamped her face and she toppled back. An unbearable ache crippled her reactions as Carl loomed over her quaking body. Hugging her bare stomach, she tucked in her knees, weeping uncontrollably.

She had to look at Marcus, to see his face, to help him, to hold him. Lifting to her haunches, she prepared to crawl her way back to his side, but a blast of pain blasted up her spine as Carl kicked her in the back with the toe of his boot.

"You were fucking him, Lana? You're just like all the rest them. I thought you were different," he spat out.

She winced in pain, almost cowering away from his stale smoky breath, until she sucked in a deep breath and prepared to fight her way back to her love. Shoving Carl sideward, she scrambled through the diluted blood stream, hoping to get closer to Marcus.

His boot slammed down on her hand, making her cry out, but she carried on regardless, driven to save him.

Each time she burst forward, Carl kicked her ribs or stamped on her fingers. The fear of losing Marcus was far worse than the bruises she gathered on her broken body.

They had only just found their way back to each other.

This couldn't be the end.

Lana had learned to watch him leave, only now she couldn't afford to accept it.

She loved him.

Tremors shook her limbs but she lunged forward for the last time. Carl seized her hair, halting her retreat with a forceful jerk.

Squatting by her side, he screamed into her face and shoved the barrel of his gun to her temple. "Move another inch, and I'll blow your brains all over this fucking room."

Her face paled as her wide eyes found Marcus, huddled in a heap. "What have you done…" the words floated past her lips, but they didn't sound like her. "Marcus," she yelled again. "Marcus, I love you."

Her heart cracked in two.

She was trapped.

Held prisoner once again.

Her hero, her lover, her protector was dying, and she was helpless. They both were.

Lana closed her eyes, giving in to the idea of death bringing her back to Marcus. Her shoulders shook as silent sobs shuddered from her chest.

"I'm supposed to be your hero, Lana. Not him. Is that why you fucked him? Because you think he's the hero?" Spats of his saliva catapulted from his lips and landed on her grey face as he pulled her up to meet his steely stare.

She cursed the tears that clouded her eyes, making her more lost and vulnerable. "I'll be my own fucking hero, you bastard." Short breaths shuddered shaky words from her mouth as she accepted the fact that Marcus might not keep his promise to protect her after all.

In a flailing swipe, her palm flew up to meet Carl's smooth jaw. Crooking her fingers, she stabbed her nails into his soft flesh. The other hand fisted, slamming into his neck.

A thud of metal hit the side of her skull. Her grip fell away, and she staggered back. Dazed and stunned, she almost lost her footing, crouching quickly to steady herself. Her blurry gaze flicked up to catch a glimpse of Marcus, but Carl stood in her line of sight.

The world had crumpled like a car wreck, leaving her smashed and twisted inside.

She craved to hold Marcus.

She would fight to be by his side.

He was too far to reach, slipping from this world to the next, on the cold wet floor in a puddle of fresh blood, all alone.

33

Lana was hoisted by her armpits to a shaky stand.

Carl pressed the glock to her tear blazed cheek, holding her wide-eyed gaze away from Marcus.

"At least I don't have to hunt you down. I got two cheating fuckers for the price of one flight." Carl smirked. "I'm going to enjoy fucking you up, Lana. I should've done it back in the garage, but you know what? I thought we could be together. Little did I know you would fuck that cocky asshole. You're tainted now. I don't want to be your hero. I'm going to be all your god damn nightmares rolled into one." His face propelled into hers with malice dripping from every word.

Lana sucked in as the pads of his fingers gripped her cheeks and the hideous familiar smoky stench left his mouth.

"Jesus Christ," Jamie roared, skidding to a halt in the doorway. His hands flew upwards, holding his head. "What the fuck have you done to my brother?" The rattle in his throat was the giveaway sign that he was holding back fear. "Marcus, get the fuck up!" he bellowed.

His startled gaze rapidly narrowed, and his fists clenched

so hard that his knuckles turned white. He bolted forward, in the direction of Marcus's still form.

"C'mon, mate," he protested with a deep set frown.

"Don't think about it." Carl turned the gun away from Lana and pointed it at Jamie. "I didn't come all this way for you to save the prick. Back off!"

Jamie slid to a standstill, lined up to precision with Carl's aim. His big brown eyes held fury while he stared in disbelief at the bloody scene surrounding his big brother's lifeless body.

"I'm gonna fuckin' kill you, asshole!" his strained words boomed through the airy room and scattered chills over Lana's scalp.

Her knees wobbled making her falter. The betrayal of her body forced her to lean into Carl. Her jaw locked as her choice to stand tall drifted away with her broken heart.

The cold steel returned to Lana, digging harder into her cheekbone. Carl shunted her towards the exit with her neck secured in the crook of his arm.

His body clung to her back and his knees banged into her legs as he walked. "Really? You're going to kill me? I've already shot a hole in your brother." His head bobbed backward, acknowledging Marcus. "I should've wrapped the motherfucker in a body bag, like a cheap gift - all tied up, just for you, pretty boy," Carl sneered. "You come one step closer and I'll blow off this little bitch's pretty face. You'll have her death on your greedy hands."

Out of the corner of her eye, she watched helplessly as Jamie's chest grew, inhaling the reality. She strained her neck, hoping to glance back, to see Marcus for one last time but Carl's hold only tightened, and he guided her further and further away.

"I promise you this, asshole, I'll blow a hole in *your* fucking ugly face if you hurt her," Jamie snarled.

Carl puffed out his chest. "Hey, hotshot. You think you're the good looking one? Well guess what, you little pussy, I'm the one holding the gun. What have you got? Your dick?"

Jamie's neck tilted with a sudden stiffness. "No, you fucking asshole. I have this…"

Whooshing smoky breath ruffled her hair. Carl's squeezing arm released her neck and the gun clattered to the floor. A loud grunt left his lungs as he wilted, sliding down her stiff back. Lana spun around to find Marcus, barely standing, with a glass ashtray in his bloodied hand.

"Put your arms around me, baby." A slow smile crept over his pale face and he clutched his side. "I told you, beautiful, I'll always protect you."

Heaving sobs racked her body. "You're alive. You're okay. You're okay," she chanted pressing her hands to her heart.

34

Carl's eyes drifted open.

A fabric bag covered his head, shrouding him in darkness. It tightened around his neck with a draw string. The smell of pig shit clung to his nostrils.

His heart beat raced as he tried to free his arms, but they were tied behind his back with a plastic cord that bit into his flesh, growing more painful as he struggled.

Rattling from side to side, he soon realised he was tied to a wooden chair that creaked under his weight. His ears pricked, and a threatening chill coursed over his scalp.

Silence.

Then from close by, the sound of heavy footsteps thumped closer, signalling there was more than one person, but he couldn't be sure.

The tie around his neck loosened and the cloth bag was abruptly ripped off his head. His eyes were slits, blinking rapidly to focus on three shadows towering before him.

As his gaze adjusted to the low lighting, he scoped the room. It was a large barn with chains hanging from railings and gulleys set out in rows.

Bringing his gaze back to his captors, he studied the figures before him. They wore balaclavas and camo combat gear. Their eyes were cold and menacing as they observed him quietly.

One of the captors leant forward. He was the tallest of the group by a few inches. A dark green jacket hung loosely at his sides and the black material covering his face bulged at the sides like his hair was braided.

His dark eyes were unforgiving. "What ya got ta say for yourself, ya stupid fuckin' asshole?" he snarled with a thick Dublin accent.

Carl narrowed his eyes, daring to stare back with an air of importance. "Who the hell are you? Where the hell are we?"

A second man chuckled. He was broad, with muscles that packed out his clothes making them almost too tight. "Don't you remember, Carl?" he sneered with a broad Belfast cadence. "You're in Italy."

The two men looked behind at the third captor who stood farther back. His eyes gleamed with malevolence.

"You're pathetic," snarled the shorter man, turning to face Carl again.

Carl's nostrils flared. He tried to sit tall even though his hands were secured at the back of the chair. "I'm not pathetic!" he spat.

"Ya really tink you could come to Italy and try ta kill Marcus?" scoffed the man with a southern Irish twang.

Carl's shoulders slumped, and he swallowed loudly.

"Have ya been ta the dentist lately?" the tall guy asked Carl with unnerving calmness.

Carl's brows snapped up. "Why?"

"We have ta burn the car out. Can't have anyone finding our DNA. When they find ya, they'll have ta identify ya by dental records." His voice took a jeering tone but hinted truth.

"You're such a looser," grunted the shorter man who crossed his arms over his broad chest.

Carl sighed with the weight of his own retribution weighing on his chest. The shorter guy flicked out his leg, booting Carl on the shin. "Bet ya thought ya were Carl fuckin' big balls?"

"No...I...just wanted to stick it to the McGraths," Carl stuttered like a naughty school kid waiting for punishment.

"Well, you're a dumb fuck and ya messed with the wrong crowd." The taller man pulled out a gun from inside his jacket.

"Who are you?" Carl snivelled.

The third man who stood on the periphery, stepped closer. "I'm your worst fuckin' nightmare, Carl." He ripped off his mask and revealed his face.

Carl's pale cheeks reddened to a shade of plum. "Marcus. You son of a bitch. Why aren't you dead?"

Marcus chuckled with an unfriendly hum. "You know how much of a fucking waste of skin you are, Carl? You couldn't even shoot to kill. The bullet perforated the skin just above my hip. It was a tiny wound that bled like a fucker. I'm only here to make sure everything goes to plan. This time your little secret society can't help. You are miles away from home and no one will miss you, Carl."

Drawing back, Marcus inhaled and tucked in his chin, then, he threw the crown of his head into Carl's nose. The crack of bone misted Carl's eyes and his ragged sob echoed in the stillness of the desolate barn. A trickle of blood ran into his gaping mouth.

The sliding metal door was wide open. Carl flicked his head towards the dark night sky, noting the tiny sparkles, far-off in another world. Each majestic little star would keep secrets hidden for eternity. Inside the barn, the smell of death permeated the steel walls and clung to the atmosphere with an unfriendly stench.

"Please, I'll give you whatever you want. I'll stay away from you, and from Lana," he protested.

Marcus pounced forward, wincing like the pain of his stitched wound burned. "Don't even say her name. Don't speak of her, don't think about her, don't even pretend she exists. When Lana goes to sleep, she dreams of me." Marcus prodded Carl's chest with his forefinger. "And when she screams, it's my name she calls." His nostrils flared, and his breathing became furious.

Spinning around, he bit out, "Ciaran. You're up. Payback time."

The shorter man reached around his back and pulled up his jacket. When his hands returned, Carl swallowed hard. He held a black gun with a silencer attachment at the end of the barrel.

Ciaran leant into Carl's crimson face. "Ya can't give me back my wife, can ya, Carl?"

Carl's eyes bugged. The man squeezed his cheeks with a firm grip. "Look me in the face, ya gobshite!" he growled. "Look into the eyes of the man whose gonna snuff out your insignificant life. A life for a life, that's the fuckin' rules!"

"No, please, let's talk about this," Carl pleaded.

Ciaran Simpson held the gun at Carl's face and hacked up saliva. The slimy spittle landed on Carl's face, clinging to his eyebrow.

"Your time for talkin' is over. The minute ya strangled my Jaqueline, was the exact minute I put a price on your greasy head."

He drew back and pressed the tip of the gun to Carl's lips. "Open up," he sneered.

Carl clenched his jaw and shook his head frantically. The cold tip nudged his teeth and the sensation rattled in his skull.

"Ya strangled my wife, took Marcus's woman and tried to murder him. Do ya accept the charges?" The tall man barked from the side like this was his sentencing and Ciaran was the jury.

Carl's eyelids almost slipped behind his eyes. He mumbled inaudible words as he kept his mouth clamped shut. The cold steel traced the seam of his lips.

"Do ya accept the charges?" the tall man asked again with eerie restraint.

Carl nodded. His face was now ghostly pale. His bright red flustered cheeks drained as he realised there was no way out now.

The gun clattered along his teeth like the keys of a piano before the short man pulled it away. Ciaran stepped back.

In a short stride, the tall man aimed the gun directly between Carl's legs and squeezed the trigger. A hair-raising scream preceded the deafening bang.

Crimson blood oozed from Carl's groin, pooling beneath the chair. Between erratic pants he whimpered and begged.

"Shut da fucker up, Mal." Ciaran nodded to the gunman.

Mal shoved an apple into Carl's mouth, spearing it in place by his teeth. The men untied his writhing body from the chair and dragged him deeper into the barn.

They tugged a rusty chain down from the metal railing, circling the icy metal around his already bound wrists. His writhing body was hoisted up by a levy with his feet left dangling.

"We'll be back later, once ya've bled out." Mal laughed as they all turned away.

The men walked a few steps from his convulsing body. Without warning, Ciaran spun back around to face him.

He pointed the silencer at Carl and squeezed the trigger, blowing a bullet through Carl's throat. "And that one's from me."

35

Seconds after Marcus had knocked Carl out cold with an ashtray, the security team arrived and bundled Carl into the back of a car.

Marcus's wound had haemorrhaged blood quicker than a burst pipe and he'd almost passed out for the second time. One of the guests came forward to help him—an American surgeon.

She doused his wound in McGrath whiskey and tightly wrapped his chest with bandages from the first aid kit, to prevent further blood loss.

Marcus knew Lana would be reluctant to let him out of her sight. His heart crashed into his aching ribs when he witnessed her fragility, helplessly watching her beg Jamie to let her go with him to the hospital.

The fact she was in shock, naked and drenched in blood was enough of a reason to force her to stay at Villa Veronica, take a warm shower and put on some clothes. Marcus kissed her cold tear streaked cheeks and ordered her to stay. It wasn't by choice that he left her again, it was a necessity.

The brothers knew what had to be done. Lana was blissfully unaware that Marcus left the hospital once his wound was patched up, and Carl Reed paid for his actions with his life.

She hadn't noticed the men trail Carl's limp body away because her entire world revolved around Marcus and making sure he stayed alive. It was only after she had showered, that Freddy told her Carl would finally be taken care of.

When Marcus returned at the break of a new day, he jogged into her open arms and kissed her ghostly pale face, fluttering warmth over her sunken eyes. Holding her close, Marcus had nodded to Jamie, signifying Carl's fate had been sealed. The weight of his responsibility drifted off into the sunrise.

The deed had been done.

He had witnessed the brutality and accepted it as the only way to keep Lana safe. Wrapping her in his powerful arms, Marcus kept her close as they watched the blazing orange sunrise light up the world, signifying a fresh start.

The future was filled with promise and most importantly, Lana. When her head tipped to his chest and her breathing turned shallow, he carried her to bed where they slept peacefully in each other's arms.

VILLA VERONICA HAD BEEN RECLAIMED AS A PEACEFUL HOME once again. Freddy was happy to cater for everyone while Marcus demanded all of Lana's time.

Every now and again, she sat up on her elbows, just to watch his golden body flow through the water with grace. His wound was covered in a waterproof dressing, reminding her of the unbearable feeling of loss she endured.

The sun was high in the sky, reflecting golden light across

the water. He rose out of the pool like an Adonis. Water droplets trickled down his muscular golden physic.

The outline of his six-pack glistened as his arms raised and his fingers swept back inky black hair. The snug black shorts hugged his glorious cock, clinging to the bulge in an enviable position.

Her breathing intensified. Her obvious gawk lingered as he sauntered her way with sparkling green eyes focused solely on her. He leant across the lounger, water dripping off his hard form and almost sizzling as it melted into her warm skin. His wet lips pressed down on hers and he indulged in a gentle loving kiss.

A balmy lemon scented breeze wafted around them. "I'd like to take you on a date," he said breaking their connection.

"A date?" She stifled a grin.

"I owe you a first date." He smiled lazily. "There's a hotel on the island of Capri with an amazing restaurant. I think you'd really like it. The views are stunning."

"Sounds perfect!" Her eyes sparkled, watching avidly as he patted his moist skin with a towel.

"We can take the Eurocopter directly from the Villa. Do you want to stay in the hotel?"

Her head shook. "Let's stay here. I don't think Jamie is ready to let you out of his sight again." She smiled with sincerity and truth.

He nodded casually. "Fine. As long as you end up in my bed later."

Lana giggled. "We'll see."

He thumbed her chin and tilted her head up. "You know you will." His face was deadpan.

"I think you know, you'll get it later. There's no doubt about that." She waggled her eyebrows. "I can't resist a hot guy in tight shorts who would take a bullet for me."

His eyes twinkled. "Really? You like what you see, beautiful?"

She hummed in her throat and skimmed the pads of her fingers over his warm damp skin. "Yeah. I like what I see."

"And what would you like me to do to you?"

"I have plans." She bit her lower lip with a gentle nip.

"Interesting...." He climbed onto her sun lounger. "There's no point in waiting, is there."

Marcus checked and double checked that she was strapped securely into the helicopter. Her heartbeat galloped and her body was rigid.

"Sit tight, beautiful. We'll be there in no time. Right, Luca, we're all good back here," he said to the pilot.

As the propellers spun at high speed, Lana scrunched her hands in the fabric of her dress. Marcus released her tight grip from the fabric and pulled her fists up to his mouth.

He kissed her knuckles lightly. "First time, huh?" he asked through the head piece.

Lana nodded, feeling gravity pull her stomach up to meet her heart as they rose into the sky. He unravelled her clenched fingers and wrapped her tiny hand in his.

With the pad of his thumb, he stroked her skin with a soothing pressure. "I'd like to kiss you for the entire journey, but the views are something else. You should have a camera up here."

"I get motion sick too," she shouted as her cheeks drained to chalky white. "Plus, there's only a bit of tin between us and the long drop to the ocean."

He squeezed her fingers and smirked. "Focus on the island ahead. We're nearly there."

Lana peered out of the small window. She fixated her gaze on the pretty island in the distance, with its green trees and scattered dwellings. The main port was in clear view, with yachts and speed boats lined up like a car show room.

Larger ferries transported throngs of visitors back and forth from Naples and Sorrento. The helicopter tilted to the side, sweeping away from the main bay.

"Oh, sweet Jesus." She squeezed her eyes shut.

"l'll look after you." He nudged her nose with his. "We're going to Anacapri. There's a hotel with an amazing restaurant. I'll buy it for you if you like it."

Her mouth twitched, staving a giggle. "If we have to get a helicopter every time, then don't bother."

True to his word the restaurant views were outstanding. The terrace had crazy paved tiles and round tables covered with white linen. They were escorted to the best seat in the restaurant, cordoned off from the rest of the guests.

"It's a pleasure to have you back with us, Mr. McGrath." Marcus shook hands with the tall maître d' who then pulled out Lana's chair.

The extensive gin list had the McGrath brand top of the list, alongside a multitude of mixers and special edible additions.

"I see they do have the best gin ever." She winked.

"It gets around." He nodded to the patient waiter who approached their table but hovered in the periphery. "The lady will try them all."

Lana gasped. "Are you trying to get me drunk, so you get me into bed?"

Marcus flipped off his aviators, sucking her in with a lazy smile. "We both know, I don't need to get you drunk, to get your panties off." His eyes darkened. "And we certainly don't need a bed."

"Seriously, I'll be sick if I drink all of those concoctions."

She looked up at the young waiter. "Just one for now. I'll go with the Raspberry Rose Gin, and please, make sure you use the McGrath Gin. Thank you."

The waiter tilted his head forward with a gentle nod. "Sì signora, nothing but the best."

Marcus ordered without a second thought. "Whiskey on the rocks."

She eyed him as he quietly browsed the menu, a moment to herself to absorb the situation. There he was, in front of her, an alluring man who could have any woman he wanted—and he chose her.

Plain and simple Lana. She felt like pinching herself to prove she was actually with the man of her dreams, the man who scattered chills across her skin with just one look.

He glanced up from the menu. "Can I ask you something?"

"Sure."

"Rory. Do you still love him?"

Her brow creased, and she inhaled sharply. "Not in that way." She paused. "It was wrong of me to accept his marriage proposal."

"It was wrong of him to ask you to marry him, when he was banging Jacqueline behind your back," he said through clenched teeth.

"I guess I was settling. The guy I wanted was a bit of a playboy who only wanted me for sex."

"It wasn't just sex."

"Yes, it was!"

"Okay. Maybe in the beginning," he conceded.

She fiddled with the edge of the menu. "It's different with you. It always has been. We have a deeper connection."

He grinned. "Like none other." Taking a deep breath, his

words waited in his throat for a few seconds. "He'll, no doubt, want to reach out to you, Lana, now he's out of prison."

Her shoulders slowly raised to her ears. "Does that bother you?"

"Yes."

"I'd like to make sure he's okay, but that's all. There's nothing left between Rory and I, Marcus. I've paid for trying to help him, especially after what he did to me when we were together. I don't think I need to see him again. That's all in the past now, where it belongs."

The corners of his mouth twitched like he was holding back a smirk of relief. He nodded. "That's fucking good to know, beautiful."

Lana took a deep quiet breath of contemplation. "Did you really come out to Italy for me, or to help Jamie?"

Marcus sighed. "He told me you were in Italy, at Villa Veronica, and all I could think about was coming out here to see you again."

"I didn't have a nightmare last night. I hate that bastard Carl." Her voice cracked.

The emotion in his eyes roiled like the stormy seas. "You don't have to worry about him, Lana. He's history. You have my word on that. It's over."

Lingering uncertainty swirled in her chest. "How did he get out of prison?"

His back seemed to straighten with slight unease, and his shoulders pulled back like a secret was trying to escape from his chest.

"Marcus?" A lump formed in her throat, and she swallowed loudly as he let out a steadying breath.

He drummed the table with his fingers. "He had contacts everywhere. After he was released, he murdered Donna

Marie. The sick fuck shaved off her hair and scattered it around her house," he said solemnly. "The police found another girl, drugged up and beaten. They showed her a picture of Carl and she confirmed he kidnapped her."

Her hands flew to her cheeks. "You're fucking kidding me. Donna Marie is dead? Jesus Christ, Marcus, when the hell were you going to tell me." Her voice cracked when she scrunched the linen napkin in her fists.

"Lana," he hissed. "I didn't want to put you through anymore shit. I didn't tell you he was out because I didn't want you to worry. Carl won't hurt anyone, ever again. Jaqueline's husband took care of it."

"But you got hurt." Tears glistened in her eyes, fogging her view of his stern expression. "I thought he'd killed you, Marcus. I died inside. Tell me he can't get to us again, Marcus, please," she pleaded.

Marcus dropped the menu to the table, leant forward and said huskily, "He will never touch you again, beautiful. You have my word on that. It's over. He's gone for good."

Lana didn't want to know the ins and outs of what had happened to Carl. She didn't care if he was dead, as long as he didn't show up unannounced again.

Anxiety left her tense muscles when his fingers threaded with hers. The sincerity in his face gave her reason to feel safe. Marcus rescued, liberated and owned her. He was her everything.

She rose from the chair, nudging it with the back of her knees. In two short skips she was on his lap, burying her tear streaked face in his neck. "Thank you."

"I made you a promise, Lana. To be honest, it's like a weight off my shoulders. Getting justice was all I could think about. It took over. Clouded my judgement and made me think you were too much of a responsibility. Even without you by my side, you were still mine to protect. I'm better off with you, than without."

His words of protection meant more than anything. He was kind, yet ruthless, sexy, yet emotionally unavailable. She secretly hoped he would let down his barriers and let her stay for good.

"What about Jamie. Did the deal fall through?" She lifted her head.

"Thankfully Falcone signed it anyway. Jamie can be quite persuasive. I taught him well."

Lana squeezed him tightly and gathered herself together before hopping off his knee and returning to her chair. While she had been wrapped in his arms, safe from the world, the waiter had rectified her seat and refreshed the napkins.

Marcus browsed the menu. His forehead was creased and his lips tight. His face was edgy and filled with emotion, like he was trying to keep himself in check.

Her heart bounced in her chest, knowing this guy had really been there for her all along. Even now, he was guarding his reactions, so he could be the stronger of the two.

Marcus had been on this journey with her, he rode the hurricane as Carl tore through their lives. It was the journey that pulled them apart, yet it was the very thing that brought them back together.

She finally felt at peace within her heart. Carl was in the past and Marcus was in her future.

A creeping arousal slowly became unbearable and a surprising slickness soaked her panties. His sparkling green eyes flicked up, locking her intense stare. "Are you okay? Do you need a glass of water?"

A slight sigh escaped her mouth. "Just looking at you turns me on." Her fingers pressed to her lips, she was heating up under the table.

His eyes blazed with lust. "Fuck, Lana. You never cease to surprise me. Do you want to go somewhere more private? I'll get us a room."

Pulling open her legs, she slid her hand down to the hem of her dress and under the blue fabric. She was free, the worry and fear had dissipated.

She knew he couldn't see her little show. He'd have to imagine what she was doing as the table guarded her self-indulgence.

Her fingers rubbed the wet lace, while her eyes gazed into the dark orbs that pierced her flesh with fire. Slipping one finger inside, she inhaled sharply then trailed her hand up to her pink lips and sucked.

Marcus's hands fisted. His lips formed a thin line as he tried to contain himself. With forced control, he shoved back his chair and stood. The napkin floated to the floor.

Suddenly, the waiter was by his side. "Is there a problem Sir?"

"Please give us some time to consider the menu. I want to show the lady around before we settle for lunch."

His demeanour was calm and collected, the only give away sign of his hunger was the pulsating vein in his throat. He grabbed Lana by the elbow and escorted her towards the main reception.

"We need a room," he growled into her ear.

She swivelled around and pressed her rising chest into his. "I can't wait that long, Marcus."

"Wait here," he ordered, then he marched over to the tall red head at the reception desk.

Within a matter of minutes, he returned with a key card. He waved the white plastic card and widened his mouth with a wolfish glint in his eyes.

He swooped her up over his shoulder, her head dangling to the floor. With a quick slap, his hand met her ass.

"You'll learn not to tease me, Lana."

The regal hotel suite was lavish, from what little she saw of it. As soon as they entered the light spacious room, Marcus flipped her onto the large bed and unbuttoned his jeans.

His fingers deftly popped open each button with speed and accuracy. His smouldering eyes devoured every curve on her body.

Lana hurriedly slipped off her panties and released the side zip of her dress, allowing Marcus to pull it over her head. He pushed down his jeans and snug boxers, and his erection sprung out, ready and begging.

"Open your legs," he commanded.

His large hands tugged her from the waist and pulled her close. "You want it?" he growled.

All she wanted in the world was his throbbing cock pushing deep inside her, but he held back, waiting for her to beg.

"Please, Marcus, please!" she pleaded.

He paused with a swirl of fire burning in his eyes. "I love it when you beg me to fuck you."

She nudged forward with the crown of his cock at her entrance. It nestled in a fraction, but still Marcus withheld. His hands smoothed over her skin and found her swollen breasts.

With a firm pressure he pushed the plump mounds together and licked each nipple in turn. Lana melted into his touch and her temperature soared as he played with her body and her mind, but she needed him, right then, no waiting.

Grabbing his wrists, she hauled herself further down the bed and speared herself on his length. Her legs immediately locked behind his back.

This was the first woman he had entered with no protection. It felt so immense that he nearly came.

"Lana…I'm not wearing a condom. I've never had unprotected sex before." He forced himself to still, beads of sweat gathered on his brow.

"The doctor gave me a clean bill of sexual health and I've been on birth control for a few years. Are you clean?" Her words spilled out with urgency.

"I get checked out regularly."

"Then fuck me, Marcus. Let me be the first."

Her eyes closed briefly when he pushed his length fully inside, so deeply it hit her cervix. The relentless pounding pushed her near the brink of ecstasy.

Her breasts jiggled as Marcus rhythmically shunted his shaft in and out.

"You feel so amazing, Lana. So tight. So ready. Just for me. I can feel right inside your fucking perfect pussy."

His eyes drank in every inch of her flawless body as it fused with his, skin to skin. Their souls combined, their flesh became one.

She was the perfect fit for his hard long length. The piece of the puzzle he didn't want to admit was missing.

While he was balls deep in her tight centre, he was on a higher plane, a spiritual journey. He lost himself in the vortex known as Lana.

His fingers found her engorged nub and he pinched it hard, sending her over the brink. His teeth grazed her flesh and his mouth ventured from her breasts to her mouth.

She screamed his name and arced her back. Her fingers tugged his mass of thick hair as her thighs shook.

Her insides clenched his bare rock-hard cock. He waited for the spasms to subside then he lifted her spent body and backed up to the headboard.

With his back to the velvet material he beckoned Lana onto his lap. She straddled his thighs and scooted closer, so his dick was at her entrance again. Their lips met in a mash of hunger and desire.

Their teeth clashed and tugged. Hungry hands guided her up and down until she took the lead, bouncing freely, ready to detonate into smithereens.

"Come inside me, Marcus," she panted. "I want to feel you explode inside me."

Her erotic request set him on fire. Marcus was beyond the state of arousal now—fucked in every way possible. He needed to claim his territory, to pump his load into the only woman he ever wanted as his own.

As Lana's jaw slackened, giving in to the pleasure, he too matched her insanity. His back stiffened and he thrust deeper. Her tight spasms clamped around him, rippling through his muscles and pushing him over the edge.

Lana pressed her forehead to his. "I'm going to need that gin now." She chuckled.

He kissed her swollen lips, he rasped, "And I need to do that again."

The corners of her mouth rose slowly, melting his heart into an unknown shape. Lana rose on the balls of her feet, letting his softened cock slip out. She stood, each foot astride his thighs, her pussy in front of his face.

"Look, baby."

With a quick intake of air, he watched in awe as his creamy liquid was expelled, clinging to the inside of her leg.

"You came inside me," she purred sexily.

"Fuck! That's so sexy, Lana. I've never done that with a

woman before. You're making me hard again." His heart was slamming against his chest and all the blood was rushing straight to his dick.

Nudging her closer, he pulled her mound to his face. He latched onto her nub until her legs quivered and shook. An immense orgasm exploded in her core.

Without realising it, Lana had just woven herself into the innermost chambers of his heart. The overwhelming feelings were so new to him, so unknown.

He couldn't decide whether his heart was going to explode with love, or if he was going to have a heart attack.

36

When they finally made it back to the dining table, fresh drinks were waiting.

A rosy glow blushed her cheeks and Marcus wore a smug smile on his gorgeous face.

Lana pulled open the menu. "What do you recommend? It all looks so good."

He cleared his throat and hesitated. "I have to go to New York tomorrow. I want you to come with me," he half ordered, half asked.

"Do we have to leave so soon?" she pouted.

"Believe me, I'd rather be relaxing with you all day, than sitting in meetings. But this one is very important. It's a life changer. I'm not leaving you behind this time." His hand crossed the table and his fingers brushed her knuckles.

"What about Fred…" Her words drowned under the shrill voice behind her.

"Oh my god. There you are. I should have known you would come here."

A loud voice like sugary syrup projected in their direction. Lana froze, catching sight of a tall slender model-esque vision of beauty who strutted towards their table.

Her slender frame donned navy shorts, with a silky red blouse tucked in neatly to show off her non-existent waist. Marcus pushed back his chair and stood.

He greeted the elegant woman with a nod. Her earthy brown hair was scattered with gold that glistened in the sunlight. She yanked off her oversized sunglasses and dropped them on the table in front of Lana.

Spreading open her arms, she held Marcus in a tight embrace. A warning flashed in Lana's mind and her chest tightened. She watched helplessly as the overly friendly gesture lingered.

Marcus broke the embrace, yet her nude glossy lips kissed both his cheeks and her hands rested on his broad shoulders. His back stiffened at the gesture. Was it because Lana was there, or did he not like the close interaction?

The scene before her was all too familiar and exceptionally rude given Marcus's failure to introduce her.

The woman grabbed his hands. "I thought you were in New York, but when I called the hotel they told me you hadn't checked in. I guessed you were either at your dad's or with your brother." Her fingers slid down the seam of his shirt.

The invaders voice nipped at Lana's skull. A combination of nausea and irritation mashed together with one massive unhealthy scoop of hate.

His husky voice cracked open her fears like a can opener. "Natasha, this is Lana." Marcus looked down at her, his eyes giving nothing away.

He introduced Natasha to Lana, not the other way around. *Did he need this woman's approval?* Natasha gave her a sideward glance.

"Hi," she managed to mutter before her eyes flicked back to Marcus.

"We were about to have lunch." Marcus jammed his hands into his pockets, upholding his usual casual sexy stance.

Her wicked cackle packed a cruel punch and was crammed with an intentionally demeaning rasp.

"Of course. Once you have finished your *business,* we can get a few drinks together. I take it you're staying at Veronica. I'll head there now and see you once this…" She waved her hand in Lana's direction. "…is done with."

How the hell does she know about Villa Veronica? Has she been there before?

Marcus nudged Natasha's elbow, beckoning her to the side of the restaurant. There were hushed words. Natasha glanced over, once, then twice and then finally turned her back to Lana.

Suddenly, the charming restaurant didn't seem so appealing. Her appetite all but dwindled and her happiness sunk to the pit of doom. Something wasn't right, and Marcus was hiding it, or her.

She needed room to breathe—away from Marcus and his captivating hold that sucked her in every time. She knew her insecurity was the very thing that pushed him away before and she wasn't about to show him how much their interaction was crushing her heart.

Escaping the restaurant, Lana bolted down the cobbled pathway and away from their cosy chat. Rationality had fallen flat on its face.

Lana couldn't let him see her fall apart again.

37

The brief conversation between Natasha and Marcus ended abruptly when he glanced back to the table, finding Lana's seat empty.

"Fuck!" he growled, startling the relaxed diners.

Natasha snatched her sunglasses from the table and quickly covered her misted eyes. She joined his side, leaning closer with a hint of hope shadowing hurt.

"Have your fun, McGrath." Her saccharin sweet smile angered him even more. "I know you. You'll forget her by next week."

"You don't know anything about me," he snapped back.

Weaving past the tables, he darted down the pathway leading to the helipad and caught sight of Lana grappling with the passenger door of the small aircraft. The propellers were stationary and the cockpit was empty.

"What the hell are you doing?" He stormed towards her with warning bells ringing in his head.

Lana spun around with red eyes and pink cheeks. "I want to go back." She choked back a sob. "Please. I'm feeling a little unwell."

He stepped forward, overwhelming her personal space.

"Please, get someone to take us away from here." Tears pooled in her eyes.

He crossed his arms over his chest and stood patiently, mustering every ounce of restraint. "What's wrong?" he asked calmly.

Lana puffed air from her open mouth. "Nothing." Lingering dread kept her hands clenched and her shoulder stiff.

"Lana?" He reached forward.

She sucked in a ragged breath with her tucked chin down, keeping her eyes low. "That woman. She knew you pretty well, like you'd been together," she said quietly.

His brow creased. "She's an old friend."

Her pretty face was so perfect. Her bright blue eyes glistened behind a watery sheen as she stared up at him.

She was lost but lustful, sexy but shy. "She doesn't look old!" Lana snipped, lowering her gaze to her twisted hands.

"Lana..." His stance widened. "You have no need to be jealous."

This was it, he had to get through this, he had to find a way to figure it out. And he sure as hell wasn't going to let her walk away this time.

Her face was the last thing he remembered before passing out after being shot, and it was the very thing he fought to protect.

Lana's head swam with love and hate.

She was lost in a flesh-eating jealousy. In love with a man whose past was filled with more sexual partners than the client list at a high end brothel. She knew there would be women creeping on the scene at some point, but after the events of the last few days, she wasn't prepared to lose him all over again.

"Lana?" Marcus ducked down, trying to meet her distant gaze.

She lifted her eyes, accepting the hold he had over her. "Did you have a relationship with her?" she asked, exuding a masked confidence.

He scowled. "We had sex, a long time ago."

Lana expelled air through her nose, a glut of uncertainty settled in her belly. "Okay then, how many times did you fuck her?"

Marcus sighed. "Do we need to do this?"

"Answer the damn question." Her misted eyes enlarged and her small voice grew louder.

Marcus shook his head. "This is crazy, Lana." He paused with a slow sigh. "We fucked a couple of times. But, it's not what you think. It was a long time ago. I wasn't into her. She offered it up on a plate every time we were in the same company. She wanted more. I didn't. End of story." He shrugged casually, like it was nothing to him. "We probably fucked, no more than two or three times. I was just fooling around, my mistake."

"So, I'm not the only one who broke your rule? You fucked her a few times, just like me. I bet she's been in Fermanagh with you too." Her stomach flipped and her head felt woozy.

His eyes flashed. "I don't fuck you, Lana. It's more than that for me. She's just a woman I know. Nothing more. It was a very long time ago. Other than my family, and Freddy, you're the only other person who has been in my home. You know that, beautiful. Come on, don't make this into something."

She desperately wanted to reach out to him, to pull him close, but her arms just hung redundantly by her sides. She was exhausted.

"I think she wants to be more than just friends, Marcus. How does she know where to find you? Why didn't you introduce me as your girlfriend?" Questions were burning in her mind, begging for answers. "It's like being with Rory all over again. Are you embarrassed to be seen with an ordinary girl like me, or are you just hedging your bets with other women?" Her face crumpled as her heart realised it was a sacrificial offering to the devil. "Perhaps this is just a cruel joke, a way to make *her* jealous. I mean, look at her compared to me. She's leggy super model and I'm…I'm just me."

In one stride, he broke the invisible boundaries keeping them apart. "Don't ever say that, Lana. This isn't fake. It's unbearably real. The most real feeling I've ever had in my life." The hard lines on his face softened and a gentle extended breath tingled her skin.

"I told you, I'm new at this. I knew I'd keep fucking it up. I didn't call you my girlfriend because I've never had one before. This is new territory.

You overwhelm me, consume me, breathe life into me, tease me, strip me of all my defences and turn me on so fucking much. When I'm not with you my heart stops beating in protest. It beats alongside yours, Lana. If I wanted Tash, then I'd have her. But I don't want her, and I never have. Everything you are, is everything I need. In fact, it's too much for me to deal with. It's driving me crazy, Lana."

He reached out and clamped her shoulders firmly. His palms dragged down her biceps. "I want *you*. The woman who broke every rule back in Belfast. I'm in love with you, beautiful. Your 'just me' is my fucking perfect." His words slipped out like honey.

Whether he meant to reveal his soul to her or not, each thoughtful word lingered between them like gifts from cupid, each one aimed for her heart. The galloping beat of her fragile heart stuttered, regulating to a rhythm that matched his.

Dazed, she gave him a relieved smile. "It will take time to get used to this feeling of jealousy." She drew in her lower lip.

His chin dipped. "I'll sell the club. The plan was to join forces with Luke Devereux, in New York. We were going to spread it worldwide but maybe this is the perfect time to get rid of it."

Her brow scrunched. "Why?"

He sighed lightly. "The whole idea of Verto Veneri revolved around helping couples—protecting them, so to speak. But look what happened. Rory cheated on you and Jaqueline was murdered, and don't get me started on Carl. If I'm still the owner, then I'm still associated with that world and we'll keep having these issues."

Her head wobbled. "I don't want that. It's part of who you are, Marcus. People are going to cheat whether they're in Verto Veneri or not. What happened with Carl was messed up, but it wasn't because of the club. It was all down to him. Maybe you should rebrand it. Instead of couples being separated, they could be brought together somehow."

"In what way?"

"I don't know, like a sex club where they discover bondage, with each other. A place where they can grow respect for each other and learn their limits together. I don't know. It's just an idea."

"And you'd be happy, knowing I was a part of that underworld?"

"If you involve me. Let me be part of it with you." His green eyes sparkled as she spoke. "Marcus, I'll go to counselling. I'll sort my head out. I can't lose you, not again. I know I shouldn't have run off just now, but we've been through so much. I couldn't deal with loosing you all over again." Her hand slid to her stomach, recalling his naked body slumped in a pool of blood.

Marcus pressed his lips to her temple. "I'm not going anywhere. Let me talk to Devereux about the club. Your idea might just take it to a whole new level."

She stared up at him. "I knew the minute you showed up at Rory's place that night, that you were 'the guy'."

Stroking strands of tickly hair away from her face, he asked, "The guy for what?"

She rocked into him. "The guy I'm meant to be with. The guy I would fall in love with."

Sliding his fingers along her scalp, he pressed his brow down to hers. "And are you truly in love with me?"

She hesitated, holding a mischievous silence. "Like you didn't know. I've already told you once and I'll not make a habit of repeating it." Her eyes glittered. "I'm in love with you, Marcus McGrath. Tread carefully because you own my heart. All of it."

He gifted her with a devastatingly sexy grin. Blistering heat simmered behind his eyes. "I wasn't ready to say it, back then, Lana." A low chuckle rolled in his chest. "I told Tash that I was in love with you, and I told her to stop showing up."

Lana grinned like a love drunk fool. Her hands came up to his neck and she fondled the short hair at the back of his head. "I didn't quite hear you." She giggled sweetly. "You're in love with who?"

He kissed the tip of her nose and forcefully jerked her into his body. Feathering kisses down her face, he landed the best one of all on her needy lips.

"I'm crazy in love with you, Lana. Fancy sharing the rest of your life with me?" he mumbled into her mouth. "Move your stuff into my place, in Fermanagh. It's filled with memories of you already, so there's no going back there without you."

Was she ready to move in?

She blinked quickly, running it over and over in her mind. "Marcus, I signed a lease for an apartment in Belfast before I flew out here. I committed to my own place."

He grinned. There was something lurking behind his playful smile that made her lips curve. "I know you did. Don't worry about it, I'll get someone else to rent it." He shrugged. "Or you can keep it."

Her heart beat wildly against his chest. "You're the landlord?" She gulped. "I knew there was something odd about that set up."

He tilted her head and took her mouth in a long deep kiss. "Yeah, sorry." His lips lingered unapologetically. "I couldn't let you shack up in some dirty hovel, even if we weren't together. I was trying to look after you from a distance."

She buried her brow in the curve of his shoulder, her grip tightened. She was speechless. He had wanted her all this time.

"Just say yes. Move in with me?" He slid his hands down the slope of her buttocks and cupped them firmly. "I'll even seal the deal with your very own puppy. I've picked one out for you already. She's called Violet."

Lana's heart exploded. Her head lifted and her lips

smashed to his. He responded to the scorching kiss, sparking her fearful soul with honesty and truth.

Her body trembled, enjoying the exploration of his greedy hands. She was resigned to the fact that Marcus made her whole again.

Taking a breath, she peeked up under her lashes. "I've always wanted a puppy." Excitement bubbled out with each word.

His emerald green eyes were brighter than she recalled, shaded with a sexy wickedness. "Which are you more excited about - the puppy or moving in with me?" His teeth skimmed the ridge of her jaw and he suckled her earlobe, nipping it as he drew away.

Her head fell into the hollow of his throat, hiding from his seductive spell. "Are you jealous of my new puppy?" A soft giggle bubbled in her throat.

Grasping a clump of hair at her nape, he drew her head back bringing her gaze in line with his serious eyes. Releasing his fingers, he cupped her cheeks.

"I'm jealous of the sunlight that dances in your eyes. I'm jealous of the rain that rolls down your skin. I'm jealous of the clothes that nestle into your sexy fucking body." He winked, covering her lips in a demanding, deep kiss.

Dizzy and shaky, she broke their heated kiss to contemplate her decision. Her lips parted and her teeth sank down on his lower lip, sucking it into her mouth and releasing it with pop. "I'm nervous about…"

He placed the pad of his forefinger over her mouth, dragging her lip out from under her teeth. "I'm not nervous about this, Lana." He licked the soft red skin of her jutted lip, sparking a shiver of heat over every inch of her skin.

"I've only got a small cardboard box of belongings. It shouldn't take long to move it." Her voice wavered.

"That's it?"

"Yup. My childhood things are in storage with my parent's furniture. It was a fresh start for them moving to France."

He hummed into her hair. "The best things come in small packages."

Rocking into her hip, his hardness nudged the angular bone. "I like big packages," she purred.

"I wonder how Jamie will take the news. This officially means I'm out of the game." Marcus smirked.

"I'll let you out to play, as long as you come home to me." She laughed, dodging his playful ass swat.

"I won't share you with anyone." His eyes danced with the truth behind his demanding words.

Her brows snapped together. "I need to have friends!"

"Fine." He simpered. "But they need to know you're mine. The world needs to know it." A devilish glint twinkled in his eyes. "I'm going to get a new tattoo on my chest. My life fell apart when my mum died. I signified her death with that tattoo. With your birthdate underneath, I can signify both life and death. You're my life, Lana."

"Really?" She fluttered her lashes playfully.

"Yup." He grinned.

"Are you sure you're ready for me to move in with you? I don't want to rush this. To rush *us*. Especially after the last time I stayed over." Her stomach clenched and she fumbled with the thick strands of his hair.

"You're not just staying over, Lana. You're moving in. It's our home now. Believe me, I've never been more certain about something in my whole fucking life. We'll make it work. I know we will, beautiful. The question is—do *you* really want this?"

"I'll have to think about it…" She paused, a hint of a grin teased her lips. "Of course I do, Marcus."

He took her face in his large hands. His mouth stretched wide with a smile that lit up her soul.

"I'll do whatever it takes to protect you, Lana. I promise to keep you safe, now and forever, no matter what I have to do to achieve it. I love you, beautiful."

A FEW MONTHS LATER...

So much had happened over the passing months. Marcus's office in The Fitz looked exactly as it had before, right down to the ochre cushions scattered on the twin sofas. Everything appeared the same, but Marcus, he was completely different.

Leaning back in the swivel chair at his desk, he studied the twinkling city lights, noting the familiar yellow cranes that signified power and dominance over Belfast. He had finally committed to one woman. It hadn't been easy, figuring out how to share his life with a woman who he would actually give his life for. Marcus gave Lana everything, and more, but he had to learn how to keep his soul in the process – to be the man she needed, not just expected.

He returned to business after signing a multi-million-pound deal, merging Verto Veneri with an influential New York business man, Luke Devereux, who was only too happy to change up the original business plan. They agreed to modify the club's ethos, and rather than encourage couples to play around with strangers, they would learn boundaries and limitations within their existing unit, pushing their sexual relationships to the peak. It was under development and an exciting new business venture. Lana had played a key role in the new terms and conditions, setting up a policy that protected members but highlighted the reality of life.

The desk phone buzzed. Marcus checked his watch before collecting the receiver in his hand. He was running late. Lana was waiting for him.

The voice on the other end of the line was familiar and to the point. "A young woman has been caught causing trouble, Mr. McGrath." His cock stirred, recalling the night Lana wandered into his office.

Pulling his shoulders back, he replied, "Send her in."

He ended the call and waited patiently for the door to open. After a moment, a light tap proceeded an entry. Marcus drew in a steadying breath as the woman strutted inside with a bold look in her bright eyes. She wore glossy trousers that looked like every curve had been poured inside a leather mould, and a tight black corset top showed off perfect cleavage. A set of killer red heels matched her sumptuous scarlet lips. Standing tall before him, she fiddled with the golden curls tumbling over her bare shoulders.

Marcus rose from his chair and rounded the desk. His heart rate elevated from calm to erratic, in zero to thirty seconds.

"You must be Mr. McGrath?" Her gaze dawdled over his navy suit trousers and lingered on his obvious erection.

Marcus folded his arms and perched his hip on the edge of the desk. "And you must be trouble?" he countered.

She nodded, sucking in her lower lip with intent. "Apparently, I'm here for punishment." Her voice was confident but a slight waver in her tone highlighted the subtle flare of her pupils.

It was all bravado.

"What kind of punishment did you have in mind?" His hungry gaze swept over her teasing attire and sultry stance.

Taking a step forward, she flicked the long tendrils of hair over her shoulders, letting it cascade down her back. "Every girl wants to taste Marcus McGrath." She stopped inches from his defensive pose. "Maybe you could break your rules, just for me?"

"I'm no stranger to breaking the rules." He almost laughed.

Drifting her hand up to her mouth, she placed her forefinger to her lips and sucked gently. "Can I taste you?" Her wet tongue played with the pad of her finger.

"I'm not available." The gruffness to his tone lacked conviction as her cheeks hollowed, drawing the finger deeper into her mouth.

Reaching forward, her nails grazed the buttons on his shirt. Instantly, he grabbed her wrist, halting the sexy torture. She sucked in a quivering breath and his composure went to shit.

Pushing off the surface, he tightened his grip and towered over the naughty temptress. "You don't get to touch me, understand."

She nodded, her big blue eyes filled with lust. Leaning down into her hair, Marcus inhaled the dangerous intoxicating fragrance. The pounding in his dick became unbearable and he quickly dropped her hand like hot coal.

"Oh, now, Mr. McGrath. You disappoint me," she whispered huskily. "Just one lick, that's all." His nostrils flared as she looked up at him under fluttery black lashes and hummed lightly. "It will be our little secret, Marcus."

Dipping back to the desk, his long fingers curled around the edge, holding back his building desire. "What exactly do you have in mind?" he half growled.

A few months later...

A sly smile curved her pouty lips and her hand met the zipper of his trousers. "Hmmm, Marcus. You're so hard for me. I think we could come up with something that would please us both, don't you think?" She winked while slowly pulling the zip down.

His breathing deepened when she dropped to her knees and gazed up at him, so ready to please, so damn fucking sexy.

"I'd like to punish *you*, Mr. McGrath." A playful smirk lifted the corners of her juicy stained lips.

The vibrations from her hand echoed in his groin when her palm wrapped his hard cock, tugging it free. "And why would *you* punish me?" He bit out like it pained him to hold back.

She darted her tongue over the tip with her eyes fixated on his, watching as they glowed with danger. "Because you're late, Marcus." Her eyes sparkled. "I was waiting for you. It's rude to keep your girlfriend waiting."

His strong hands ploughed into her blonde locks, jerking her head back so he could see the pulse thrum in the hollow of her fragile neck. "I know, beautiful. I was on my way down, until a fucking amazing woman entered my office, and pulled out my dick."

She purred under his unyielding spell. "Perhaps you would rather wait until we got home, Mr. McGrath?" she said playfully. "After all, the pups are waiting for us. I bought them more treats…"

"Finish," he growled, threading his hands through her long lengths. "Fucking finish it."

"Hmmm, I'll think about it." She giggled.

In one swoop, Marcus slotted his hands under her arms and heaved her off the floor. Spinning around, he lifted her onto the desk, so she rested on her buttocks. "I should've

A few months later…

done this to you the first night you walked in here and licked my heart with that dirty little tongue of yours. I should've fucked you, right here, on this desk, Lana."

They had been to hell and back, yet they stood stronger together for it. The sweet little Lana who he met all those months ago had shown herself to be a powerful, strong sexual woman – the love of his life.

Her teasing game had ended. All she could do was gaze into his eyes and let him rip off her clothes.

"I love you, Lana."

"I love you, Marcus."

The End

Continue reading The Unforgettable series and meet Jamie McGrath the Northern Irish billionaire in book 3, His Addiction.

What readers are saying about His Addiction

'I feel like I need to forewarn you about the STEAMY AND THE PASSION in this, because it will blow your mind! Romantic with a twist! Autumn has a way of writing darker romance that satisfies you fully!'

'I wanted to slap him just as much as I wanted to kiss the hell out of him. He's... refreshing. Yeah, it's a weird adjective but it fits. He surprised me with his bluntness, unapologetic cockiness and his overall delicious wickedness. And oh, is he wicked.'

'This was one hot book. Had some really steamy parts. Had really awesome characters. Loved the McGrath men. Spicy hot.'

A cold-hearted billionaire hiding out in the jungle finds a scientist lost in the wild.

She's a threat to his kingdom, and a new obsession.

Enjoy this dark romance in Kindle Unlimited

ALSO BY AUTUMN ARCHER

Romantic Suspense

The Unforgettable Series
His to Steal, #1
His to Keep, #2
His Addiction, #3

K. Bromberg's Everyday Heroes World Project
Call Out

Dark Romantic Suspense

Vow Duet
Vow of Revenge
Vow to Protect

Jungle Oasis
Fever
Fall
Flame

Contemporary Romance

Miles from Home (Standalone's)
The Chance
The Photo
The Right Guy
The Star

My True Heart Series

Also by Autumn Archer

Wild Heart #1 - Autumn Archer
Fake Heart #2 - Britney Bell
Rodeo Heart #3 - Coming soon

Sign up to Autumn Archer's Newsletter for more details on upcoming releases.

www.autumnarcher.com

ABOUT THE AUTHOR

Autumn is a USA Today Bestselling Author from Northern Ireland, best known for romancing the darkness. She's a teen wrangler, dog slave and matcha lover who thrives on the written word.

Her novels delve into the darker element of life at times, giving her romantic suspense books a curious edge, with alpha men who have to work hard to win over strong women. That being said, she also loves to write sweet and swoony books under A. Archer depending on her mood.

Autumn's books follow her soul, with equal parts playful to enigmatic.

"When there is darkness, the light will always follow."